PIRATES AND PATRIOTS

The New World Nautical Series
Book One

David Field

SAPERE
BOOKS

PIRATES AND PATRIOTS

Published by Sapere Books.

24 Trafalgar Road, Ilkley, LS29 8HH,
United Kingdom

saperebooks.com

ISBN: 978-0-85495-023-2

1

March, 1554

Francis Drake was on his fourth journey across to Boulogne under the command of Thomas Crayshaw, who never ceased to demonstrate his resentment at having to include the precocious fifteen-year-old in his crew. Francis, for his part, was living out his boyhood dream of being a sailor, following holidays with his Hawkins cousins in Plymouth. While wandering the mudflats and navigable reaches of the Medway Estuary, Francis had prevailed upon his mentor John Tench, owner of the *Bonaventure*, to let him take to sea with the basic knowledge he had acquired in the Hawkins family's shipbuilding yard.

An unseasonable easterly had taken command of the vessel's two mainsails the minute that they'd left the Medway at Sheerness and turned the *Bonaventure* south-westwards as they hugged the French coast. Francis was gazing up at a flock of seagulls that was tailing their vessel when Captain Crayshaw ordered helmsman Jim Bunting to take their vessel a few more points to starboard to keep her well off the coastline. There was a cracking noise, and a loud curse from the helm, and Francis looked back inboard, to where John Bunting was staring helplessly at the wheel in his hands. It had sheared clean away from the spar that joined it to the rods below the waterline, which were connected to the rudder.

'What happened?' Crayshaw demanded.

Bunting stared back at him with an expression of frozen horror. 'She just sheared off, Cap'n,' he explained unnecessarily. The vessel lurched landward on the south-easterly gale that would drive them onto the rocks beneath the headland, now that they had no way of steering to starboard.

'Lower the mainsails!' Crayshaw ordered, and several deckhands ran for the main masts.

'Hold!' Francis yelled instinctively, and Crayshaw rounded on him angrily.

'Who are you to countermand my order, boy? I'll report you for mutiny, or perhaps just run you through now and lob you overboard!'

'If we lower the sail, we'll be even more at the mercy of the current,' Francis said, 'and it's driving us straight onto those rocks ahead.'

Crayshaw stared at him disbelievingly. 'We just lost steering! What use is sail without steerage?'

Francis jerked his head towards the stern. 'The rudder runs proud of the stern rail, doesn't she?'

'So?'

Francis spotted his friend Jim Short among the deckhands. He yelled to Jim to bring him a hammer and a length of wood, and was shortly instructing a protesting Captain Crayshaw to hold the length of wood steady over the top edge of the rudder while he hammered in ten heavy nails. He then pulled it hard towards him. Almost immediately the ship lurched to starboard, towards mid-channel, and then the opposing pressure from the protesting keel and rudder threatened to pull Francis off his feet. He yelled for Crayshaw to add his weight to the horizontal bar of wood.

Slowly and painfully the *Bonaventure* creaked, bucked and heaved its way further out into the open sea, the chasing wind tearing noisily through the rigging as the full sails billowed outwards. Ten minutes later, they passed the tip of the cape. A ragged cheer of relief could be heard from the deckhands standing amidships, shivering with a combination of relief and the heavy spray that was blasting on board as the vessel continued to cut across the heavy current from the full tide.

Their first port of call after they moored in Boulogne and set a guard for the cargo was a local inn, where Captain Crayshaw ordered a bottle of rum, which he shared with all hands. He reluctantly handed the bottle to Francis for him to swig from, but Francis shook his head.

'Too holy to drink, are we? I suppose you're feeling very virtuous right now, having saved the *Bonaventure*? What *was* that inspired piece of woodwork, anyway?' Crayshaw demanded.

'It's called a whiplash, and it's the latest way of steering,' Francis explained. 'My cousins, the Hawkins family of Plymouth, build ships, and they're fixing them in all their new ones. But, as you saw, it takes strength to operate — more than is needed for a wheel, anyway.'

'Before you think of boasting to our employer about how you saved his ship,' Crayshaw warned Francis almost under his breath, but still contriving to breathe rum fumes all over him, 'remember that you countermanded my order. The first rule on board ship is to obey the captain's orders, right or wrong. To refuse to do so, or to question any order, is mutiny, and you're lucky you're not dead.'

'We're *all* lucky that we're not dead,' Francis riposted as he nodded towards the others.

Crayshaw gave Francis a meaningful look of triumph. 'Before you even *think* of telling our employer what transpired, or how he came to be the proud possessor of a lump of wood nailed to the top of his rudder, bear in mind that if I report you for mutiny, you'll never mince back on board the *Bonaventure*, because I'll refuse to sail with you. We'll get the wheel repaired in harbour here, so you won't even have the evidence to support your story.'

'I was thinking of going back to Plymouth anyway,' Francis replied with a hint of defiance.

'Tired of the sea-going life, are we?'

'No — tired of sailing under your command. To my mind, a captain's first duty is to his men, not his reputation.'

'Out of my sight, boy, before I run you through!' Crayshaw spat back at him.

Francis made a hasty departure. His comrades on the next table gave him a round of applause as he scurried past them, head bowed.

The return trip was uneventful, and after their mixed cargo of shoes, paintings, wall hangings, brandy and salted herring had been unloaded, Francis walked back home with his eyes on the ground ahead, contemplating his future. It was only a matter of time before he and Captain Crayshaw came to blows, that was obvious, and if Francis had the measure of his opponent, it would likely end with him dead or in prison. He was gloomily considering his options as he opened the front door to Upchurch Vicarage, which the Drake family occupied by virtue of his father Edmund's ecclesiastical office. He was immediately surrounded by younger brothers eager to learn about his adventures, who were swept impatiently aside by their mother, Mary Drake, as she embraced Francis.

'Your father's got something to tell you,' she whispered.

At that moment, his father, Edmund Drake, emerged from the front parlour in which he composed his sermons, no doubt attracted by the disturbance at the front door. 'Welcome home, son, but the news isn't so happy, I'm afraid,' he began.

'What do you mean?'

'John Tench has not been well while you were away, and it seems he's taken to his deathbed. He was asking to see you, so you better not waste any time.'

'He's going nowhere until he's had some supper!' Mary insisted. 'You can see for yourself that the weight's fair falling off him. Time enough to go visiting the sick in the morning.'

The sun was well up in the sky before Francis awoke from his longest and most comfortable sleep for a week, tucked into a hearty breakfast, then walked down the village's only street to the large house owned by John Tench. Although a single and childless man, he'd bought the house a few years previously in order to demonstrate his success in life, and employed an elderly woman, who according to rumour had been something more than a housekeeper in her prime. It was she who admitted Francis to a house that smelled of camphor and old men and ushered him mournfully up the panelled staircase and into the rear bedroom, whose window commanded a view of the upper Medway Estuary.

Propped up in bed like a scarecrow from the field was the man who'd given Francis his start at sea, looking every day of his sixty-odd years. He waved with an age-spotted hand for Francis to sit on the side of his bolster.

'Looks like I'm not long for this world, my boy,' John Tench wheezed, then coughed. Wiping the sputum from his chin, he managed a grin as he fixed Francis with a stare from rheumy blue eyes. 'I hope I didn't steer you wrong by giving you your wish to go to sea.'

'Not at all,' Francis assured him as he gripped the cold hand. 'I owe you everything, but now I think that I should return to

Plymouth, where my cousins have their own fleet. Perhaps they'll give me command of one of them.'

'Is that because of Tom Crayshaw?' Tench asked, and when Francis looked hesitant, torn between loyalty and the truth, the old man smiled. 'No need to tell me, lad — I hear tales from the other men. But think on, afore you go running back to Plymouth. Is it better to captain a vessel, or to own one, would you say?'

'Both, I would think,' Francis replied after giving the matter a moment's thought, and Tench grinned conspiratorially.

'Then both it shall be, young Francis. I never had a son — for that matter, no children to provide for at all. The *Bonaventure* is all yours.'

When Francis's jaw dropped in amazement, the old man chuckled.

'I wish you all the good fortune that a man ever wished the son he'd never had. Now, you'd best leave me to prepare myself for God — your good father promised to visit before sunset, and I can feel the shadows lengthening.'

Francis allowed the tears of sorrow and gratitude to roll down his face as he walked slowly back to the vicarage.

2

William Hawkins looked up from where he had been supervising the launch of an ocean-going vessel into the water beside the slipway on Plymouth's Sutton Wharf. The man striding towards him was familiar enough, and the two armed men who accompanied him left little doubt that the man was both wealthy and important. Important to Spain, certainly, since he was Don Simon Renardo, Spanish Ambassador to the Court of Queen Mary. He had made the voyage to England a year or so previously, bearing Philip's proposal of marriage to Mary in a Hawkins vessel he had commissioned while it lay idle in Cadiz Harbour between cargoes.

'Good day to you, my Lord Ambassador,' William called out as the distance between them narrowed, but Renardo — or 'Renard' as the English called him — had eyes only for the massive vessel in the water. On her deck, William's younger brother John was instructing deckhands in the lashing of the mainsails to the masts, ahead of her first test run down the Sound and out into the Channel.

'A fine vessel,' Renard commented.

William nodded. 'Our first carrack, built in our yard across the road there. We had to remove the roof of the barn in order to accommodate her aftcastle. We've named her the *Rose of Plymouth*.'

'How many state cabins does she have?' Renard enquired.

'How many do you need?' John asked as he jumped from the deck back onto the greensward.

Renard smiled. 'You anticipate the reason for my visit. I wish you to journey once more to Spain, there to take on board your most illustrious passenger yet, along with his companion and interpreter. But you will bring them back to Portsmouth.'

'Why Portsmouth?' John asked. 'Why not here, to Plymouth? Or — if he is that illustrious, as you assure us — why not London?'

'Because,' Renard replied, 'Portsmouth is the closest to Winchester, where your exalted passenger will be married to your queen. How soon will this vessel be ready? Will one thousand gold Spanish ducats be sufficient for your trouble?'

'For that amount of money, she'll be ready yesterday!' William grinned.

John was less enthusiastic. 'She needs to be tested for seaworthiness before we can commit ourselves to the responsibility of carrying a king,' he told Renard.

Renard nodded. 'Your brother has a greater awareness of the affairs of your nation than you do, Master William. Your passenger will indeed be Philip of Burgundy and Spain, shortly to become Philip of England. And on your return to Portsmouth you may anticipate being met on the harbour by half the nobles of England.'

'We need to run her to the Isle of Wight and back,' John said. 'We leave on the morning tide and will return tomorrow evening. Then we need to fit out the state cabin, so shall we say Saturday, on the mid-morning ebb tide?'

'You must be back here with my master by no later than the twentieth of next month,' Renard insisted, 'since the marriage is to be celebrated in Winchester Cathedral on the twenty-fifth. This will cause you no difficulty?'

'Not half as much as it will cause Philip himself,' John muttered under his breath, then winced as William kicked his ankle. John might find it amusing to joke about Mary Tudor's reputed lack of comeliness, but this man's employer was about to marry her, and William was anxious to acquire the custom that came from being the preferred carrier of diplomats to and from Spain.

The round trip proved uneventful, and the *Rose of Plymouth* lived up to all expectations as she slipped in and out of Corunna, returning with His Imperial Highness, who spent the entire return voyage in his stateroom in prayer. William mused that the reason for his prayers might stem from doubts about the seaworthiness of a vessel that had yet to be tested in an angry sea, but John suggested sourly that it was more a matter of preparing his immortal soul for the ordeal of climbing into a marriage bed with Queen Mary, whose plainness of feature was the talk of every sailor who'd laid eyes upon her.

Fortunately, he was not able to share his unflattering opinion with Philip himself, who in any case spoke no English and left all matters of conversation to his aide and mouthpiece, Gomez de Silva. From him they learned that there were several Spanish ships behind them, bringing Philip's personal attendants, priests and household minions, but that when they moored at Portsmouth those waiting to welcome them would be the elite of the English Court, in attendance on Queen Mary.

'Better warn the men not to swear when they miss the bollards with the mooring ropes,' John grinned, and William wondered if his younger brother would ever take affairs of State seriously enough to benefit from the trade it could bring them.

Even though they'd been warned in advance, the two brothers were overawed by the glittering company that awaited them on Camber Dock, and the collective noise of fifes, cornets and tambours that drifted over as they floated in on the tide. Only their mizzen mast provided additional wind power as John, at the helm, steered her carefully towards where the gaily coloured throng stood waiting.

Having unloaded their precious passenger, William and John were seated on bollards on the harbour wall, arguing over which alehouse to grace with their custom, when they were approached by a distinguished-looking man with two attendants. He nodded down at the deck of the *Rose of Plymouth*. 'Is this your vessel?'

'It is, but she's not for sale,' John told him bluntly.

'Who built her?'

John, becoming irritated, replied brusquely, 'My brother here, but he's too pleased with himself at the moment, so don't go drivelling on about how good she looks, because the measure of a vessel is how she handles on the ocean.'

'Indeed it is,' the man replied, 'and perhaps you'd be inclined towards greater politeness if I introduce myself, as I should have done from the start. I'm Sir Benjamin Gonson, Treasurer to Her Majesty's Navy, and I'd be honoured if you two gentlemen would join my daughter and myself for supper at my humble inn this evening.'

'We'd be delighted,' William confirmed before John could say anything rude, making a mental note of the inn in question. Having risen for long enough to bow as their new acquaintance departed, he turned back to look down at John with a frown. 'Had he been the queen herself, you would no doubt have enquired as to her reason for taking the air without her attendants. You really must learn to be more polite to people who matter.'

'And why does *he* matter?'

William clicked his tongue in frustration as he replied. 'Because I suspect that he wishes to buy more carracks than we can possibly build. Now, get off your arse and clean yourself up in anticipation of a good supper, if nothing else.'

'This lamb is exquisite!' John enthused as he and William sat opposite Sir Benjamin Gonson and his daughter Katherine, a sparkly-eyed and lively brunette with a captivating smile.

'As you are no doubt aware,' Gonson told the two brothers, 'our late King Henry took great care to expand and improve upon the Navy that his father had created. Given our sad history of warfare with the French, that was clearly advisable. In addition to the dry dock in Portsmouth that I visited in my official capacity earlier today, we now have naval dockyards at Woolwich and Deptford, both on the Thames, and Chatham on the Medway. But King Henry's son, the late King Edward, let matters slide in his obsession with religious reform, and it is to be feared that Her Majesty sees no threat to us from the sea, given her alliance with Spain in the person of its heir apparent.'

'But the French threat remains?' William asked.

Gonson nodded. 'Not just the French threat, but — and I should be grateful if you would not repeat what I can disclose to you — the threat from any nation that can use our period of inactivity in shipbuilding in order to build up its own navy. Chief among these are the Spanish themselves, closely followed by the Portuguese, and if Queen Mary should die prematurely...' He looked behind him nervously before continuing. 'I do not suggest that this will happen, you understand, but my point is that should we cease to be protected by the might of Spain, then we shall be seriously outnumbered in matters of not only warships, but the skilled men needed to crew them.'

'You have presumably expressed these fears to Her Majesty, perhaps in more suitable words?' William asked.

Gonson nodded. 'Indeed, I have, but she will hear nothing of what she regards as the provocative policy of increasing the number of our warships. However, she *is* prepared to listen to suggestions regarding the expansion of trade in those new markets that the Spanish and Portuguese have opened up across the Atlantic.'

'The Americas?' William confirmed. 'But surely they lie beyond the range of the average barque, whose low tonnage could not justify the weeks at sea, and whose supply holds could not contain enough victuals for the crew during such a lengthy crossing?'

Gonson smiled. 'Hence the importance of your new carrack. Do you intend to sail her west in the foreseeable future?'

William frowned. 'I don't have the navigational skills, neither are there any charts of which I'm aware. If the Spanish and Portuguese have them, they're keeping them close to their chests.'

'As for the navigation, I am very friendly with a man called Dr John Dee,' Gonson told them. 'He's a diviner of sorts, and some say a necromancer, but he is also a skilled mathematician, and he has devised a means of navigation by the stars that wants only some brave mariner to test it on the open ocean.'

'Even then,' William persevered, 'we don't know how the Spanish would be likely to react, were we to interrupt their hitherto sole trading in the Indies.'

Gonson nodded. 'Now we come to the nub of it. Do you carry armament on your carracks?'

'We've only built the one so far,' William said, but Gonson was not to be diverted from his main point.

'Were you to build new ones, could they carry cannon?'

'They could carry anything,' William assured him, 'but above decks everything has to be securely lashed down.'

'And below decks?' Gonson asked without relaxing his smile. When William had no answer, his host reverted to his earlier point. 'Her Majesty, as I already advised, is not minded to invest in new warships. But she *is* prepared to finance an expansion in overseas trade, making use of carracks just such as yours, but exceeding four hundred tons in dead weight. It is hoped that they will be able to carry large cargoes and cross mighty oceans. I wish you to build such vessels. The *Rose of Plymouth* approaches three hundred tons, by my reckoning?'

'You obviously know your ships,' William whispered, deeply impressed, and Gonson nodded.

'I also know a well-built one when I see it, and I was encouraged by what I saw. I would require as many five-hundred-ton carracks as you can launch from your yard, but the additional one hundred tons in dead weight would already be accounted for.' William raised his eyebrows in a silent request for further enlightenment, and Gonson obliged. 'Cannon. Below decks, one level down. I have in mind what might best be called "armed merchantmen" that can be converted into warships with a naval captain in command on its afterdeck.'

William thought deeply before enquiring, 'Can you let me have the detailed specifications for any that already exist?'

Gonson shook his head. 'That is why I have come to you. There are, of course, warships at Deptford and here in Portsmouth, and you can copy their design for the placing of the gun deck. Our current warships are more along the lines of Portuguese caravels, but they are not adapted to long voyages. If you could build a mighty carrack of over five hundred tons in dead weight, it could then be employed to carry men and cannon as well as cargo.'

'I would need some time to copy the design, and I would need to speak with those skilled in the use of the guns that would be placed below decks,' William told him. 'I assume that they are above the waterline, making the vessel lower in the water, and also less able to carry cargo?'

'They are indeed,' Gonson confirmed, 'and they have what the sailors call gun ports, through which the cannon may be fired. "Holes in the sides of the vessel", if you prefer that description.'

William glanced sideways at John, who was eyeing Gonson's daughter. 'Perhaps my brother could be allowed to study these cannon placements? He can then bring the design back to Plymouth for me to instruct my shipwrights on how to include them in the final vessel.'

'You are the one mainly responsible for the building of your vessels?' Gonson asked, and when William confirmed that this was the case, Gonson nodded across the table at John. 'Then what does he do, apart from leering at my daughter?'

'He is the sailor in the family,' William said as he slapped John gently on the back of his bonnet to remind him that there were two other people around the table. 'It is John who advises me on matters such as how the vessel sits in the water, and how she responds to the winds and currents — the invaluable wisdom of a man accustomed to life on deck.'

'Then it is he who could advise on how your new gun decks can be placed on your carracks so as to best employ them?'

'Indeed,' William confirmed. 'That is why it should perhaps be he who remains here in Portsmouth to study your warships.'

'Would he not be better coming to us at Deptford?' Katherine asked without taking her eyes off John.

Gonson looked across at John's mesmerised facial expression and chuckled quietly. 'Indeed he would, and if I judge the situation correctly, he would deem it no hardship.'

'I would embrace such a proposal as both a privilege and a God-given blessing,' John murmured, 'and I can also learn something of gunnery while I am there. This may, I fear, take some time.'

3

When John and William returned to Plymouth, Francis was waiting for them with a request to be allowed the command of one of their new cargo vessels. He briefly recounted his changing fortunes since they had last met, and his eyes lit up as John advised him of their new commission for the Navy.

'Just imagine,' Francis enthused, 'being in command of one of Her Majesty's men-of-war, and firing shots across the water at the enemy!'

'Do you know how it's done?' William asked as they sat swilling local ale in a harbour-side inn that never closed as long as it had customers.

Francis shook his head. 'It must take much practice and skill — knowing when to load, and when to fire at a moving target on a rolling ocean.'

'Would you like to learn?' William asked, and when Francis nodded eagerly, William turned to John. 'You must take Francis with you to Deptford, to learn this great art.'

'I thought I was being sent to do that,' John said. 'By this means, I shall have greater time and more excuse to pay court to Mistress Katherine.'

'John has lost his heart to the daughter of the Navy Treasurer,' William told Francis with a smirk. 'It comes to us all in the end, and thank God that I chose wisely in that regard.'

'You don't say that when you come to the yard bleary-eyed after the children have kept you awake all night,' John teased him, then turned to Francis. 'I shall tarry as long as I can, learning the design of gun decks on carracks, while you master the skill of sinking enemy ships with iron balls fired from cannon. We shall travel to Deptford together.'

'Not just yet,' William corrected him. 'We haven't completed the sea trials of the *Rose of Plymouth*, and until Master Gonson pays for his first armed carrack, we must continue to put food in our mouths. I need you both to take the *Rose* to Antwerp during a rough westerly, then acquire a heavy cargo that will test her across the water into the Thames. Sell the cargo in Deptford, then bring the *Rose* — and the proceeds from the cargo — back here to Plymouth.'

Two weeks later the *Rose* was tacking up the Thames, heavy with Flanders cloth bales. She finally dropped anchor mid-channel in Greenwich Reach before being granted a mooring inside the Naval Dockyard in Deptford Strand when John sent word of their arrival to nearby Trinity House, the office and town dwelling of Benjamin Gonson and his daughter. While Francis took a wherry across the water to Thames Street, where he sold their cargo at a favourable price, John presented himself to Sir Benjamin Gonson and announced that he was ready to begin his inspection of naval carracks, while his cousin and fellow mariner Francis Drake was eager to learn how merchantmen could become warships in all but name.

Both men had something to celebrate. For Francis, it was his first voyage to Antwerp, where so much money was to be made from cargo trading, while for John, the cause for celebration was the warm smile of welcome that he'd received from Katherine Gonson behind her father's back as he enquired after John's health. He invited the men to supper that evening, and left John and Katherine to gaze wistfully at each other as he opted to get the measure of the athletic-looking young cousin that John had brought with him to Deptford.

'I assume, Francis, that you have no experience of ships' cannon?' Gonson asked.

'No, sir, but I am eager to learn.'

'For what reason, and to what end?' Gonson asked.

'I intend one day to sail around this entire globe that we live on, and it is my belief that I will be opposed in that by mariners of other nations. I will therefore need to defend both my ship and my crew.'

'This will of course remain strictly between us,' the older man assured him, 'but do you have any formed opinion as to where that opposition might come from?'

'Clearly, those nations that consider that they have already laid claim to the new worlds that are being opened up for their riches every day. Spain and Portugal, to name but two.'

'And yet we have a Spaniard married to the queen who will shortly become the King of Spain also,' Gonson argued. 'Does that not alter your view of things?'

There was an awkward pause before Francis replied. 'Forgive me for further candour, but it is rumoured abroad that King Philip is not well accepted by some of our nobles, and that he means only to add England to his swiftly growing Habsburg Empire. If that be true, and he is first and foremost intent upon adding to his conquered nations, will he sit easily by and allow England to exploit them for itself?'

'But if England is part of his empire, as you hypothesise, then will he not welcome any growth by *any* part of that empire?'

'There is also the matter of religion,' Francis added, avoiding a direct answer to the last question. 'Many of those, like me, who may seek their fortunes across the sea, may be of the Reformist persuasion. How would it be for them to settle the lands to the west with Protestant farmers, when the Spanish and Portuguese who have so far led the way have enforced Catholicism on the people they have discovered, or those they have left behind to plant their flags?'

'Our current queen would not countenance settlement by Protestants,' Gonson reminded him.

'Hence my need to be skilled in the firing of ships' cannon.'

Gonson chose not to respond to this virtually treasonous remark. 'Tomorrow, I shall acquaint you with Master Ralph Innes, who is in charge of gunnery training here at Deptford. He in turn will acquaint you with the basics that you will require in order to ensure that your cousin's proposed new carracks are appropriately constructed to take on board our new cannon.'

'In what way "new", pray?'

'They are made of iron, rather than brass. We have converted the old foundry here at Deptford into a repair workshop only, and down the road at Woolwich is a set of furnaces in which iron is melted into cannon moulds. Iron cannon do not last for as long as brass ones, because they rust, but by this new process we can make more cannon more quickly, and we can be surer of the accuracy of their diameters. As you will learn, we can now choose from between four and forty pounds of weight for our shot. Given that they are also moulded from molten iron, we can be more accurate in their size, and prevent disasters such as over-sized shot becoming stuck in the cannon and blowing half the ship away.'

'Is it necessary for the gun deck to be specially strengthened in order to take the weight of these new ordnance pieces?' John asked during a brief lull in his optical conversation with Katherine.

Gonson shrugged. 'For the answer to that you will need to ask our royal shipwright, Peter Pett, whom you should lose no time in seeking out tomorrow.'

'Where will I find him?' John asked.

Katherine was swift to answer. 'May I take him and introduce the two, Father? I rarely get an opportunity to see where you work, and I will surely come to no ill if I am escorted by such a brave young man as Master Hawkins here.'

'Very well,' Gonson conceded. 'Ten of the forenoon, by our front entrance here.'

'You got the faintest idea how these work?' Ralph Innes asked as he and Francis stood on either side of the medium-sized cannon on the workshop floor.

'Only that they fire iron balls that smash into enemy vessels,' Francis grinned back, to be met with a serious face from Innes.

'Just remember that if they're not fired proper, they can kill the men using them,' he growled. 'This little beauty's called a "culverin", an' she fires a twenty-pound shot that can travel over a thousand feet. So, for example, if we took it down to the waterfront an' fired it across the river, we could likely blow an 'ole in the wall o' the Tower.'

'Or the side of an enemy ship,' Francis reminded him with a gleam in his eye.

Innes looked down with a grimace. 'You probably noticed I'm missing a leg. You can thank a weapon like this one, what cut me leg clean off when it jumped back an' bit me. You've got a lot to learn, young feller me lad. Nah, pay attention.'

For the next ten minutes Francis listened closely as Innes explained the sequence of events, beginning with the pouring of loose gunpowder into the barrel, followed by a tightly compacted collection of rags called a 'wad'. Then came the cannonball itself, prior to the gun being run forward on something called a 'carriage' so that its barrel protruded beyond the side of the vessel through a hole called a 'gun port'. When everything was prepared, more powder was poured into the 'touchhole' in the rear upper surface of the cannon, then ignited with a flame from a long wooden fuse known as a 'linstock'.

'If you are lucky, the gun goes off, an' the ball goes flying at the enemy at the same time as the cannon comes flying backwards, an' takes your legs off if you're in the way,' Innes added encouragingly. 'Then you 'as to wash the barrel out with a swab afore you can reload 'er. Any idea why that might be?'

'Gunpowder residue left in the barrel?' Francis ventured.

Innes smiled for the first time. 'We'll maybe make a gunner of you, if you're that bright. So, show me what I just taught you.'

Without any hesitation, Francis repeated the sequence of procedures that he'd just been taught, and Innes smiled again. 'Any more questions?' he asked.

Francis nodded. 'Why is the cannon mounted on a swivel?'

'So's you can tip the barrel upwards, for two reasons. The first is so that she's more easily loaded when she's leaning backwards, an' the second's to do with range. If you're close to your target, you just fires with the gun flat to the carriage underneath 'er, but if your enemy ship's a good distance away, you needs to tilt the barrel backwards, so that the shot goes further. Got it?'

'In theory, yes,' Francis told him. 'But it must take a long time to learn the art of finding your range.'

'You're a smart lad, in't you? Like to see gunners being trained 'ow to do that?'

Thirty minutes later, and a mile or so downriver, Francis was one of a dozen men below decks on a specially equipped carrack, gazing down a long galley just above the waterline that was lined on both sides with culverins of the type he had examined earlier. They were laid in a 'herringbone' formation, each on its own carriage, so that no two guns were directly aligned with each other. Innes explained that this was to prevent the cannon from colliding with each other when they ran back after firing. 'You'll see the powder boy doing a little jig between 'em in due course, so as to make sure that 'e still 'as two legs when it's all over.'

'There are six guns on either side,' Francis pointed out. 'Is that a normal configuration?'

'Depends on the ship,' he was advised. 'I've seen as many as twenty on the big 'uns — ten on either side. But best to keep it simple while the men's in training.'

If this was simple, Francis told himself as he watched the intricate series of movements — almost like a May Day dance on the village green — then he'd need time to absorb it all before he called upon his own men to do something more complicated. One shattering explosion after another rocked the vessel from side to side as the guns on the port side blasted off in series, followed by each of the starboard guns after a few seconds' delay. As he peered through the smoke and coughed as the acrid fumes drifted his way, Francis observed that the overall effect was one of regulated mayhem, and he was mightily impressed by the progress that the trainee gunners were already demonstrating.

Eventually, Innes called a halt with a few words of grudging acknowledgement. He then ordered that the vessel be held where it lay at anchor, its port beam facing the widening channel as the Thames meandered its way towards the Essex marshes on one side and the first low range of Kent hills on the other. He turned to Francis. 'Take a look through one o' them gun ports and tell me what you sees.'

Francis did as instructed, and further downstream, seemingly at anchor in the middle of the channel, was a battered old fishing hulk that he realised must be the target. Then another thought struck him, and he turned to Innes. 'What were we firing at before?'

'Nowt,' said Innes, 'since the cannon was laid flat to minimise the range. The shots fell into open water on both sides. Mind you, that don't stop complaints about the noise, so we doesn't do it every day. We ain't got the shot to spare neither, to be honest with you. But now we got a target, as you can see. 'Ow far away d'you reckon she is?'

Francis ducked again and squinted through the gun port. 'About five hundred feet, I'd reckon.'

'So 'ow far up would you raise the barrel?'

Francis puzzled for a moment, then inspiration dawned. 'If the overall range of one of these balls is a thousand feet, and the target is half that distance away, then common sense suggests that the barrel should be raised halfway.'

'Let's see if you're right,' said Innes, then called three men down the aisle by name, and pointed to Francis. 'Master Drake 'ere reckons as 'ow you need the barrel at half upwards. Let's see if 'e's right, and while 'e's at it, let's see if 'e remembers the sequence. When you're ready, Master Drake.'

Francis grinned self-consciously as he ordered the barrel to be swabbed with a wet rag on the end of a 'rammer', then ordered the loading of the new powder, followed by the wad. Then he picked up an iron ball from the line to the side of him and ordered the barrel to be raised half upright. When this was done, he rolled the ball down the barrel and called for the cannon to be pushed as far as she would go through the gun port once it had been lowered. It was then re-raised through forty-five degrees, and Francis added powder to the touchhole before holding out his hand for the linstock and applying the smouldering flame to the tightly packed hole. For a moment he thought it had misfired, until a shattering roar filled the air around them, and the cannon shot backwards three feet along its carriage. From somewhere he heard a muffled cheer, and he ducked down to eye level with the gun port in time to see the target listing heavily to its starboard side, taking in water from the sizeable hole that his cannonball had blown in it.

'Well, Master Drake,' Innes said, 'any time you wants to sign on as a Navy gunner, I'll remember this morning.'

John was standing back from the *Dreadnought*, in dock for routine maintenance, when Francis joined him.

'Can you build one?' Francis asked.

'Probably. But if we do, can you load her with guns, and do you know what to do with them when you do?'

'There are two questions there, John, and to answer both of them I need to return to Plymouth. I suggest that I take the *Rose* and its crew ahead of you, leaving you to return by road. How long behind me will you be?'

'As long as I dare,' said John. 'Mistress Gonson has given me cause to hope that she might consent to my hand in marriage, should I offer it.'

'Have you approached her father?'

'Not as yet, which is why I must remain. Tell William that I will have full drawings for him on my return, but that he may begin laying the keel for a boat exceeding five hundred tons in deadweight. And wish me luck!'

4

Francis was hailed from the quayside at Plymouth as he supervised the mooring of the *Rose* at a berth reserved for Hawkins's vessels. It was William Hawkins, and he frowned as he looked down at the deck.

'You set sail with my brother on the *Rose*, and now you return alone. What has befallen John?'

'He's in London, learning how to make ships that carry the guns I have recently learned to fire. He is but a few days behind me, detained by a gaoler of the heart.'

'The young Gonson woman? It would have been obvious to a blind pedlar that something was going on there. Did he entrust you with the money from the latest cargo?'

'He did indeed, but it will cost you a fine supper and a flagon of your cider.'

'Willingly. You may also prepare yourself to meet with a mysterious man who has been calling at the house daily for news of John's return.'

'Who is he, and why me?' Francis asked.

'He won't say, but he dresses like a nobleman, and he insists that he comes on royal authority. Speaking with John would be his preference, but since he mentioned the need for transport to the Low Countries I told him about you. As you are back first, and in command of the *Rose*, perhaps you can see to his requirement.'

The mystery visitor revealed his identity the following morning, when he called at the Hawkins house in which Francis was lodging, asking for either John or Francis. Francis rose as the man was admitted by the family's steward, and the visitor gave the slightest of bows.

'Do I address Master John Hawkins or Master Francis Drake?'

'The latter.'

'As I believed, since I am advised that Master Hawkins is approaching his thirtieth year, while you appear to be a mere youth. I am Robert Dudley, Gentleman of the Privy Chamber to King Philip, who has an urgent need to travel to the Low Countries in order to suppress some uprisings there. He is no sailor, but he has the pleasantest of memories of crossing for his marriage to Queen Mary in a new carrack commanded by Master William Hawkins. He assures me that he is currently too busy building ships to be in a position to command one, but since King Philip wishes to cross to Antwerp by the same vessel, he will make it available with either his brother or yourself in command.'

Francis's face lit up. 'You refer to the *Rose of Plymouth*, which is back in harbour here in Plymouth. Your master may board her once we have made the state cabin fit for his occupation.'

Dudley frowned. 'My master is currently in Portsmouth, where we were lately reviewing the troops that will land at Antwerp ahead of him, to clear his path. When do you expect the *Rose* to be ready?'

'Whenever you wish it to be,' said Francis. 'It merely requires your master to journey here.'

And so word was sent by fast horse to Portsmouth to make ready for travel, and a week later the *Rose* was mid-Channel, travelling east on a stiff westerly with Francis at the helm. After supper, and with Philip as usual at his prayers in the state cabin, Dudley wandered above decks and, for want of anything else to do, he stood beside Francis at the stern as they watched the lights of Calais drifting past on their starboard beam.

'I hesitate to calculate how many English lives have been lost defending that miserable town,' Dudley observed. 'And yet again it is under siege, this time from the Duke of Guise. By siding with Spain we have of course unleashed the French against us, and it is no doubt they who will be stirring the Dutch into rebellion, necessitating that my master look to his other Habsburg realms at a time when his queen needs him most.'

'There is word that she is once again with child,' Francis remarked, 'and England needs an heir. It is to be hoped that this new lying-in proves more productive than her last. Tell your master that I will hold the *Rose* in readiness for when word is sent from Antwerp that he judges the time right to return in order to be by her side.'

It fell quiet for a moment, then Dudley spoke again in a lowered tone. 'This is for your ear only, Francis, since it is important that you know. The queen may not be preparing for childbirth, but for death. It is unlikely that the *Rose* will be required for any return crossing other than mine.'

Francis was too stunned to reply, but Dudley continued.

'Queen Mary's physicians advise that there is some sort of blockage where there should be a child, although Her Majesty had not been so advised when we took leave of her. My master, whether out of grief, an inability to watch her further suffering, or for whatever reason, has chosen this time to see to his possessions in the Low Countries, but should the queen die while he is away, it is unlikely that he will be welcome back in England. However, I will need to make a speedy return, to be at the side of our new Queen, Elizabeth. Should you not be available by that time — and I understand that vessels such as this should not sit idly at their moorings — I will need to take the first available crossing to London.'

The crossing was completed uneventfully, and Francis set his sails to tack his tedious way back to Plymouth, mindful that under his feet was the current pride of the Hawkins boatyard. He therefore lost no time in completing the journey, and was about to hail William, who was standing watching their drift up the Sound, when John appeared from behind his brother with an excited expression on his face.

'I have something amazing to show you, Francis!' he yelled. 'And by the way, we have a new queen.'

As they hurried down Sutton Wharf, heading for the Hawkins' boatyard, Francis called out to John, who was ten yards ahead of him in his enthusiasm.

'Slow down, John! I'm still getting my land legs back, remember, and when you've seen one Hawkins carrack, you've seen them all.'

'It's not a vessel,' said John as they reached the entrance, 'although we have a new one of those as well. But what you are about to see will make a further fortune for us all!'

As they stepped into the semi-gloom, Francis's eyes rested on the massive wooden cradle that was supporting an enormous carrack nearing completion. He focused on the wide beam and the row of gunports just above the waterline, and he was mentally assessing how many cannon she would eventually boast, and how they might best be lowered below decks when John interrupted his thoughts. 'Well?' he demanded testily. 'Say something, if only to blaspheme.'

'She's amazing,' Francis murmured, 'and I was just wondering how to get the cannon on board her.'

Satisfied with his assessment, John led him back to the Hawkins family home. Once there, they sat down with William and the mother of the Hawkins brothers, Joan, to share a meal.

'John tells me that we have a new queen,' Francis commented as he helped himself to another slice of pickled fish. 'I assume that it's the sister of the last one?'

'Correct,' William told him. 'They say Elizabeth is comely, and as tall as most men, although very few have yet seen her, and the tales of her beauty come from tradesmen who saw her progress into London some weeks ago now. But it is also said that she is Protestant in her persuasion, so that should be an end to the burnings.'

'That will come as a great relief to my father,' said Francis, 'since he was ever fearful of being tied to a pyre and lit like a torch.'

'It's no joking matter,' Joan chided him as she reached over to place more wine in the centre of the table. 'I heard that it's the most horrible thing a person can ever witness, and it escapes me completely 'ow them what professes to love God can do such things to a fellow Christian. Your father's a brave man, to 'ave continued to preach in the English form, and you've hopefully inherited at least some of 'is stubborn courage.'

'Which brings us to the matter of the *Judith*,' said William. When Francis looked blank, William explained, 'Our new carrack — the one you saw earlier today. Named after my wife, which for once brought a smile to her face. She's ready for her sea trials, and in due course she'll be fitted out with cannon. We wish you to take her down the coast to Deptford and supervise the purchase and laying of eight pieces of ordnance.'

'While there, you should also seek out a man called John Dee,' John added. 'He's said to possess the art of charting

33

one's way by the stars, which we can add to what our father told us about trade currents that can be ridden all the way to the Americas, transporting blackamoors from the coast of Africa. We wish you to learn Dr Dee's secrets and bring them back in order to teach them to me.'

Francis looked uncomfortable as his eyes dropped to the board. 'You would trade in human souls?'

John smirked in reply. 'No more than your father has done these past few years.'

'That is not the same thing!' Francis protested. 'I will have none of it.'

'I don't recall offering you the opportunity,' John smirked again. 'There are already enough wealthy merchants in this town who have expressed a wish to invest in this latest venture. And, as we already advised you, we wish you to sea test the *Judith* and bring back both the cannon with which she will be armed, and the secrets that Dr Dee can impart to you regarding navigation by the stars.'

Relieved that he was not being asked to trade in human cargo, Francis's thoughts drifted to other matters that might keep him more humanely occupied. He looked across at William. 'Would it be in order for me to take the *Judith* across to Antwerp before I sail her into the Thames?'

William nodded. 'Of course — if anything, that would be preferable, since she will spend more time at sea. But think you of bringing back a cargo?'

'A human one, perhaps,' Francis replied, 'but not of the type that John has in mind. When I took that man Dudley to Antwerp some weeks ago, he spoke of the need for a swift return should Elizabeth become queen. If I lose no more time, I may place the *Judith* at his disposal.'

'Do that, and with our blessing,' William confirmed. 'The *Judith* should be in the water by the end of the week, and it wants only a crew.'

'Are any of the men from the *Rose* still in Plymouth?' Francis asked, and it was John who answered.

'There's one left, at least — name of Short. He was here earlier, looking for you and his next voyage. He's lodging at the Seamen's Rest, next to the Custom House.'

'Excellent!' said Francis. 'Jim Short will be just the man I need when it comes to arming the *Judith*. He's wasted on general deck duties, and he's a man after my own heart.'

'Talking of hearts,' said John, 'remember me to Mistress Gonson when you're back in Deptford, and assure her that I'm well on my way to my first fortune.'

5

Two weeks later, Francis strolled purposefully through the Place Hanséatique towards the office of the Harbourmaster of Antwerp, with Jim Short trotting behind him and assuring him that he didn't speak a word of either French or Dutch. There were several people seated on benches inside the front entrance, but Francis ignored all of them as he strode up to the front table, behind which sat a clerk. He then asked, in loud and carefully pronounced English, whether or not a gentleman from England called Robert Dudley was still to be found in the town, and whether or not he might be seeking an urgent passage back to London.

The man behind the bench looked blankly up at him, so Francis began yelling more loudly, using the simplest phrases he could conjure up. Following his fourth attempt with 'Dudley', 'Boat', and 'England', a man seated on the benches near the entrance called out to him.

'You seek Master Robert Dudley?'

Francis turned to address the man — a wealthy merchant, by the look of him — and nodded. 'Lord be praised that someone in this place speaks English! You know Dudley?'

'By sight only,' the man replied. 'But I can advise you that he took ship to London two weeks ago. We've been waiting for another vessel ever since that day, because he commandeered the one we had chartered, claiming that he did so in the name of Queen Elizabeth of England. That was several days before news came of the death of the late Queen Mary.'

'I thank you for that knowledge,' Francis said with a bow, 'even though I am now without the paying passenger I had been seeking.'

'But you have found two more, if you journey to London,' the man told him, and for the first time Francis noticed the frail-looking girl who was huddled at his side, pale and sniffling into a cloth. He raised his eyebrows, and the man introduced himself.

'I am John Newman, bookseller, formerly of The Fleet, and more recently La Place du Valois, here in Antwerp. This is my daughter Mary, who enjoys indifferent health, as you can see. I wish to take her back to abide with my married sister in Chelsea, where the country air may benefit her delicate constitution.'

'Might I enquire why you left London in the first place?' Francis asked suspiciously.

Newman shrugged helplessly. 'My books are those of the Protestant and Reformist persuasion,' he explained, 'and the London of Queen Mary was not a safe place to conduct such a trade. Here in Antwerp they are less inclined towards Old Church bigotry. But now that Elizabeth is our queen, it is said that such persecutions will cease. Moreover, there are rumours that the Spanish King Philip's grip has tightened over the Netherlands, and that Protestants may expect to be rooted out and put to the question. I must also consider my daughter Mary, who would not survive one day without my wealth and my loving concern for her welfare. If you will convey us to London, you may name your price.'

Never one to take advantage of those at his mercy, Francis agreed a moderate fee for the two passages, and gave his own stateroom on the *Judith* to the father and daughter. But the girl, for all her delicate health, seemed determined to expose herself to the elements in order to savour the experience of being on board a vessel crossing a rough sea. Francis handed over the helm to Jim Short as he stepped down onto the main deck to assist the poor girl, who was heaving her meagre breakfast onto the planking.

'You should perhaps go below, mistress,' Francis suggested gently as he placed a comforting arm across her shoulders.

Mary looked up at him. 'It's worse down there, since the air is so still and confined. I'm sorry for throwing up on your beautiful vessel.'

'Think nothing of it,' Francis assured her, 'since even the hardiest of sailors sometimes do it. But they find it more convenient to do so over the side, and into the sea. Is this your first ocean crossing?'

'The first I can remember,' Mary replied. 'My father tells me that I was a girl of but four years of age when we came out from London, but I have no memory of it, since I was — or so I am told — somewhere below the deck, asleep in my mother's arms.'

'Your mother is no more?' Francis asked gently.

Mary's eyes began to fill with tears as she shook her head. 'The fever took her two winters ago. Her name was Catherine.'

'And you will be living with your aunt when we reach London?'

'So my father tells me. I have never met her, but I'm told that she has a fine house with servants, and that her husband, my uncle, is a brewer of ale. Perhaps I shall be put to work serving customers in their ale shop.'

'If they are anything like the ones that sailors frequent, then it is to be hoped not,' Francis replied kindly. 'Do stay here while I bring you some bread and wine.'

'I will only throw it up again,' Mary protested, and Francis gave in to the urge to tousle the fair hair that was peeking out from under her tightly fastened bonnet.

'Take the advice of an old sailor, Mistress Newman. It is far better to throw up when there is something down there waiting to come up than it is to do so on an empty stomach.'

'You are not so old,' said Mary. 'But you are very kind, like my father. God shines through your eyes.'

As Francis stepped onto the harbour wall at Deptford, the reflection of the sun's dying rays from the west bounced off the mullioned windows of the building that served as a residence and an office for Navy Treasurer Gonson. He sought admittance, which was quickly granted.

Inside the main hall, where a fire had been lit against the impending evening chill, he was welcomed by Ursula Gonson as she bustled into the room with a swiftness of gait that took Francis by surprise. His face presumably registered that, because Lady Gonson grinned broadly as she held out a warm hand in welcome.

'Master Drake, your return will be well received by my husband. He tells me how much he hopes to advance the cause of England's naval supremacy through your skills and contacts, and he has never been known to tell untruths about anything concerned with his work for the nation. Unlike what he tells others about *me* — you were advised that I was in delicate health, were you not?'

'Not I,' Francis conceded, 'but my cousin John Hawkins was left with that belief, certainly.'

Ursula clicked her tongue. 'This may explain why Master Hawkins has not seen fit to grace us with a return visit. My poor daughter is beside herself with apprehension, in case his heart has wandered elsewhere.'

'She may rest assured that it has not,' said Francis. 'Were it not in connection with so gracious a young lady, his constant chatter regarding his hopes to marry Mistress Katherine would drive his listeners to distraction.'

'This is all to the good, since we must lose no time in arranging the wedding, before my dear child explodes with the sheer tedium of waiting.'

'But John has not yet made his fortune,' Francis reminded her, 'and my return to Deptford is partly in connection with that.'

Ursula gave him a penetrating look. 'As the daughter of the Treasurer to the Navy, Katherine is of course a considerable catch. She regrets her mendacity where your cousin is concerned and were he to sail back up the Thames tomorrow, he could claim his bride with our blessing, and to Katherine's rapturous delight.'

'I regret that it will be some time before I can return to Plymouth with those glad tidings,' Francis said, frowning. 'I must secure cannon for the new ship that lies moored in the Strand out there, after I disembark my honoured passengers and seek a wherry to convey them down to the nearest river steps to The Fleet.'

'And who might your passengers be?'

'A former London bookseller, lately returned from Antwerp, along with his daughter, a girl of fifteen or so years. Name of Newman, as I recall.'

'They shall be welcome to take supper here with us,' Ursula enthused. 'We receive so few visitors who are not sailors, and it will be a welcome distraction for me to be able to converse with a man of letters, rather than a promoter of naval warfare.'

Ursula lived up to her own expectations as she dominated the conversation around the supper table to such an extent that John Newman was almost overcome by her enthusiasm for the written word. He had already agreed to remain in Deptford for a few days with a view to seeking a site for a new bookshop before the first course had been replaced with fresh salvers of cold meats and freshly baked loaves. Francis had devoted his time to encouraging young Mary to eat something, if only to build up her strength, and felt himself falling into the role of a solicitous older brother as he carved lean slices from the roasts, placed them on her dish and gently insisted that she eat.

As the meal came to an end, and the servants began removing the salvers, Mary placed a small, cool hand in Francis's, thanked him profusely for what she called his loving friendship, and kissed him demurely on the cheek before retiring to her chamber for a long sleep. Ursula insisted on sending for a chart of the local area beyond the docks, from which John Newman might identify a possible street for his bookshop, once his many boxes of them had been offloaded from the *Judith* and transferred into storage on the dockside. This left Francis and Sir Benjamin Gonson free to discuss the real reason for Francis's return.

'I have been sent to load cannon onto the specially constructed gun deck of the *Judith*,' Francis announced, 'but before I do that, I need further training in their use by your man Innes. I must also seek training for my second-in-command, Jim Short, who I suspect will be the man left to fire them, should that ever be required.'

'If he possesses half your natural ability and instinct in that regard,' Gonson smiled back over his port, 'then Master Innes will be only too happy to oblige. He was most impressed and urged me to take you into the service of Her Majesty's Navy as a gunnery officer.'

'A flattering gesture only, I fear,' Francis blushed. 'And if the truth be known, the thought of such explosive devices upon a delicate wooden structure holding so many men sends chills of apprehension down my spine.'

'This is as well,' said Gonson, 'since we lose too many men and ships through disregard for the basic precautions, and lack of respect for ordnance. If you are free to recommence your acquaintance with culverins, I shall make Master Innes available tomorrow, for as long as you require his wisdom and experience.'

'There is also the matter of loading the guns down onto their deck,' Francis reminded him. 'You presumably have the means to do this, here at Deptford?'

'It would be a poor naval dockyard if we did not,' Gonson replied. 'I'll have the pulleys drawn alongside, and the cannon and their shot brought down from the foundry. There is no need for any payment, since my arrangement with Master Hawkins Senior is that he will defray the cost of building your vessels, and Her Majesty will arm them at her expense. Hawkins may keep the profit from his brother's voyages, and Queen Elizabeth will acquire a new navy at no cost to the royal purse. I am happy to be this conduit between Her Majesty and the Hawkins family, since my wife assures me that we shall shortly become related by marriage.'

'I will undertake to bring my cousin back without delay,' said Francis, 'in return for your effecting an introduction to a Dr Dee, who I am advised has a system of navigation that relies upon the charting of the stars. Or was someone jesting?'

Gonson chuckled. 'There are some who regard John Dee as a harmless old halfwit, but it is said that his ability to predict the future is relied on as much by our new queen as it was by her sister. And it is true that he claims to be able to employ the stars in the firmament as an aid to navigation of the ocean. But you should be warned that he also claims to have communicated with the God Apollo.'

'I would still meet with him,' Francis insisted.

'And so you shall,' Gonson reassured him, 'but you cannot later claim that I did not warn you, should he turn you into a toad or something.'

Francis winced as the final cannon was lowered through the hatch on straps attached to a pulley, and thudded heavily onto the wooden boards of the gun deck. The *Judith* sank even lower in the water, then rocked fore to aft as the culverin was trundled on its carriage into place behind the open gun port. Five hundred tons was definitely the minimum capacity for a carrack if it was to boast a complement of eight cannon — along with its accompanying case of balls and sack of gunpowder — while carrying any sort of cargo that would make a voyage financially worthwhile. He was making a mental note to discuss with William Hawkins the wisdom of going to seven hundred tons or more when Benjamin Gonson appeared at his elbow with a smirk.

'Your Court magician has arrived and awaits you in the hall, armed with charts and suspicious-looking equipment. Either he intends to teach you the science of navigation, or he is about to summon up the Devil. Either way, you are welcome to join him, while I ensure that these oafs we hire by the day do not breach this fine vessel of yours by their clumsy actions.'

Francis smiled to himself as he walked purposefully into the hall of the Gonson residence and announced himself to the strange-looking man who awaited him. John Dee wore robes that were emblazoned from shoulder to hem with symbols of the sun, moon, stars and cabalistic devices whose true import were presumably known only to members of the man's close circle of adepts. Dee gazed at him over a long white beard that was perhaps meant to impress, but succeeded only in making the learned old sage resemble a scholarly goat.

'You wish to learn the mysteries of navigation by the stars?' Dee asked. 'I was told that this was why I am summoned here.'

'Indeed I do,' Francis confirmed, 'since it is my chosen destiny to one day sail round the entire globe.'

'You do not share the lingering belief of some that the earth is flat?' Dee asked with a hint of mockery.

Francis shook his head. 'Were it so, then the oceans of the earth would have long since emptied over the sides.'

'An intelligent response,' Dee conceded, 'but if it is indeed round, then would the oceans not empty out even more quickly, down the sides? Have you ever wondered why this doesn't happen?'

'No, I merely rejoice that it does not,' said Francis.

Dee nodded towards a huge chart lying before him, all but covering the entire table. 'Are you familiar with the stars of the firmament?'

'I am when they give me light by which to sail close to shore and judge my distance by the glow from the breaking surf.'

'You sail by night on occasion?' Dee asked, clearly impressed. 'This takes both courage and skill, they advise me. I have also been advised that you are one of the best.'

'The flattery would be welcome, were I not about to display my total ignorance of matters of which I have no experience,' Francis replied ruefully.

Dee pointed a bony finger down at the chart on the table. 'Behold the stars in the firmament, which for our purpose may be regarded as fixed. I am of course aware of the opinions of those who argue with the Bishop of Rome regarding the movements of the planets around ours, but we may discount those for the purpose of your education today.'

The reference to 'the Bishop of Rome' alerted Francis to the fact that he was dealing with either a hardened Protestant or a doubting Atheist, but either would suit his purpose, so he simply nodded and tried to look alert as he fixed his eyes on the chart. Then, to his surprise, Dee asked him to look up at the ceiling.

'Pick some feature on the vault above you — some prominent knot in the wood, or some point at which the beams intersect with each other — then fix your eyes on it and walk slowly towards it. Then tell me how it appears, to your untutored eye, to change in appearance as you do so.'

Francis did as instructed and stopped immediately under the large joint between a heavy 'down' beam and one of the 'stretchers' that ran across it. From behind came the enquiring voice of his tutor.

'How has the point you selected changed, to your eyes?'

'Clearly, I am much closer to it,' Francis replied, somewhat at a loss to understand how this might be significant.

Dee chuckled knowingly. 'How can it be closer, when the distance between the floor and the ceiling has not varied between the point at which you began your walk, and the place where you now stand?'

'I have become closer to it by walking along the floor, obviously,' Francis replied, wondering if perhaps his visitor really was as disordered in the mind as some contended.

'You would therefore concede that while progressing along what we mathematicians call a horizontal plane, your vision of something that remains at a fixed height above you in its opposite, or vertical, plane, somehow seemed to change?'

'Did I not just say so?' Francis countered, now becoming a little irritated.

Dee invited him to return to the table and pointed down at the chart. 'Welcome to what the Greek scholar Euclid named "geometry", Master Drake. Now, regard this chart of the stars, which I already postulated must be regarded as fixed where they appear to us as we look up, in the like manner of that fixed point in the ceiling that you followed with your eyes a moment ago. So we may regard the sky, with its stars, as our ceiling, yes?'

'Yes,' Francis agreed, already beginning to feel like his five-year-old self back in the schoolroom in Tavistock.

'And the ocean on which you sail may be regarded as your "floor", even though it moves up and down?' Dee persisted, and again Francis conceded the point.

'So, as you sail towards this fixed star in the firmament, your view of it will alter, in the like manner of your view of your point on this ceiling a moment ago?'

'Yes, but...' Francis began, then stifled his objection when the old man raised his hand in a gesture for silence. 'One more question, then you may engage me in debate. Do you by any chance recall what happened to your head as you walked towards your fixed ceiling point?'

'I was hardly well placed to view my own head,' Francis replied testily.

'You may take it from me that it slowly moved back on your neck, as the relative positions of your eyes and the object changed through the horizontal plane. You may not have been able to see it, but would you concede that in order to see something immediately above your head, you must tilt your head backwards, whereas from a distance you need only raise it slightly? And that in order to see something on that far wall — one of those tapestries, for example — you need not raise your head at all?'

'So where does that leave us?' Francis demanded, resentful of the man's increasingly condescending manner.

'It leaves you with a stiff neck, and me with a proven point. That point being that as you walked towards the point at which your chosen object was immediately above you, the position of your head relative to your neck varied with each step forward. Put another way, one could tell how close you were getting to your target point by the position of your head.'

Francis's eyes began to widen as the first glimmer of understanding broke through, and Dee, encouraged, pushed home his point.

'The mathematician Euclid termed this relationship between your eyes and the chosen object an "angle", and he gave it mathematical values, which for the moment we need not concern ourselves with. But can you now see that the angle of your head towards the object will vary according to how close you have come to being immediately beneath it?'

'Yes!' Francis enthused. 'And the reverse must also be true — namely that I may judge how far away I am from being under a fixed point by the "angle" of my head!'

'Precisely!' Dee encouraged him. 'You can perhaps now see that if we assume a given star to be at a fixed point, we know how close we have come to the ocean beneath it by the angle at which we view it. It now only needs you to become familiar with the positions of each of the stars, relative to the land that you are seeking to journey to, and you can calculate how close you are coming to it.'

'Does every land on earth have a star conveniently shining above it?' Francis asked eagerly.

Dee shook his head. 'It is to be regretted that it is not that easy. You sailors normally follow a coastline, do you not?'

'We do indeed,' Francis confirmed, 'since without being able to see the land on our beam, and without charts to advise us of the name and location of what we can see, we would be lost.'

'So were you to sail out into the middle of the ocean, with no land in sight, you would have no idea of where you were?' Dee persisted.

Francis nodded. 'That is why so few of us venture to cross open ocean in order to visit the Americas. But if you can show me on this chart of yours which star to follow, this would make the crossing that much easier.'

'To the best of my knowledge, there are no charts showing where all the lands of the earth lie,' Dee advised him. 'Without knowing where the lands lie, how can I locate any stars above them?'

'But if I were able to supply such charts, and if, in addition, I could advise you of how many days of sailing it took to reach each new land I discover, you could allocate a star to follow?'

Dee's smile of superiority turned to one of pleasure. 'I believe that between us, Master Drake, we could open up the entire world to English navigation.'

'Only English?' Francis cautioned. 'What is to prevent the Spanish or Portuguese making use of our discoveries?'

'That is for you to ensure. Her Majesty trusts not the Spanish — or, for ought I know, the Portuguese — so when and if we complete our joint venture to chart the entire world, we must keep it close to ourselves.'

Francis nodded towards the chart on the table. 'I shall begin with the Americas — do you have a suitable star to assist in that, at least?'

Dee picked up a long, pointed rule that he had earlier propped against the side of the table, and pointed to something in the centre of the chart. 'You see this collection of stars that most resembles a serving spoon? It is known to those of us who make a deeper study of these things as "Ursa Major". We calculate that the one furthest to the left must be halfway down the great ocean that divides us from the Americas, which are said to be vast and cover most of the globe from north to south. If you set your eyes upon that, and wait until it is immediately above you, then turn to the west, you will almost certainly be destined to reach the far shore.'

'This will be fine enough by night,' Francis pointed out, 'but by day?'

Dee gave him another schoolmaster's smile. 'Where does the sun set daily?'

'To the west — everyone knows that,' Francis replied, and then he comprehended. 'Of course — I simply follow the sun by day, and this star of yours by night?'

'Exactly,' Dee confirmed, 'but I have not yet fully explained how you may use this star to the fullest advantage.' He picked up a curious implement that resembled a spy glass mounted on a horse's bridle.

'If you look through this small glass object, then raise the piece of metal on which it sits until the star comes into view, you will note a number exposed to view on the metal. You need not concern yourself with the mathematics involved and must pay attention to only two of these numbers. When you are a third of the way towards being immediately below the star, the number shown will be fifteen. Then, when two-thirds of the way there, the number you will see will be thirty. But always remember that being underneath this star will tell you only that you have travelled far to the south, and may then turn west for the Americas. It will not tell you how far away they are, because I have not yet been advised which of these stars sits above them. Perhaps you might bring me back this knowledge, in return for the valuable lesson I have imparted this day and the gift of this sighting device.'

'I shall not fail to do so,' Francis assured him, as he looked proudly down at the strangely shaped device that he was probably the only sailor in England to possess. Placing it carefully inside the small felt bag that Dee also handed him, he thanked the old man for sharing his precious learning. He then made his farewells before walking back outside to the Strand and seeking out Jim Short, who had been undergoing his first gunnery training.

'How went it?' Francis asked of a white-faced Jim, who grimaced.

'They're deadly, and I'm not sure we should be taking them aboard a ship.'

'Such a pity,' Francis teased him, 'since I was hoping to make you my master gunner. Perhaps, upon our return to Plymouth, I might ask Billy Marley if he wants the rank.'

'I didn't say as 'ow I wouldn't do it,' Jim hastened to explain as he rose to the bait, 'just that you 'as to be careful where you puts that there gunpowder, an' where you fires them there cannon.'

'Hopefully you'll never have occasion to learn,' Francis chuckled, 'but if the culverins have all been lashed down securely, and the *Judith* is fully provisioned, we must lose no time in taking the benefit of the tide and returning to Plymouth.'

Several hours out from Plymouth on their return voyage, they dropped anchor in mid-channel. Having carefully ensured that there were no passing vessels, Jim was allowed to select three men and take them down onto the gun deck, where shortly afterwards the ship was rocked in the water by the recoil from three explosions, as heavy shot skidded across the wave tops before sinking from sight.

'Maybe that weren't ser bad after all,' reported a proud Jim, flushed in the face.

Francis ordered the helmsman to turn to starboard as he stood on the high stern deck and studied the coastline carefully for the tell-tale sight of surf breaking on the headland that marked the eastern approach to Plymouth Harbour.

'Was that you playing with your new toy, or are we being invaded?' asked John as he helped Francis ashore.

'They are now your toys,' Francis told him, 'since they lie in the *Judith*. I must speak with William without delay, since the need to carry ordnance has greatly reduced her capacity, and his next carrack must be a minimum of six hundred tons in deadweight. But before the pair of you get your hands dirty with that, you must travel with me back to Deptford.'

'Out of the question,' John protested. 'I have investors lining up eagerly for my first voyage in the *Judith*, and they grow impatient to double their investments.'

'There is also a young lady in Deptford impatient to become your wife,' Francis replied. When John looked both puzzled and elated at the same time, Francis explained how the Gonson family had merely been testing his resolve, and that Katherine could become Mistress Hawkins whenever John could be bothered to lift his thoughts above keels and gun decks.

51

The news was greeted with genuine delight in the Hawkins household, and Joan was particularly enthralled by the prospect of another woman in the house, given that her older son William had established his own family in a cottage in nearby St Budeaux. Joan therefore excitedly demanded that her second son John make his married home with her in the old family house in Plymouth, so that Joan might at long last have a daughter-in-law and grandchildren to keep her company.

Judith's petulant reaction to the news of John's impending wedding in Deptford was to forbid William to attend, and an embarrassed but anxious John was obliged to ask Cousin Francis to act as his groomsman and chief witness. Francis agreed without hesitation, since he would welcome a further opportunity to obtain training in gunnery and navigation at the Royal Dockyard. Suitable communication was sent to London by fast horse, and two weeks later the *Judith* set sail once more, mooring in Deptford Strand. John was barely off the side of the vessel onto the wharf before he was bundled into a warm embrace by Katherine Gonson. This was accompanied by urgent advice that their wedding day was only three days away, and a demand to know why it had taken him a further two weeks to follow up his letter of proposal with a personal appearance.

Francis was still wiping the smirk from his face as he looked up and saw John Newman and his daughter Mary approaching, accompanied by Benjamin and Ursula Gonson. As the distance between them narrowed, Mary Newman slipped from her father's side and raced towards Francis, skidding to a halt and grabbing his hand.

'Katherine says I can be her maid of honour, and since you're to be the groomsman for the groom, that means we have to walk down the aisle hand in hand, doesn't it?'

'Please forgive my daughter her forward manner,' John Newman said with a smile that eliminated any possibility that he might be annoyed by it. 'She falls too heavily under the influence of the bride-to-be, I fear.'

As they sat at supper, Francis learned that during his absence Katherine and young Mary had become almost constant companions. Mary had even been afforded her own room in the Gonsons' home in Deptford. John Newman was on the point of opening the new bookshop in nearby River Lane, and since this occupied not only all of his time and attention, but also Ursula Gonson's, the two distracted parents were content for each of the young ladies to act as a companion to the other, despite their age difference.

'I would deem it a great favour if you would undertake the role of protector of my somewhat precocious daughter when she journeys south to Plymouth as companion to the new Mistress Hawkins,' John Newman announced out of the blue.

Francis shot a startled look across the table at John, who blushed.

'Forgive me, Francis, but we had only settled on Plymouth as our married home shortly before supper commenced, and I had no time to mention it. However, I was unaware that Mistress Newman was to accompany us.'

'We have become the dearest of friends, as you have learned,' Katherine Gonson reminded him. 'Since John advises me that he fully intends to desert me almost as soon as we have made our new home, in the hope of finding his fortune in foreign parts, we had hoped that you would be our protector in his absence, Francis. Master Newman also advises that the sea air will be good for Mary's health.'

'I had rather hoped to sail with John myself,' Francis objected as the colour rose in his face. He checked himself as he felt a soft, cool hand slip into his on the tabletop.

'You would not leave us unprotected, would you?' Mary wheedled as she gazed up at him adoringly with wide brown eyes, forcing a smile to Francis's face.

'How could I resist such a plea?' was all he could manage, as he struggled to understand how such a small creature as Mary could so melt his resolve to go to sea on his first great voyage, putting his new knowledge of navigation to the test.

It was all decided before the board was cleared. In the excitement of discussing the arrangements for the forthcoming wedding ceremony in the local parish church of St Dunstan in the East, Francis all but forgot his ambition to be a sailor.

The wedding was celebrated with all the dignity consistent with the bride being the only daughter of the Treasurer of the Queen's Navy, and two days later Francis held out his hand in a gallant gesture to assist Mary Newman on board the *Judith* as she wiped a solitary tear from her eye after bidding her father farewell. He looked into her eyes enquiringly.

'I had expected more tears, mistress.'

She looked up at him knowingly as she held on to his hand. 'Why tears, when I am going to a better life? I long to see Plymouth and make my new abode with a new friend and amidst a new family. Here in London my life would be dry books, dirty streets and smelly lodgings, whereas by the sea I will enjoy ruder health and may find a strong, seafaring man to be my husband.'

'Take my advice, mistress,' Francis told her as he finally freed his hand from hers. 'The life of a sailor's wife is a lonely one, with no guarantee that his latest voyage will not prove to be his last.'

'And how many sailors' wives have you spoken with?' Mary challenged him. 'For that matter, you have no wife of your own, so whose wife has been complaining to you of her loneliness? And it is to be hoped that you did not take advantage if she did.'

Francis's blushes were spared by the shouted command from John on the afterdeck that the deckhands should push the *Judith* back from the wharf, while the oarsmen in the naval cutter took up the strain and eased her out through the Middle Watergate and into the mid-channel of the Thames. Here John proudly spun the wheel as the outgoing current caught her stern and she began to ease downriver, to the faint cheers of the farewell party whose waved kerchiefs rapidly faded from sight. As they passed Canvey Island on the port beam, the order was given for the mainsails to be unfurled. Francis sighed with pleasure as he felt the familiar lift under his feet when the *Judith* responded to the westerly and lifted her bow, almost in a further salute.

Late the following afternoon, John handed the helm over to Francis and stood at the bow with his arm around Katherine, the two of them dodging the occasional spray while John pointed out the coastline features that they were following on their way to their new home. Mary slipped from Katherine's side and came to stand next to Francis.

'They wish to be alone, I suspect, so you will have to make do with me as your companion.'

'I don't need a companion in order to steer this ship into Plymouth,' Francis told her. 'Just a little peace and quiet, so that I may concentrate on following the navigation channel.

That is assuming that you don't wish us to run aground and be cast into the ocean.'

'When you next go to sea, may I come with you, to preserve both of us from loneliness?' Mary asked innocently.

Francis looked indulgently back down at her. 'At the helm of an ocean-going vessel, with the fate of thirty or forty men in your hands, one has little opportunity to be lonely. And are you not supposed to be acting as a lady's maid to the new Mrs Hawkins, or something?'

'I'm her companion, not her maid,' Mary pouted.

'Even so,' Francis went on, 'it will not be your part to be crossing the ocean like a common sailor. And there are some who say that it brings bad luck to a vessel to have a woman aboard.'

'Yet you have two,' Mary replied. 'Do you not believe the superstition?'

'It does not apply to passengers, in my experience, unless they distract you from your navigation,' Francis replied pointedly, and Mary finally took the hint and went below.

The entire Hawkins household was assembled at Sutton Wharf once word came to Plymouth that the *Judith* had been sighted off Salcombe Head, tacking for the incoming passage up the Sound. They waved and shouted a greeting, silhouetted against the setting sun. Francis stood back while John guided his new wife up the rope steps onto the mossy quayside, where she was immediately smothered by his mother Joan and introduced to the family servants one by one. Once Francis had seen to the fore and aft moorings, he looked round for Mary, who had been sitting on a coiled rope amidships. He held out his hand, which she grabbed eagerly as he hoisted her onto the rope ladder. Francis climbed up after her to find that she had already been introduced to Joan, and was eagerly enquiring whether the somewhat elderly head of the family would teach her how to cook. Joan looked across at Francis with a grin.

'You've brought me a right bright 'un 'ere,' Francis. Do you want me to teach 'er 'ow to make your favourite cod pie?'

'Yes please — start with that!' Mary enthused, and Francis shook his head with a laugh.

6

'Are you sure you don't need lessons in navigation?' Francis demanded testily as he watched the last of the provisions being loaded into the *Judith*. Two other vessels were already at anchor in the Sound, awaiting the command to raise their anchors and take advantage of the outgoing tide.

John smiled. 'You forget that my father navigated the waters we'll be sailing when he made the first Hawkins crossing to the Americas some thirty or so years ago. He bequeathed me the charts from that voyage and took advantage of a trade current that is said to run all the way from Guinea or thereabouts. Once we find it, we follow it, and your pictures of the stars will not be required.'

Francis was still smarting from John's refusal to give him command of one of the accompanying vessels as he made his first voyage south. William was beginning to feel his years and wanted Francis by his side during John's absence, in order to assist with the construction of a six-hundred-ton carrack, and thereafter its provisioning with cannon. Added to this was the need for at least one man to remain in the principal Hawkins household as a protector of its three women: the elderly mother Joan, John's pregnant wife Katherine, and her somewhat lively companion Mary Newman.

Francis had faced a chorus of protests and objections when he announced his original intention to be part of the fleet, and he had eventually tired of raising arguments in his own cause as new reasons were advanced for why he should remain. The final one was that he was in no position to contribute finance towards the expedition that could have been provided three times over by local Plymouth merchants eager to buy into a new form of commerce. Deep down, although he would not admit it, Francis was also moved by Mary's wide-eyed pleas not to leave her at the mercy of the rough sailors of the town, given that William had to give priority to protecting his own household in St Budeaux. The same pleas had been voiced by Joan and Katherine, but somehow it had been Mary whose innocent appeal to his gallantry had finally won him over. Next time, perhaps he would go, but for the foreseeable future Francis would be helping to construct large carracks and making regular sailings back to Deptford in order to arm them, accompanied by Mary on visits to her father.

Almost a year later, Francis was pacing nervously up and down outside the Hawkins house as if he was the father to be, rather than Cousin John, who was God knew where when he was most needed by Katherine's side. Francis had been exiled to the rear garden while Joan, who vaguely knew what she was about, and Mary, who didn't have the first idea, fussed around Katherine as she moaned and swore through her first childbirth. It finally ended with a scream that could probably have been heard across the Sound a good mile away. Then it suddenly went quiet, and Francis said a silent prayer.

He opened his eyes to see Mary standing before him with tears rolling down her face.

'Is aught amiss?' Francis asked fearfully.

Mary shook her head and rushed into Francis's arms before he could hold her back. 'It was quite the most amazing thing I've ever seen — dear Katherine seemed to be in a good deal of pain, but then this little infant slid out, and she's now a mother. It's a boy, and they plan to call him Richard.'

'God be praised!' Francis murmured as he instinctively held Mary closer to him, and she rested her head on his chest.

'I think I'll be ready to have one of my own soon,' she announced.

'And your father would no doubt run through the man responsible,' Francis chuckled, 'given that you're still wanting sixteen years of age.'

'Women have babies at that age,' Mary insisted.

'Only married ones, and even then it tends to be a bit of a scandal. I know nothing about women and babies, but I've heard tell that a woman should be at least in her twentieth year before she has her first, and no older than forty when she gives birth to her last.'

'That doesn't give her very long,' Mary complained. 'I think I'd like to have no more than five. But I'll have to find a husband first.'

'Indeed you will,' Francis confirmed, as he pushed her gently away from him, 'and you're more likely to find someone of whom your father approves back in Deptford. Which reminds me — we're overdue another visit, and I have to take the *Solomon* for cannon before much longer.'

'Do you think my father will insist on choosing a husband for me?' Mary pouted. 'The only men I've ever met through his book trade were as dry as the parchment from which their books were made. I think I'd much prefer a sailor.'

'I warned you before about sailors,' Francis reminded her. 'And come to that, how many do you know? And of those, who — if anyone — would make you a suitable husband?'

'There's one,' Mary whispered as she stood on tiptoe, leaned forward, and kissed his cheek.

'Back into the house, and see what comfort you can bring to Katherine,' Francis instructed her firmly as he pushed her away again.

A few days later, Francis stood on the quayside of the inner dock at Deptford, where he was greeted by Benjamin Gonson.

'They tell me that I'm the grandfather of a healthy young boy,' Gonson observed sourly. 'At least, I am thus advised in my daughter's letter, and I suppose I must take comfort from the fact that I learned the glad tidings before the father did. Do you have any idea when — or indeed *if* — he'll be returning to us?'

Francis shook his head. 'These things are always in the laps of the Gods, as you must have known when you gave your consent to the marriage.'

Gonson shrugged. 'As I recall, I did not so much "consent" as give way to the insistent demands of my wife and daughter. I had hoped that Katherine would journey here with you, in order that we might at least hold the child before it grows sturdy enough to resist such things. However, enough of that — you are here for more cannon?'

'Indeed I am. The *Solomon*, as you can no doubt see for yourself with your experienced eyes, exceeds six hundred tons in deadweight, and she will be the new flagship of the Hawkins fleet. It is fitting that she be armed, since no doubt John will lose no time in heading back to sea in search of more riches, such is his nature. But before you chide his seeming unconcern for his new-born son, you should reflect that it is his wealth that finances the new vessels that carry Her Majesty's guns.'

'I made that very point to the queen on her recent visit here,' Gonson nodded. 'I argued until I was quite short of breath that we should be commissioning new warships, either here or at

Portsmouth. She replied that she had been reliably advised that her new merchant vessels could be turned into men-of-war at a moment's notice, and that we had no immediate cause to fear any foreign power.'

'The vessels, perhaps,' Francis conceded, 'but whence will come the men to command them? Experienced captains such as myself can cause ships to cross oceans, but we have no experience of battles at sea, hence my desire to learn all I may regarding the art of seaborne gunnery, which I may then pass on to the men who serve under me.'

'England is fortunate to have men such as you and my son-in-law,' Gonson said ruefully, 'but I begin to feel that my days as Navy Treasurer are limited. The Navy I knew and understood was a King's Navy that transported men-at-arms across the Channel, in the days when wars were fought on land, and ships were merely the means of transporting knights and their horses to the battlefields abroad. Then it became a matter of using ships merely for trade, and men forgot that an island nation such as ours requires ships for its protection. There are those who urge Elizabeth to look to the nation's defences against either France or Spain, but her response is ever that we have not the finances for a fighting Navy for as long as we cannot trade with the Americas, as Spain and Portugal do. Until someone persuades Her Majesty to invest in warships and men, we are doomed to be the paupers of the high seas. Ironically, the only one with such foresight among her closest councillors is her Master of Horse. Anyway, I digress. We must arrange for you to recommence your gunnery training under Master Innes.'

Francis paused briefly, then seized the moment. 'Might it be possible for me to hire some of your gunners for my own ships?' he asked tentatively. 'We shall soon have several heavy carracks armed with eight culverins apiece, which will remain just dead weights unless we have men skilled in firing them. I have so far only managed to pass on my knowledge to one of my senior crew, and he is doing his best to teach others, but it is a slow process. If I had dedicated gunnery officers, and not just boatswains with gunnery as a part-time distraction, I would feel more confident in our armed power.'

Gonson thought deeply for a moment, then looked enquiringly back at Francis. 'What if I were to allocate men on loan to you? Men who could teach your crews as part of their naval service, then return to Deptford when their mission is accomplished?'

'That would be an excellent arrangement,' Francis replied, and the two men walked back towards the Navy Treasury Building for an early supper.

7

Francis turned from watching the cannon disappearing below decks on the *Solomon* and walked through to the armoury yard, where Jim Short was in conversation with three men as they stood around a culverin in the centre of the dirt floor, with a supply of cannonballs around their feet.

'We're going out to sea, to do some *real* gunnery!' Jim enthused, and Francis smiled as he recalled Jim's original unwillingness to become involved with cannon aboard ship. 'This is Alan, an' the other's two's brothers — Tom an' Edward,' Jim continued. 'They bin sent to teach all the other blokes in our fleet 'ow to blow the enemy out of the water!'

'That's what I like to hear,' came a voice from behind, and Francis turned to welcome a familiar face.

'Master Dudley! Delighted to renew our acquaintance — do you require another passage to Antwerp? I went looking for you there after the old queen died, but I was informed that you'd already taken ship to England.'

There was only the hint of a smile as Dudley lowered his head in recognition. 'I am now *Sir* Robert Dudley, and the Master of the Queen's Horse.'

'Yet you come by barge?' Francis responded by way of a weak jest, then wished he hadn't as Dudley's face remained expressionless.

He nodded to the group of men in the centre of the dirt floor, on which the sun shone down in the absence of any roof to the armoury — or perhaps it had been blown off in an earlier mishap. 'How ready are these men to operate ordnance?'

'Three of them are master gunners already, or so Sir Benjamin Gonson assures me,' Francis told him. 'The ruddy-faced one with the hair that looks as if it was cut with a scythe is the boatswain of my vessel the *Solomon.*'

'She is your vessel?' Dudley asked.

Francis shook his head. 'I am merely her captain. The true owners are William and John Hawkins, my cousins from Plymouth. John is currently engaged in an expedition to the Americas.'

Dudley nodded, then invited Francis to walk with him out of the armoury, while Jim Short and his new-found companions prepared to put to sea for gunnery training.

'When do you expect your cousin John's return?' Dudley asked as they walked side by side along the wall that separated the Thames from the Dockyard.

Francis shrugged. 'Who can judge? He set sail for new lands and new fortunes. He may even have been attacked by Portuguese rivals.'

Dudley stopped suddenly and turned to face Francis. 'I know you are a man who can keep confidences, Francis, so I tell you privily that it is not the Portuguese you should fear. It is the Spanish.'

'Spanish or Portuguese, they both resent English traders travelling to the Americas, do they not?' Francis countered.

'But Philip of Spain has other causes to feel resentment towards England,' Dudley told him as he looked carefully around to ensure that they were not being overheard. 'Queen Elizabeth rejected his offer of marriage and is sending what assistance she can to the Dutch, who are seeking to overthrow Spanish domination in the Low Countries. We fear that the Spanish are planning to invade our shores in retaliation. The queen wishes us to have the means to resist them, but we as a nation do not have the finance to equip a proper navy.'

'Gonson said nought about this to me, and he is the Navy Treasurer,' Francis lied tactfully.

Dudley's face set in a sneer. 'Sir Benjamin belongs in a former age, Francis, when our enemy was France, and his ships were used solely to transport armies. He has taken ill to the modern way of firing ordnance from below decks in order to sink foreign vessels. He has served England well, but he will soon need to be replaced, and we need as many armed ships as we can construct. Unfortunately, we have not the means to pay for these, hence the importance of the work that is performed in the Hawkins boatyard in Plymouth, the need for such wealth as John Hawkins can bring back from foreign parts, and the desire of Her Majesty to have men like yourself skilled in blowing enemy vessels clean out of the water.'

Francis let all that sink in before attempting to summarise it. 'So you need William Hawkins to build the ships, and me to arm them and convert them into floating fortresses, while John Hawkins lays the riches of the New World at the queen's feet?'

'You have the matter well within your grasp, Francis. But Her Majesty must not be seen to have a hand in your actions — any of you. If need be, she will deny that any of your deeds were conducted with her authority, in order to maintain what remains of our once good relations with Spain.'

'So she desires the spoils, but not the risk?'

Dudley's face darkened. 'Do not besmirch the loyalty and integrity of Elizabeth Tudor, Francis, or you will answer to me,' he hissed. 'We have been friends since childhood, she trusts me in everything, and you may rest assured that what I put to you is designed for the greatest benefit of England, which is Her Majesty's only concern.'

'I meant no disrespect,' Francis hastened to reassure him. 'I merely express my concern that my cousins are required to hazard their own fortunes, but bring the spoils back to share with the nation. It is the normal way of things for the profits of any overseas venture to be shared with its investors, who are the ones taking the risk.'

'Think you that Elizabeth is so grasping?' Dudley frowned. 'My reason for calling upon you today is to convey you to Greenwich, there to take command of perhaps the largest vessel you have ever sailed in. She is called the *Jesus of Lubeck*, she is some seven hundred tons in deadweight, and she boasts twenty cannon. She came to England as a gift to the late King Henry, and she is currently coated in barnacles. She probably requires much other work done on her besides, but she is yours to command. You are to take her westwards in search of the fabled riches of the Americas, and she will be the queen's contribution to the next Hawkins venture. Her Majesty requires a one-third return of any profit, which will be converted immediately into finances for more ships like the *Jesus*. These will of course be commissioned from the Hawkins yard.'

Later that day, Francis stood awestruck by the magnificence of the giant carrack with which he had been entrusted. Then his brain began to race through the many matters that needed to be organised if the *Jesus* was to be transferred to Plymouth. Dudley had departed after instructing the Greenwich dockmaster that Master Drake had the queen's authority to commission such work as might be required.

The barnacles were completely removed from the ship's hull two days later by a team of day labourers hired from the murky streets that lay behind the docks. She was then re-caulked, fitted with new sails, and provisioned for five days, which by

Francis's estimation would be more than enough time to run her down the coast to Plymouth. Only then did it occur to him that he required not only a crew, but also some means of returning the *Solomon* to her home port.

His ultimate solution was to leave the *Jesus* where she was, and return to Plymouth in command of the *Solomon* in order to await John's return. After that, they could return to London with a fresh crew as additional passengers who could then take the *Jesus*, under John's command, back to their home port in preparation for a fresh voyage of discovery and acquired wealth. This was, of course, assuming that John was still alive, wherever he might be now. Francis's thoughts drifted to other vessels lying at anchor or tied up on the wharves at Plymouth, and another idea began to form.

8

Mary Newman was led to the ladder by her father, and Francis took her hand to help her down the several rungs to the deck. She smiled just before he was about to let go of her hand, then kissed him warmly on the cheek before glancing back up to make sure that her father had been watching. Then she imitated a flounce of sorts before heading down the gangway to the captain's cabin, carrying her clothing bag.

Francis put her out of his mind as he supervised the several delicate processes that took the *Solomon* out into the mid-Thames ebb current, then he turned her stern-on to the stiff breeze and ordered full sail. Avoiding the occasional sandbanks that lurked only a few feet below the falling water level, their presence betrayed by the whirling eddies just above them, he only relaxed when the *Solomon* had cleared Margate on her starboard beam, and he had pointed her bow well clear of the treacherous Goodwins. The wind was westerly, so he set a long tack to port with his eye on the cliffs of Cap Gris Nez, smiling as he always did at the memory of the day he had saved the *Bonaventure*, which he regarded as his first day as a true mariner. Once he had cleared the Cap, he could take a long, slow reverse tack towards the far-off Lizard, ahead of which lay Plymouth and home.

Shortly afterwards, Mary appeared on deck, negotiating the regular rise and fall of the vessel with ease as she stepped up onto the rear deck and handed Francis a mug of cider. 'Didn't spill a drop,' she announced proudly as she reached into the pocket of her gown and produced some cold meat and bread, wrapped in a clean cloth. 'Let me know when you have a hand free from that wheel, and I'll give you your dinner.'

Francis laughed. 'I remember your first journey, from Antwerp, when it was I who brought you some bread and wine. It was all you could do not to throw up on my deck.'

'I was but a young girl at that time,' she reminded him, 'with a constitution born of the dust of bookshelves and the miasma of foul street alleys. Thanks to you and the good Plymouth air, I am today of much sturdier frame, and ready to begin the life of an adult woman in a man's world.'

'You are still barely sixteen,' said Francis, 'and yet your father advises me that you have adopted the air of a lovelorn woman lost in romantic dreams. If some man has captured your affections, you must advise me, in order that I may warn him against mistreating you in any way.'

'You need have no fear, big brother,' she giggled gleefully, 'since he who has captured my heart cares not for women, for all that I am aware. I just hope that he does not prefer boys, because if so he will be foregoing such a flood of passion that would drown him faster than the ocean that he ploughs as his first love.'

'Very poetic,' Francis replied. 'You have clearly been reading quite the wrong sort of book.'

'In truth,' said Mary, 'I have no time for reading, since I am learning from Mistress Joan all that there is to be learned regarding the keeping of a fine house, so that the man I intend to marry will not be able to fault my skill.'

'You should also take instruction from William's wife, Judith,' Francis advised as the smile faded from his face, 'since she aye complains of the absence of her husband, and the difficulty of raising children alone. No doubt Mistress Katherine will be making the same complaint when we reach

Plymouth. She has a squawking infant and a husband who has been gone for over a year. That is the true nature of the life of a sailor's wife.'

'You have no urge to marry and have children?'

'I do not prefer boys, if that was the true import of your question.' Francis said as he summoned the sternest expression he could. 'It was, wasn't it, if truth be known?'

'Such conceit!' Mary replied mockingly. 'But that is at least one obstacle out of the way.'

'Out of the way of what, precisely?' Francis asked shakily.

Mary tapped her nose. 'Have no regard for the witless ramblings of a girl who, according to my father, is a "lovelorn woman lost in romantic dreams". And since you appear not to be hungry, I'll leave this food down on the deck, for when you have a hand free. When you have *two* hands free, ask again regarding where my lovelorn thoughts are fixed.'

With that, she strode sedately back down to her cabin, leaving Francis's mind in such a turmoil that for once he failed to note the passage of Cap Gris Nez. He only noticed when it lay far behind them in the misty spray. Quietly cursing himself for being so easily distracted, he turned the wheel gently to starboard and set a course for Plymouth.

Francis gave a cry of delight several hours later as he had the *Solomon* towed gently into a berth at the Hawkins quay, and he noted that the *Judith* was back at her mooring. He lost no time in ordering the crew ashore when they berthed, and he hurried, with Mary, through the back lanes that led to the Hawkins' house, where he and John embraced like long-lost brothers. John breathlessly recounted his adventures on the Western Ocean, and proudly announced that his investors would see a triple return on their original capital. But Francis could not help noticing the sour expression on Joan Hawkins's face as

71

she laid out the pewter dishes for supper, while Katherine sat, subdued, in a chair by the fire, nursing infant Richard, whose squirms and protests suggested that he'd prefer to be set free to crawl around the hearth.

The conversation around the supper table was stilted, and the reason for this swiftly emerged. Even though he had been back barely two weeks from his first expedition, John was already planning a second, much to the displeasure of the two women in his life.

It was only when he seemed to be running out of breath that Francis deemed the time appropriate to enquire after the health of William and his family, but John seemed incapable of diverting his thoughts to anything other than ocean-going vessels.

'Wait until you see the *Pelican*, Francis!' he shouted. 'She's smaller than the *Solomon*, and only takes three hundred tons, but she's faster than any other vessel on the water, and she could take at least ten cannon, William reckons. Plus she has a massive afterdeck along Spanish lines, with two staterooms. She'd be ideal as an escort ship to the *Judith*, or even the *Solomon*. We can use the larger ships for the cargo, and the *Pelican* to guard them against Spanish or Portuguese resistance.'

'I almost forgot, in all this excitement,' Francis replied, 'that while in Deptford, I was visited by Robert Dudley, Master of the Queen's Horse. Her Majesty has this massive carrack berthed at Greenwich, which she wishes to loan to us by way of her investment in our next expedition. She's called the *Jesus of Lubeck*, and she has a deadweight of seven hundred tons with a fit-out of some twenty cannon. I promised to take you to collect her and bring her back to Plymouth, while I return with the *Solomon*.'

'In all this excitement,' Katherine muttered grumpily from John's side, 'do you bring news of the health of my father and mother?'

Francis's face reddened with his embarrassment at the rebuke. 'Yes, please forgive me — they are both well, and send their love. They are also looking forward to meeting their grandson ere too long.'

'If you are planning to sail back to Deptford so soon, John, in order to play with your new toy,' Katherine announced sourly, 'then I shall accompany you, along with your son. His name is Richard, in case you'd forgotten.'

It was John who broke the embarrassed silence as he turned back to Francis with raised eyebrows. 'You mentioned "our" expedition — do you wish to apply to join it?'

It was Francis's turn to regard John with a disgruntled stare. 'Do I have to make application, now that you've grown so wealthy and — it has to be said — so vainglorious?'

John nodded. 'I already have more would-be investors than I can possibly satisfy — including, or so you advise me, the queen herself.'

Francis's face grew red with displeasure. 'You will need captains for your escort vessels, and in particular this new one — the *Pelican*, did you say she was called? If she's meant to be your gunship, you also need men about you who can fire cannon, and I have lately become more skilled at that. I have also brought back with me three naval gunners who will be put to training our own crews in how to deploy shot against enemy ships. What did you discover that made your trade so profitable?'

'Where I landed, there were vast sugar plantations,' John replied. 'I also secured animal hides, and enough raw pearls to decorate the gowns of all the ladies at court three times over.'

'So I would captain this new vessel of William's when you next set your course to the south.'

'I shall require three hundred pounds,' John declared. 'It is the minimum share that I have been charging those merchants who have already signed up, and it is only meet that I ask that of you.'

'Even though I will be providing protection for your entire fleet?' Francis protested. 'You drive a hard bargain, cousin, but you shall have your three hundred. Now, if you would excuse me, the air in here proves not to my liking, and I will take a turn in the garden.' He made a point of closing the door unnecessarily hard as he disappeared from sight.

A few minutes later, as he paced up and down the grass, he saw Mary crossing from the scullery door to join him. He halted, but Mary simply smiled back at him reassuringly.

'Don't let me get in the way of you walking off your anger, Francis. And you have just cause to be angry. John has become an arrogant pig, and he treats Katherine and their child abominably.'

'Do you now believe what I tried to tell you about the perils of being married to a man whose first love is the sea?'

'That depends upon the man, and the woman who chooses to make her life with him,' Mary replied with a wisdom beyond her years. When Francis remained silent, she added, 'So you intend to become as bad as John, and desert us all, leaving the women in your life with no protector?'

'There's always William,' Francis replied weakly, not convinced that this was an adequate answer. 'But if we are taking Katherine to Deptford when we journey to collect the *Jesus*, will you not be accompanying her in order to be reunited with your father?'

Mary grimaced. 'For one, I ceased to be any companion to Katherine some time ago. She clearly regards herself as the second lady of this house, and is forever making disparaging remarks about Plymouth, and the London life she is missing. I fear that when John takes her back to that dreadful Deptford, she will insist on remaining there. For myself, my future lies here, in the refreshing salt air; were I to return to the world of books, dust and dirty back alleys, I would lose the robustness of constitution that I now enjoy. So go back to London, and I will await your return. But perhaps before you do, you should equip me with a sword and teach me how to use it, so that I may defend what you leave behind.'

'Perhaps I should,' Francis replied with a stern face, 'since once we return, we shall be planning our next voyage.'

'Can you raise three hundred pounds?' Mary asked.

Francis nodded. 'I have a vessel I can sell. It's high time I did, before the barnacles get her.'

'So you do not mean to profit from trading in human lives? You clearly recoil from such business, yet you intend to join with John — are you so eager to leave me behind?'

'No, Mary,' Francis replied as he took both her hands in his. 'I have, since I was a boy, dreamed of devoting my life to an exploration of all the oceans of the world, and I have joined forces with a wise old man in London who can assist me in charting them all, so that English sailors may rule the seas.'

Mary's face set in a determined effort to hide her disappointment. 'So any wife you may deign to take will be expected to wait here for you, as Katherine waits for John, giving birth in your absence, and measuring the passage of time by your departures and returns?'

Francis retained her hands in his. 'Yes, I suppose that is how it must be. Now do you wonder why I have not thus far thought of taking a wife? I would not subject any woman I loved to that sort of life.'

Mary leaned in and kissed him warmly and lingeringly on the lips, then broke the contact to look him up and down. 'You have also, it would seem, given no thought to whether or not a woman would accept you on those terms, regardless of your wealth. But I know of one such, and you need only ask. Now, let us return to the company, before they suspect us of something.'

Mary's gloomy predictions proved all too accurate when Katherine was back in the family home in Deptford. Her parents fussed over their new grandson and took him, along with his proud mother, on an almost regal tour of the houses of the nobility who they classed as their friends. It came as no surprise to John or Francis when Katherine announced her firm refusal to journey back to Plymouth, and instead insisted that John set about finding them a London residence appropriate for the daughter of the Navy Treasurer and her son Richard.

'Clearly you have some important matters to consider,' Francis told John as they strode aboard the deck of the *Jesus of Lubeck* for the tenth time in as many days. They surveyed her sleek lines with approval, prior to going down to inspect her massive holds that to Francis resembled merchant warehouses. 'Why don't you remain here for as long as married duty requires, while I take the *Jesus* back to Plymouth and arrange for new men to be hired and trained as gunners on the *Pelican*? You can follow in the *Solomon* in due course, and by the time you return I can have both vessels ready for our departure, along with the sister ship to the *Judith* that William told me would be ready for our return.'

'You forget the small matter of three hundred pounds,' John reminded him grumpily as he realised that Francis had rightly assessed his state of virtual house arrest in Deptford.

'That is not a sum that could be easily forgotten,' Francis assured him, 'and it is being held to my credit by Robert Bridges, the chandler who has that secure vault in Church Lane.'

'Who did you rob?' John asked.

'I've sold the *Bonaventure*.'

'And not before time,' John chuckled. 'She was becoming a nuisance, taking up one of our berths and growing barnacles. So, cousin — we finally set sail together in search of our joint fortune.'

9

By Plymouth standards it was a large crowd that gathered at the Hawkins quay to wish the flotilla of four vessels 'Godspeed' as they drifted down the Sound on the afternoon ebb tide. In the lead was the *Jesus*, with John proudly at the helm preparing to call for full sail once the navigable channel led them directly into the open sea. Behind her Francis had command of the *Pelican*, looking almost insignificant as she followed in the gentle wash of the *Jesus*, apart from the high poop that made her look more Spanish than English. The third and fourth vessels in the line were the *Solomon* and another heavy cargo vessel, the *Lady Joan*, both commanded by Plymouth men with years of service in Hawkins-built ships.

On the main deck of the *Pelican*, enjoying the last rays of the sun, were five men who were less experienced seafarers, although none of them was undertaking their first voyage. Each of them had been hired for a purpose that Francis was hoping would not be required, since they were the recently recruited gunners, Navy-trained and anxious to prove their worth should they be put to it.

Francis left the navigation of the outgoing channel to his tried and trusted boatswain Jim Short as he kept his eyes on the diminishing white flutter that was Mary's unfurled coif as she strained to keep the *Pelican* in sight in the fading light. Nothing had been said, but he had held her hand as they'd walked from the house to the quay. They had then shared a farewell embrace and a final kiss.

Francis was now cursing himself for not proposing to Mary on one of the many occasions when she'd left herself wide open to it. He could not bring himself to contemplate a situation in which he might be obliged to choose between a wife and family and the beckoning ocean, as seemed to be John's fate, but neither could he bear the thought that Mary might transfer her affection to another. They were likely to be separated for a year, such was the uncertainty of the events that lay ahead of them as they entered the open Channel, and set a course for Portugal on the first leg of their voyage. They did not intend to make landfall in Portugal, but John stoutly maintained that from a league off the entrance to the port of Lisbon he knew which course to set for Tenerife, using his father's old chart and his memory of the previous year.

As John ordered that the *Jesus* be moored at the governor's official wharf in Santa Cruz, while the other three vessels dropped anchor in the outer harbour, his smirk faded when he was informed, in the Port Office, that the previous regime with which he had done business had been replaced by a less corrupt one, and that he should lose no time in casting off back whence he had come, because the King of Spain had banned any form of trading with English mariners. John's plea that he was only there for fruit and fresh water fell on deaf ears, and it was a considerably deflated John who had himself rowed across to the *Pelican* to conduct a council of war with Francis.

'Where is the water held?' Francis asked, to which John replied that when he had filled the barrels of the *Judith* a year previously it had been from an enormous vat in the centre of Santa Cruz, to which fresh water was delivered by channels cut into the side of the surrounding hills in order to catch the rain as it fell, and from which it might be extracted by pulling one of several levers. After a moment's thought, a slow smile crossed Francis's face.

'From what is this vat constructed?'

'Some sort of mud, which has been allowed to bake hard like our crudest pottery.'

'So if it were subjected to a barrel of gunpowder, the entire town would have no water?'

'Indeed not,' said John, realising what Francis was planning. 'Get four men, arm them with pistols, and bring them with you in order to carry a keg of powder into the governor's office when we meet with him to argue the justice of our cause.'

Two hours later, after the governor had accepted the logic of their argument, the crews of all four vessels were detailed to fill the water barrels necessary to see them back across the Atlantic to the west coast of Africa. Meanwhile, Jim Short and Robbie Gregory from the *Pelican* were sent with coin into the marketplace, where a delighted street trader sold his entire supply of oranges before the heat of the day could begin to rot them. Then, with a cheery wave to the governor, and a rude message for King Philip of Spain, the convoy of English ships drifted out on the tide and set a course east-south-east to the aspect of the voyage that was niggling at Francis's conscience, but which he had to go along with.

The voyage back east to the African coast took a week longer than anticipated when the wind dropped. They were running low on fresh water when John raised the flag to indicate that all four vessels should drop anchor in the bay that he thought he recognised from a year previously. But the landing jetty was now a skeletal ruin, and the line of huts behind it had been replaced with what at first resembled a row of round haystacks, but which on closer inspection through an eyeglass revealed themselves as native huts constructed from some sort of bamboo. Francis looked on anxiously as John ordered the lowering of the cutter from the *Jesus*.

Francis called Jim Short, Job Hartop and Ralph Pendennis down to the gun deck, and gave them his orders in a quiet but firm series of commands. 'We line the *Pelican* up broadside to the beach, about five hundred feet out from the shoreline. The pitch should be about halfway up the barrel swivel, and we load Numbers One to Three. Jim, Job and Ralph, you man them in that order and load them ready, lining up with one of those native huts each. I'll bring down a lit fuse and hand it to each of you in turn. As soon as you get it from me, you light the touchhole then give me back the fuse, so that I can give it to the next man. If all goes well, we'll have three going off in turn, with a few seconds between each of them, and the natives will be looking for somewhere else to live. Any questions?'

Three slightly pale-faced men shook their heads, and ten minutes later three loud roars shattered the peace and quiet of the bay, and three native huts were blasted to shreds. One of them caught fire, and forty or so frantic natives began beating out the flames in order to prevent the conflagration spreading.

'Now what?' a triumphant Francis demanded of John, who was still aboard the *Pelican*.

John nodded towards the chaos on the foreshore. 'We take a dozen men, each carrying trading items, and each armed with a pistol, and we reinforce the terms of trade.'

'And if that fails?' Francis demanded, but there was no quelling John's elation at what he had just witnessed.

'Then we run like rabbits back to the ships and try our luck somewhere else.'

The cluster of armed men who waded ashore clutching clothing, cheap jewellery and old boots found themselves confronting a muttering, but clearly fearful, band of thirty or so Black warriors, minus their weapons this time.

Once they reached the compound, the crew members were instructed to lay all their trading goods in a large pile in front of the native chief.

'How much do you calculate you will receive?' Francis asked as they sat at supper in John's state cabin on board the *Jesus*.

'That will depend upon local trading conditions,' John told him, 'but the price we got in Plymouth for that last lot of sugar will make it all worthwhile, given the hold capacity of our four vessels. The Spaniards where we're heading seem to have slight regard for the stuff, and if they've had a rich harvest, they'll be only too glad to trade it to stupid Englishmen, and we should be able to get a favourable exchange. Hopefully we can buy a few raw pearls as well, using the English money I've brought with me, and thanks to current courtly fashion I'll be able to multiply my investment fourfold. We just have to hope that we get a better reception in Hispaniola that we've enjoyed in the other two ports of call.'

It wasn't native hostility that proved the problem at Santo Domingo, but a lack of fresh water. The whole of the island appeared to be suffering from a lengthy drought, and John was not prepared to risk the health of his men by taking into their barrels the muddy residue that was trickling down the mountain streams that ran through the wooded hillsides. To make matters worse, the genial (when suitably bribed) previous governor had been replaced by a younger, more ambitious man who advised them curtly that since the settlers for whose welfare he was responsible to King Philip of Spain were facing a drought, it would be more than his appointment was worth to allow English traders to take what little water was available.

When Francis appealed, in a mixture of English and sign language, to his humanity and his duty under God to fellow humans, the governor grudgingly suggested that they venture due south, where they would find the small Spanish colony at Borburata and might be blessed with fresh water in greater quantity.

Francis, commanding the *Pelican*, was assigned the vanguard role in the fleet, and he gazed in awe at the land that came slowly into view on their second day out of Hispaniola. He quickly realised that they had sailed through what was essentially an inland sea and had finally reached the fabled mainland of the Americas. It was with an already light heart that he saw the rain clouds ahead of him dumping torrential lines of water onto the wooded hills, down through which fast-flowing streams could be seen through his eyeglass.

Discretion being the greater part of valour, Francis agreed to hold the *Pelican* at anchor in the bay, along with the *Solomon* and the *Lady Joan*, of which he was given overall command. Meanwhile, John moored the *Jesus* along the inner dock of the small port, where she appeared massive and threatening compared with the humbler fishing boats that seemed to be the only other vessels in harbour. He then took a hundred or so men, recruited from all four ships, and marched them down to the governor's house, each of them waving a pistol in either hand, while for good measure Francis was instructed to fire a salvo of cannon shot into the low wooded slopes just outside the town, felling enough timber in the process to build an entire township. By the time that John arrived at the governor's front gate, the Spaniard had already signed a blank document granting trading rights, on this single occasion, to a group of mariners who were in danger of death by thirst if not allowed to load their barrels from a nearby forest stream.

Everyone was content for a few hours, until a new danger loomed from the open ocean.

They had just completed the final loading when they heard the sound of a ship's cannon, and John looked at Francis in alarm. 'Was that one of yours?' he asked.

Francis shook his head and nodded out to sea. 'It came from that,' he told John, and indeed the last few wisps of gunpowder residue could still be seen drifting over the waves in the outer ocean. A massive carrack the size of the *Jesus* was heading towards the remaining three English ships, back at anchor having taken their turn at mooring up in order to take on their precious supplies of water. It had clearly been intended as a warning shot, but all four vessels of their fleet were now in danger. Francis was about to take his cutter back to the *Pelican* in order to return fire if necessary, but John instructed him to remain and ordered the crew of the *Jesus* to climb back onto the harbour jetty, armed with everything they could lay their hands on.

To their considerable surprise and relief, the Spanish did not fire any shot beyond that first warning of their approach, but dropped anchor in the middle of the bay, blocking the *Pelican* where she sat. Then a procession of ship's boats were lowered, and some forty Spaniards were rowed ashore, led by a rotund man dressed as if he were being presented at the Spanish Court, in a garish red tunic with gold braid, topped off with a yellow bonnet. In broken English, he harangued the fifty or so English sailors standing around in a surly-looking group on the rickety jetty.

'Which is *el primero*?'

John and Francis exchanged puzzled looks, just as Don Angelo, the Spanish governor, came waddling down the quayside, sweating heavily and looking nervous. The Spaniard yelled furiously at him, and he paled as he looked across at John.

'He says, who is the leader of you?'

'That must be me,' said John, and a further exchange took place between the two Spaniards, at the conclusion of which Don Angelo addressed John again.

'He is Capitan Don Alfonso de Carrero, and he says it is not lawful that you trade here.'

John smiled as he replied, 'You had already advised us of that, but you traded with us nevertheless. The appropriate response from you now would seem to be to tell Capitan Don Alfonso de Carrero to blow his order out of his canary-coloured bonnet.'

A further bad-tempered exchange between the two Spaniards resulted in an order from the Spanish captain for the English to hand over the sugar that they had obtained, on pain of being arrested and taken back to Spain as prisoners. There was an angry muttering from the English sailors grouped behind John, who turned back to address them.

'I have reason to believe that none of you wish to either forfeit our booty or surrender as prisoners to this peasant. Am I correct?'

A rousing cheer confirmed that he was, following which John stepped forward, pulled the yellow bonnet from the captain's head and trampled it into the wet mud of the jetty. Ten minutes later there were three dead Englishmen, but over double that number of Spanish seafarers oozing their life's blood into the mud, and the remainder of the Spanish land crew raced for the safety of the mud huts and lean-to wooden sheds that constituted the harbour buildings of Borburata. The Spanish captain was badly wounded himself; he lay crumpled on the ground with several sword wounds to his torso, the blood from which was forming dark stains on his already red doublet. He raised one hand in a gesture of defeat, and spoke in a painful rasping voice to Don Angelo, who translated.

'He says he surrenders.'

'And what of his ship, which is blocking the departure of one of mine?' John demanded.

Following a further exchange, the governor informed them that the captain had made another obliging concession. 'He surrenders the ship also.'

'I wonder what cargo they're carrying?' Francis mused as he ripped off part of his shirt and tied it tightly around a flesh wound on his arm. That question was answered within the hour, as several chests of Spanish gold were transferred below decks on the *Solomon*. Francis watched the hatches being sealed.

'It seems to me, cousin,' he observed, 'that we may simply wait for more Spanish ships on their way over here — or perhaps on their way back to Spain. Either way, there is more to be gained from allowing the Spanish to bring their wealth to us once they have created it.'

10

Word had come back via a training ship in the Thames Estuary that the *Jesus* had been sighted off Margate, along with her escorting flotilla, with the *Pelican* in the lead as the spray broke over her bows. By the time the *Jesus* had been towed gently into a spare berth in Deptford Sound, a small crowd had gathered on the quayside. In its front row was a woman whose face was streaked with joyful tears as she clutched the hand of the tiny boy, who was demonstrating his newly discovered skill of standing upright.

John leapt onto the quay and raced forward to embrace Katherine as she flung her arms around him, shouted praises to God and pleaded for her husband's forgiveness for past cross words. Francis had already moored the *Pelican* and was looking out from the centre of the small group of onlookers, who were admiring her sleek lines and enquiring how she handled in mid-ocean. He imagined in how much he would cherish a welcome home like that from a young woman who was hopefully thinking loving and faithful thoughts of him back in Plymouth. As he continued to observe the happy couple, he noticed Katherine's face falling and caught John looking back over his shoulder to shake his head in Francis's direction.

'There is bad news?' he asked of John. 'Please God, nothing bad from Plymouth?'

'No, only here,' John reassured him. 'My father-in-law is laid low with an ague that has plagued him at various times throughout his life, and which he blames on a fever he caught as a sailor in the Low Countries many years ago. He is like to recover, but Katherine wishes me to remain here to assist with his Treasury duties.'

'I had assumed you would be biding here anyway,' Francis said reassuringly, 'since this is surely your new home. Once we have unloaded the spoils, I shall take the *Pelican*, along with the *Judith* and the other vessels, back to Plymouth, and bring news of our safe return. I shall also set about supervising the construction of another *Pelican*, if William does not object.'

John laughed. 'William looks with trepidation on his forthcoming fiftieth birthday, and he is aye complaining of the aches in his bones that are the legacy of so many years exposed to the southerly gales, so I have no doubt that he will welcome your return as a shipbuilder. And, unless I miss my mark, there is also a young lady in the old family home who will wish you to learn the art of being a husband, so lose no time in getting back to Plymouth. But before you leave, we must plan for another voyage, must we not? Or do you consider that the tripling of your investment from the sale of the *Bonaventure* has secured you a living for the rest of your days?'

'Far from it,' Francis replied, 'neither has our recent foray lessened my desire to see the whole of the world, rather than just that part of it dominated by the Spanish and Portuguese. I hope to impress on those who advise the queen in such matters that we must strengthen our Navy in order to enforce our claim to the oceans.'

On the following day he was able to take the next step in those ambitions. Sir Robert Dudley arrived in order to take possession of the queen's share of the wealth they had brought back. As they sat at supper, he announced that Her Majesty sent not only her thanks, congratulations and good wishes, but also more tangible tokens of her esteem for their efforts.

'As for you, John, she has instructed that you be allowed to assume a coat of arms, as befits your station as one of our most successful merchants. She has also bid me request that you assist in the administration of the Navy Treasury, at least until such time as your wife's father is restored to full health. In that time you may best assess where our limited resources could be most effectively expended in the building of more ships.'

'I have given that matter much thought,' Francis chipped in, 'and I have nothing but the highest commendation for the vessel that I had the honour, pleasure and privilege of commanding during our recent voyage. She sits at her mooring out there, and she is named the *Pelican*. I would see more of her like made available.'

'I had occasion to see her as I came in on my barge,' Dudley nodded, 'but is she not too small for extended cargo trading in the Americas?'

'That depends upon the cargo,' Francis told him. 'Raw sugar, certainly, but Spanish gold?'

'That surely belongs to Spain,' Dudley replied enigmatically.

Francis winked. 'It does until we intercept it on the high sea. We had occasion to relieve a Spanish captain of some of it during our last foray, and I could have loaded five times that amount in the hold of the *Pelican*. But she has other advantages, to my thinking. She is faster than any cargo carrack, lower in the water and sleeker by far. Only her afterdeck provides a suitable target for enemy cannon, and were we to reduce its height, the enemy shot would whistle for yards above the rest of her, even should they fire in a flat line. I propose that more like her be built in the Plymouth yard, and that I be commissioned to supervise such construction.'

'That is not to say that we shall not venture forth again shortly, in order to trade for sugar, and aught else that we can scavenge,' John added, avoiding the disapproving looks that this announcement earned him from Katherine. 'It would therefore be as well that we build more ships like the *Jesus* and the *Judith*.'

Dudley frowned. 'We have not the dockyard capacity here at Deptford to introduce such a policy, and it would perhaps be best if we sent some of the construction to either Chatham or Portsmouth. This would also serve the purpose of keeping its true extent hidden from foreign spies.'

Francis immediately volunteered to sail to Portsmouth on Dudley's behalf, but Dudley shook his head.

'It is not wise for my hand to be seen in all this, since it is too closely associated with the queen's bidding, and she is anxious not to provoke Spain at this time. Better that it come from the Navy Treasury, which of course Master Hawkins can now arrange, given his assumption of duties here. And it might be better were he to concentrate on those, rather than venturing across oceans that the Spanish claim as theirs.'

'Does that same stricture apply to me?' Francis asked. 'For one, I would relish the task of flying England's flag on every land I can discover, while bringing its riches back to England to lay at Elizabeth's feet. For another, I tire of hearing Spanish claims that they command all trade with the Americas.'

'Your loyal zeal is much admired and appreciated, Francis,' Dudley assured him, 'but you must understand that should you do ought to annoy Philip of Spain, Her Majesty will publicly deny any knowledge of, or complicity in, such actions. Matters between us and Spain are in a delicate state of late, and we cannot provoke any sort of invasion.'

'Better, then, that we be well prepared for any such attempted invasion and repel the Spanish if they set their sails for England,' said Francis. 'We can begin such preparations by building a strong fleet, fully armed, and by training men to fight in it.'

'There really is no dissuading you from your self-appointed mission, is there?' Dudley said approvingly. 'Privily I may advise that this is precisely the reaction that my queen was hoping for. Wherever you may travel across the globe, you go with her private best wishes, although not her formal encouragement. I will have a note sent here that will serve as your letter of introduction to the dockmaster at Portsmouth, and you may begin such shipbuilding as Master Hawkins here advises that we can afford.'

'At least while he is doing that, neither of you can risk your lives again in acts that are little short of piracy,' Katherine acknowledged grudgingly.

'You call us pirates?' Francis demanded testily, and Dudley raised his hand in mediation.

'We must think of some appropriate word to describe your new trade, which in truth is what might best be described as private enterprise reinforced with cannon. The term "privateer" suggests itself, and I will discuss this with Her Majesty. And now I must take my leave, in order to reach Westminster Steps before the royal bargeman falls asleep across his oars.'

Six days later, Francis's spirits soared as Salcombe Head came into sight on his starboard beam, and he judged that the tide was still full enough to permit a gentle glide up the final approach to Sutton Wharf, where there was the usual bustle of activity, and a shout of welcome from several men working on the wharf when they recognised the *Pelican* heading for a berth. One of them ran up the stony street that led to the Hawkins house, no doubt eager to bring the news to them of the safe return of at least one of their menfolk.

Francis walked triumphantly in through the scullery door, where Mary was bent over a tub of hot water, armed with a rough stone with which she was scraping a shift clean. She looked up with a disinterested face as Francis stood there waiting for her to throw her arms around him, and he chose to be the one to break the painful silence.

'Rather a different welcome home, after the warmth of your farewell. Are you not gladdened by my return?'

'We knew of your safe return by way of a letter from John,' she announced coolly. 'Sent by fast horse, to advise us that you were all in London. Why did you not call into Plymouth first? Or did you have a woman waiting in London?'

'It was necessary to unload our riches in a safe place,' Francis explained slowly and deliberately as his ire rose at the challenge to his freedom of choice. 'And, of course, John had a wife and son eagerly awaiting his return.'

Mary turned with tears forming in her eyes. 'While you had a heart no less true awaiting your return to Plymouth. If wives and children are to be given preference, then perhaps I should submit to marriage with you, and let you fill me with babies.'

'When the time is meet for me to propose marriage to you, you will hear of it,' Francis replied coldly as he made to pass behind her in order to gain access to the kitchen. A wet hand shot out to grab his shoulder, and in a single action Mary spun towards him and kissed him passionately on the lips as tears rolled down her cheeks.

'Forgive me, my love,' Mary gasped. 'I felt that I was being regarded less highly than your ships, and your business in London.'

'And you must forgive me for my distraction,' Francis replied. 'But perhaps you now see why those tasks that I have set myself must be completed before I may commit to the responsibilities of a wife and family.'

'I see, but I do not understand,' Mary mumbled as she fingered the front of his doublet suggestively. 'Perhaps not marriage yet, but could you not at least give me a child that would occupy my days while you are away seeking your fortune?'

'You forget that my father is a minister of God, and that I was brought up with a fierce aversion to sin,' Francis replied.

Mary leaned forward and kissed him again as her body trembled with anticipation. 'And you forget that I am now a grown woman,' she said hoarsely.

In the days that followed, the tension between them became unbearable, even for Joan Hawkins, who merely had to witness it. Given that the household was now so small, it was impossible to ignore, and Francis took himself off to the boatyard every morning before Mary had even risen, foregoing breakfast in his eagerness to avoid her. William was more than happy to accept a commission for the building of another *Pelican* that would be paid for by the Navy. Francis insisted on supervising her construction unnecessarily in order to be back home for a very late, cold supper that would be left out for him on the kitchen table.

This went on for the best part of a week, until one evening he heard the kitchen door opening creakily behind him, and he looked up from his supper to find Mary standing there in only her nightgown. She smiled invitingly as she nodded at the meat and bread that Francis had half consumed. 'Hopefully it will give you the energy.'

'Energy for what?' Francis asked as his throat went dry and he reached for the cider mug.

'Your bedding required a wash today,' Mary told him, 'and I deliberately chose a wet day, so that it would not dry. There is only one other bed available, but it already has a woman in it. Or at least, it did until I came downstairs.'

'I have a bed on board the *Pelican*,' Francis told her with all the self-control he could summon, 'and tomorrow I must journey to Portsmouth. The tide will be at ebb before sunrise, so I can make an early start.'

Mary shot him a contemptuous look and slammed the door behind her.

The dockmaster at Portsmouth raised his eyebrows when he saw the specifications for the new vessel that the Master of the Horse had commissioned. 'Can we afford her?' he asked.

Francis nodded. 'The more important question is whether or not you can build her,' he replied. 'She will be a sister ship to the *Jesus*, which currently lies at Deptford undergoing repair after her long voyage to the Americas. She can be fitted with cannon in London once she is completed, and we will test her on another run to Hispaniola.'

'We?'

'Master Hawkins, the son-in-law of Navy Treasurer Gonson, who is currently in Deptford learning the secrets of naval administration. See to it that word is sent to me in Plymouth when she is ready to be taken to London.'

On his return to Plymouth, Francis was alarmed to find the Hawkins house silent and seemingly empty. Realising that he had left two women behind with no-one to defend them against robbery — except the elderly lady who came in twice a week to assist the ageing Joan with cleaning tasks — he walked urgently to the foot of the somewhat rickety staircase that led to the upper rooms. 'Aunt Joan? Mary? Where is everyone?' he called out.

'Mary's gone,' came the familiar voice, and Joan appeared at the head of the stairs.

'Gone where?' Francis asked.

Joan shook her head in admonition. 'Gone to stay with William an' Judith, 'til you come to your senses. She reckons as 'ow Judith can give 'er lessons in being the wife of a man what puts ships afore wives, and God knows she couldn't be expected to stay around you, the way you treat 'er.'

'I haven't mistreated her in any way!' Francis protested, provoking a derisive snort from Joan.

'You reckon not, does you? You reckon that she should be content to 'ang around waiting for you to be so gallant as to propose marriage to 'er, does you? I may not be your mam, Francis Drake, but I'm as near as dammit, an' I'll tell you some home truths, whether you likes it or not. She's a grown woman, an' grown women 'as needs, doesn't they? If you're not careful, me lad, someone'll supply them needs behind your back while you're too busy playing at being the king o' the high seas.'

'Is she planning on staying with William and Judith?' Francis asked fearfully, earning himself another snort.

'I would, if I were 'er,' Joan replied, before disappearing from his line of sight.

In the days and weeks that followed, Francis drove William to the point of distraction with enquiries as to Mary's health and welfare, until one day he squared up to Francis and yelled back at him.

'I'm sick and tired of being subjected to your daily inquisitions, Francis! If you want to know how Mary's keeping, go out to St Budeaux and ask her yourself. You might manage one question before she throws a pisspot at your head, which according to Judith is what you deserve. For God's sake, Francis, either marry the woman or put her out of her misery, so that someone else can!'

Francis was on the point of taking his advice when word came that the new heavy carrack was awaiting his sailing instructions in Portsmouth, and he sailed the *Pelican* up the Channel to collect her, then left Jim Short to take her back while he hired an experienced crew and sailed the new addition to the fleet proudly on the ebb tide down the Solent and east to London. Word had been sent from Sir Robert Dudley that she was to be named the *Minion*, and by the end of the week she was lying at a mooring in Deptford Sound, being loaded with twenty cannon and suitable quantities of shot and powder.

The *Minion* and the *Jesus* were taken down to Plymouth, where it was decided that the *Judith*, now suitably armed and with Jim Short in charge of the gun deck, would accompany the two mighty cargo carracks, along with the *Kittyhawk*, a sister ship to the *Judith*. They lost no time in provisioning all the vessels, and William promised to alert Mary to the fact that Francis was about to set sail again in search of his fortune. There was no response, either by way of a message of goodwill, or Mary's presence at the quayside, where William and Joan Hawkins were the only well-wishers to wave them down the Sound.

At the helm of the *Judith*, Francis recalled the several other voyages he had made in her and reflected on his self-appointed mission to rule the seas in England's name. Try as he might to keep the darker thoughts suppressed, they kept bubbling to the surface like a bad dose of stomach bile. He might, as ever, not survive this latest voyage, but if he had finally managed to turn the loving, loyal and comely Mary against him, did he want to live any longer anyway?

11

As they sat at anchor in the wide bay, half a day's sailing south of where they had acquired their previous supply, Francis had himself rowed over from the *Judith* to the *Jesus* in order to take dinner with John in his cabin in the stern. Through the side window they could clearly see a promising collection of buildings on the shore that probably housed a trading camp of some sort, and John was all for putting ashore and acquiring as many goods as they could cram into the holds of the *Jesus* and the *Minion*. But Francis was more cautiously inclined as he nodded to where a stately caravel was moored alongside what appeared to be the only available jetty, flying a flag from her stern that he believed to be Portuguese.

'It seems that the captain of yon vessel had the same idea, and it's likely that his hold is already full of the best of them,' he pointed out. 'Added to which, a Portuguese trader is not likely to take kindly to our appearance.'

'He knows not why we are here, surely?' John argued. 'And from what we have been able to see, he and his men have been too busy loading their cargo to have been able to pay much heed to us.'

'When you've finished eating,' said Francis, 'let me bring the *Judith* round to leeward of you. We'll raise the English flag that Dudley gifted to us and see what response we receive.'

'Probably a broadside,' John observed sourly, 'assuming, of course, that she's armed.'

'There's one sure way I know of finding out,' Francis grinned as he stood up, opened the cabin door and called for his cutter to be made ready. Thirty minutes later, he had the *Judith* broadside to the shoreline several hundred feet away, her red and white striped Tudor ensign flowing proudly in the stiff breeze from the poop. He also gave instruction for his gunner Jim Short to hold ready with a primed linstock and a supply of gunpowder and shot, awaiting any command that Francis might shout down through the hatch to the gun deck.

Following the exchange of several waved signals, John raised anchor and turned the bow of the *Jesus* towards the shore, as if intending to land. This provoked loud shouts from the deck of the Portuguese vessel and the foreshore beyond it. When these were ignored, a fusillade of cannon shot fell all around the *Jesus*, most of it into the sea, although one lucky ball took the top few feet off her foremast. This was all the excuse that Francis needed, and on his shouted command, Jim Short ran down the line of loaded culverins and applied the linstock. A series of ear-splitting roars reverberated around the bay as the vessel moored on shore received several severe hits to her superstructure, and her mainmast shattered into three pieces and flew up the sand beyond the jetty. For good measure, a storage hut on land exploded into a fountain of bamboo and palm leaves, and several men ran from it for their lives.

It fell silent as John steered the *Jesus* gently to the shoreline, where a handful of his men, heavily armed with swords and daggers, untied the damaged Portuguese vessel without any resistance from the men on board her. She drifted down towards a promontory of rocks, and her deckhands were too busy preserving her from shipwreck to offer any opposition, or even protest, as the *Jesus* replaced her at her mooring. Francis steered the *Judith* in behind her, while the captains of the *Minion* and the *Kittyhawk* dropped anchor only a few yards out in the bay.

They took advantage of the same westward trade current from which they had benefitted greatly on their last crossing from Africa to the Americas. Their sails were soon billowing in the face of a favourable wind towards the line of islands that seemed to form an outer reef that guarded an inner ocean with a continuous land mass behind it.

After a long discussion over supper in John's cabin on the *Jesus*, the four captains agreed that rather than turning back once they'd passed between two of these islands, they would continue to the mainland beyond, in search of a substantial town or city — no doubt Spanish controlled, as everything seemed to be in this part of the world. Thus it was that they made their first landfall at a recently constructed jetty in a place called Rio de la Hacha, where they were able to trade for an impressive quantity of pearls that were to be found in abundance in the shallow waters that made up the coastline, and were acquired daily by native divers who had been trained to the task since childhood.

The reason for their nervous reception in Rio de la Hacha became clear once they dropped anchor further down the coast at Cartagena. They were advised by a red-faced harbour official that the Viceroy of 'New Spain', from his administrative base in Santo Domingo, and acting on the orders of King Philip of Spain, had issued a decree banning all trade with England in the new Spanish Empire, and had ordered all colonial officials beneath him to seize any English ships and their cargos.

A swift bribe enabled John and Francis to offload their remaining cargo at an advantageous price, and the massive cargo hold of the *Minion* was crammed almost to the point of overflowing with sugar, spices and pearls as the small English fleet set its sails for a northern voyage behind the string of islands that formed a protective barrier against the rougher seas of the open Atlantic. It was their intention to re-enter the open ocean once they reached the next port of which they were aware to the north, St Augustine in the land the Spanish called La Florida. But then the weather reminded them of its awesome power over their pathetic constructions of wood and canvas.

The hurricane hit without warning, causing the fleet to separate in order to avoid collisions as each of their captains turned their bows into the mountainous seas. The heavily laden *Jesus* incurred the most damage. By the time that the shaken and sleep-deprived captains gathered around the table in John's stateroom, he was able to advise them that her bow was heavily warped, and she had lost much of her caulking to the wild elements.

'We need to put into shore somewhere,' he told them. 'We are badly in need of repairs, in addition to the food and water we had planned to take on board in La Florida. We must also raise her in the water by transferring cargo to the *Minion*. The *Jesus* was wallowing like a sick cow while riding out that storm, and she is in no condition to cross the ocean back to London, if we are to return her to Her Majesty in one piece.'

'La Florida is but two days' sail to our north,' Francis reminded him, then jerked back in alarm when John's fist crashed down on the table.

'It may as well be a *month* to our north!' he bellowed as he glared back at Francis. 'The *Jesus* will be matchwood if we venture more than a few hours further without making the necessary repairs. You claim to be a navigator, Cousin — find us a port to which we can put in for repairs. And do so *now*, for the love of God!'

Francis scuttled out of the stateroom, and for the next few hours scanned the shoreline to port through his eyeglass until he spotted what he had been praying for — a cluster of seabirds whirling and swooping over what looked like a small, but inhabited, settlement. He gleefully yelled his good news down the hatch to where John was conducting a tense conversation with Robert Barret, the man who was officially captaining the *Jesus* while John used it as his flagship, although the Tudor flag that had been proudly fluttering from its mainmast was now somewhere in the bay after being torn away by the hurricane.

As the fleet resumed formation with the *Jesus* at its head, it began to look as if Francis's distance vision might have been playing him false. What he had taken to be a port was in fact an island that appeared to have been created by human hand, using local rocks. There were jetties after a fashion, but it was obvious that the main township that they had reached lay further inland, at the far side of a stretch of water between it and the pile of rocks that passed for its port.

Uncomfortably aware of what they had learned in Cartagena regarding the likely outcome of any English attempt to trade in Spanish-held territory, John and Francis ordered the five ships in their humble and storm-battered fleet to drop anchor midway between the town and the island port. They then had themselves rowed ashore, along with Robert Barret, to a cluster of buildings on the mainland that promised to be some sort of administrative office. They were still a few yards from its main door when it opened, and out walked a serious-looking official in a garish uniform. He was accompanied by four guards wearing slightly less gaudy attire, but their authority was emphasised by the large swords that hung from their belts and the firearms they carried in each hand.

The man in command addressed them in Spanish, and when he received no reply his face set in disdain, and he issued a sharp command to his armed escort, who moved forward so as to surround the three newcomers.

'English pigs?' the man demanded.

The colour rose in John's face, but he kept his voice even. 'English, certainly. We do not seek to trade — merely to repair our vessels and take on food and water.'

When the official shook his head in ill-tempered exasperation, Robert Barret coughed politely from behind John and Francis and asked, 'May I, sirs?'

'You speak Spanish?' John asked in surprise.

'Enough, I think,' Robert replied, and addressed the Spanish official in his own tongue. Instead of the torrent of angry abuse that they had been expecting, the man's face softened as he replied, and Barret translated for John and Francis. 'He is flattered that one of us took the time to learn Spanish — which sadly I had time to do while languishing in chains in one of their gaols in Corunna — and he says that we may moor on yon island for long enough to make repairs, and we may acquire food and water in exchange for coin. But no trading.'

'Tell him that we are in his debt,' John replied.

'Best not use a word associated with trade,' Francis corrected him. 'Tell him, rather, that we are grateful for his humanity.'

They were informed that they were free to purchase supplies in the small trading posts that lay behind the colonial offices, and to fill their water barrels from the small lake towards the rear of the township, which they were advised was called Veracruz. While men were deployed on these essential tasks, John sent Robert Barret up the wooded slope behind the town to find tree bark and other stringy substances that might be boiled down, along with old sacking, into passable caulking with which to repair the bow of the *Jesus*. They had just started work on that, with the *Jesus* taking up most of the island mooring, when they heard the sound of cannon and looked out into the bay. There was a massive caravel flying the Spanish flag, surrounded by armed carracks, lowering sail and preparing to drop anchor.

John and Robert Barret broke off from supervising the repairs to the *Jesus*, and took to its cutter, stopping briefly to allow Francis to climb down the rope from the gunwale of the *Judith*. The three men presented themselves on board the newly arrived vessel, where a tall man with a military bearing came up on deck to survey them with a patrician stare and a few imperiously delivered questions in a tone that was businesslike, but hardly warm. Robert improvised with his halting Spanish, and finally translated.

'I think we just found ourselves in the wrong place, sirs,' he told John and Francis. 'This man gives the name "de Almanza", and he claims to be the Viceroy of New Spain, on his way further south. It seems that his vessels encountered the same storm that we did, and they needed to put in for repairs.'

John thought quickly before replying, 'Tell him that, as one mariner to another, I respect his need for a berth here in this somewhat limited sanctuary. However, since we were moored first, I would propose that we be allowed to complete our repairs, following which he has my word that we will once again set sail, leaving the island as we found it, and available for him.'

The terms of the uneasy truce were further negotiated and sealed with a glass of wine in the viceroy's spacious and elegantly equipped stateroom. It was agreed that the two small fleets would be kept well apart, that their crews would not be allowed to fraternise, and that the English would remove the armament from the *Minion* and lay it, along with its shot and gunpowder supply, on the island foreshore, in a further gesture of non-aggression. This somewhat uneasy arrangement lasted for two days, until Francis, from the poop of the *Judith* moored alongside the other English vessels in mid-channel, began to grow anxious regarding certain actions he noted on the Spanish side.

The first was the steady stream of armed men being rowed across to the mainland in ships' boats that pulled away from the carracks surrounding the Spanish flagship. It was as if these carracks had been transporting only armed soldiers, and after only several hours there was a sizeable army of them in front of the administrative building where they had recently spoken with the local administrator. Then, to his further alarm, he saw them raising the anchor on a massive hulk called the *San Salvador*, which slid between the remaining vessels in the Spanish fleet, collecting large quantities of weapons as it slowly passed each of them in turn. It then dropped anchor at the edge of their line, so as to be only a few feet away from the *Minion*, the closest of the small English fleet to the foreign flotilla as all but the *Jesus* sat bobbing at their anchor points.

Francis called hurriedly for the *Judith's* boat to be lowered and had himself rowed the hundred or so yards to where the *Jesus* was moored, calling loudly for John. After a brief council of war, Robert Barret was sent in the *Jesus's* boat to the viceroy's flagship with a stern request that he order the opening of the hatches of the *San Salvador* in order to reveal whether or not, as was suspected, it was hiding an attacking force. Francis and John watched in horror as, from a distance, they saw Robert being restrained with ropes at his wrists before he was led below decks. Any remaining doubt that may have remained regarding the perfidy of the Spanish was dispelled when a trumpeter appeared on the deck of the flagship and blasted out what was obviously a pre-arranged signal.

Armed Spaniards appeared as if by magic from the hold of the *San Salvador*, from which they leaped onto the deck of the *Minion* and began engaging in hand-to-hand combat with the startled English crew. Despite being taken by surprise, the English tars gave better than they got. Although they were soon outnumbered, it reached a stage at which further boarders from the *San Salvador* could not be sure of a secure or empty landing point on the deck of the *Minion* as it began to fill with the bodies and blood of both nationalities.

In the meantime, boatloads of heavily armed Spaniards had been hastily transferred from the mainland, and they quickly overpowered the token crew that had been left in charge of the ordnance on the island harbour. Those of the English sailors who were not slaughtered hastily scrambled back on board the *Jesus*, then turned in order to repel the pursuing Spaniards who boarded her with blood-curdling yells and whoops of triumph. The contest was as bloody as it was brief, but at some point during the melee a quick-witted pair of deckhands cast the vessel off from its moorings. As she began to float slowly downstream, the marauders found their escape route blocked. They could no longer rely on reinforcements from the harbour boardwalk, and as their numbers began to dwindle by attrition, they were no match for the enraged defenders on board the *Jesus*, who were incensed by their treachery and the loss of so many comrades.

Once the deckhands were no longer required to give priority to boarders, the order was given to raise the mizzen in order to give some power from the light westerly. Slowly but surely, the *Jesus* moved out into mid-channel in an attempt to come alongside the *Minion* as a sort of barrier against the cannon fire that was now being blasted at it from their own ordnance, now in Spanish hands on the harbour side. This manoeuvre saved the *Minion* and its precious cargo, but after only a few minutes the *Jesus* was rapidly becoming a wreck, her masts blasted to shreds. She also had a large hole below the water line that took in such a surge of seawater that she began to list heavily in the first indication that she was headed for the ocean floor.

John yelled the order to abandon ship. He then dived overboard alongside some two dozen men who swam furiously towards the ropes that were hastily dropped from the deck of the *Minion*, allowing them to scramble up. The remaining English ships bobbing at anchor became the next targets of the shore batteries, and over a hundred sailors took the only action available to them and dived off their sinking decks. A few drowned, but the vast majority of them made it to the *Minion*, and John ordered full sail in order to take her beyond the range of the enemy cannon on shore. Francis ordered the same and guided the *Judith* out of the strait immediately behind the *Minion*, spraying the enemy on shore with fire from his own cannon as they glided past. He saved his final bitter salvo for the *Santa Clara*, the Spanish galleon that had been the viceroy's flagship, and a faint cheer rose from the seamen who had just returned from their perilous sally up the masts in order to unfurl the sails of the *Judith*.

When they were finally convinced that the Spanish had finished with them, and were not sending any vessels in pursuit, John signalled from the grossly overcrowded deck of the *Minion* that he was about to drop anchor an hour north of Vera Cruz, and Francis did likewise. He then joined John on the *Minion*, where they shakily assessed their position and considered their options.

'Thank God we transferred our booty to the *Minion* when we did,' said John as he raised his cider mug with a shaky hand. 'But Her Majesty will not be best pleased at the loss of the *Jesus.*'

Francis glared at him in contemptuous disbelief. 'We just lost the best part of a hundred English souls to the treacherous Spaniards, John! We will need to explain that to their wives and children if we ever make it back to Plymouth. Since you will no doubt choose to sail on to London without putting into any Devon port, it will no doubt fall to me to break the news. And all you can mourn is the loss of some cargo and your damned ships?'

If John's conscience was pricked, it didn't show. Instead, he jerked his head towards the ceiling of his state cabin, above which was the stern of the main deck. 'Talking of lost souls, there are far too many men on deck for us to make it back home with the provisions we have. I propose that we continue to La Florida, to load up on fresh supplies of food and water, and disembark half of those sitting above our heads.'

'*Disembark?*' Francis screamed. 'You mean "abandon", do you not? Have you a single shred of Christian conscience left in you? These men risked their lives to save your precious cargo, and now you propose to hand them over like sacrificial lambs to the enemy?'

'They are not officially our enemy,' John replied weakly as he dropped his gaze to the table.

'They are now *mine*!' Francis yelled, as he turned and hurled his cider mug at the panelled wall and stormed back on deck. As he waded through the crowd of displaced mariners on the main deck, many of them still nursing wounds, he ordered that his boat be lowered, then turned to address the men.

'Pray to God for your salvation, men, because Christian charity seems to be in short supply on this seaborne warehouse! Your commander cares more for the cargo in his hold than the men on his deck!'

12

Once they had sailed clear of any further Spanish attack, and once the cousins had resumed talking to each other — Francis in tones of anger and bitterness and John with his usual focus on commerce — it had been agreed that Francis would sail home alone to Plymouth in the *Judith* with the most valuable part of their cargo crammed inside the limited hold, while John would follow behind in the more ponderous *Minion* with the heavier portion of the booty that had cost them so much in men and ships. The *Jesus* and three attendant vessels lay somewhere on the seabed off the coast at San Juan de Ulua, and well over a hundred men had been abandoned by their commanders, put ashore on a rocky coastline where they would either die of thirst and starvation, or be captured by Spaniards. It was hard to tell which would be the worse fate, but Francis doubted whether any of those men would ever see England again.

The voyage home was uneventful, if gloomy, and Francis left most of the navigation to Jim Short as he sat in his cabin, brooding over the fate of so many mariners, some of them Plymouth men. He was obliged to face their wives and children when the *Judith* finally docked, and eager faces scanned the decks for their returning menfolk. Joan was on the front row and eagerly embraced Francis like a long-lost son as she enquired after the other ships, and in particular her second son John.

'He was fine when I last saw him, Aunt Joan, and he's some weeks behind me with the *Minion* and the remainder of the riches we brought back.'

'What about the men?' demanded a stout lady with three young children clustered around her legs. 'Where's Tom Dunkly? An' 'ow come there's only a handful o' you back 'ere?'

Her enquiry was echoed by at least a dozen other women — wives, sweethearts and mothers. Francis had to tell the truth — that some of the men had been killed, and others had been taken prisoner by the Spanish. Cries of horror and anger mingled with wails of misery when Francis was also obliged to admit that he could not supply any further information regarding the fates of men who had been on other ships in the fleet, and who he didn't know personally.

'But what about Rob Barret?' demanded a tear-streaked matron with greying hair tied under an untidy hood. She was surrounded by children of varying ages and had a bulge in her gown that indicated the imminent arrival of one more. 'You must know 'im, surely to God, since 'e were second-in-command on the *Minion*.'

'Mistress Barret?' Francis replied. Acid hit his throat as he remembered the last time he'd seen Robert Barret. The woman nodded, her hand held fearfully to her mouth, which was insufficient to stifle her tortured scream when Francis had to advise her that her husband of fifteen years was yet again a prisoner of the Spanish. There were angry shouts from the sizeable crowd, and the front row of women surged forward as if to hang Francis from his own yardarm. Then Joan Hawkins stepped in front of him.

'I'll thank you to let me nephew go in peace, neighbours! It's not 'is fault if the Spanish've got some o' you menfolk, an' knowing Francis I'd stake my life that 'e did 'is best to bring 'em home. So, take a step back, if you'd be so good, an' let me take the poor boy home for 'is supper.'

The crowd began to disperse to echoing tears, wails and a few muttered oaths, and Francis hugged Joan gratefully round her shoulders.

'Thanks for that, Aunt Joan. I need to stay and see the cargo safely stored away, but I'll follow on as soon as I'm ready.'

'Mind that you do,' Joan smiled back up at him conspiratorially. 'It's your favourite fish pie, an' a special cook has worked all day to make it, since you was seen coming up by St Austell.'

An hour later he was still sitting by the boat, head down, listening to the familiar sounds of cargo being unloaded as he inwardly cursed the Spanish, berating himself for being the cause of so much family grief, and wishing that God had selected him for a foreign prison instead of Robert Barret. He became dimly aware of a sturdy pair of leather pattens on the dusty ground ahead of him. He looked up, and there was Mary, a quizzical look in her eyes.

'Do you want this fish pie or not?' she asked in mock censure. 'I spent the best part of the day choosing the fish and beating it into submission. Or are you so enamoured of your ship that you can't leave her, even when on dry land?'

Francis smiled palely through his drying tears. 'Thank you for coming down to meet me. And for even speaking to me. I don't deserve it.'

'Don't get too proud of yourself,' said Mary. 'I'm only here to make sure that my fish pie doesn't go to waste.'

That night Francis was wrapped inside a dream in which Spanish soldiers were twisting his broken arm and attempting to encase it in splints made out of sword blades that were still running red with English blood, while his mother was nursing his head in her bosom and crooning soothing words. Then his eyes flew open with the recollection that his mother never smelt of lavender, and he found himself staring straight into Mary's eyes, barely inches from his as she cradled his head and urged him gently to have no fear.

'You were crying out in your sleep,' she explained.

'How did you know?' Francis asked sleepily, then recoiled as he felt her hot, naked body through his nightshirt.

'Because I was lying here next to you,' she explained coquettishly, 'and what is more, your aunt knows where I am — and why. So to preserve our reputations, you'll need to marry me. Sorry — except I'm not.'

'But we haven't sinned — have we?' Francis asked.

'Not yet,' Mary replied as she lifted his nightshirt and reached for his groin.

By the time that John returned briefly to offload those of his remaining mariners who called Plymouth home and transfer the cargo that had come ashore on the *Judith* into the hold of the *Minion*, prior to casting off for London and his own home, plans were well underway for the long-delayed wedding of Francis Drake and Mary Newman. It was to be in the parish church of St Budeaux, a few yards from William and his family's cottage along the main street, and Francis and Mary had chosen a similar one around the corner, across from the village inn. The date was fixed for July, and all that remained was for Francis to notify the guests who would be invited to attend both the ceremony and the lavish celebration thereafter. He was also uncomfortably aware that he needed a groomsman, and everyone seemed to assume that this would be John.

However, not only was John back in London, but he and Francis had never resumed the natural friendship that they had enjoyed until that fateful day when they had parted company

113

with words of bitter recrimination off the shores of New Spain. During John's two-day visit to Plymouth, the two men had walked warily round each other, and the atmosphere in the Hawkins house had been uncomfortable whenever the two men were both in it at the same time, which they made great efforts not to be. John's reaction to what should have been the joyful tidings of the forthcoming wedding had been a surly, 'You finally got *that* right, at least,' and there had been no further reference to the forthcoming celebrations. Mary was back residing in her own chamber in the old Hawkins house and tried to raise Francis's flagging spirits by suggesting that he ask one of his own brothers to act as groomsman, which only served to depress Francis further when his conscience plagued him over his lengthy absence from Upchurch, where his family lived.

There were less than two months to go before the wedding when a casual enquiry from Aunt Joan regarding how many mouths from Kent she would be required to feed finally convinced Francis that he had put it off for long enough. Reassuring Mary that he would be back within the month, he quickly gathered a small crew led by Jim Short, kissed Mary goodbye on the quayside, and ordered the deckhands to cast off into the midstream current, setting a course for Dover. He hugged the Kent coast until the incoming tide brought the *Pelican* up the Medway with all but her mizzen sail lowered. Having disembarked, Francis was once more walking down the familiar Upchurch street towards the vicarage.

The first indication that things had changed was the fresh paint on the scullery door as he knocked impatiently on it, anticipating being hugged tightly by his mother when she opened it from the inside. Instead it was a maid, and when he asked for Mistress Drake, he was told to wait where he was until an older woman appeared with the information that he would find Mistress Drake in the cottage next to the smithy at the far end of Church Lane.

'Edmund Drake?' he asked hoarsely.

'The old minister?' the lady responded, unaware of who her visitor was. 'He died a year or so past, and now my husband has the care of the parish flock. Are you seeking spiritual guidance, or is it perhaps a wedding or a funeral?'

'None of those, thank you,' Francis replied as he gritted his teeth against impending tears. 'Edmund Drake was my father.'

'Don't remember seeing you around these parts,' the lady replied, 'so you must be the sailor son he was always boasting about. Your mother will be glad to see you home, no doubt.'

'No doubt,' Francis mumbled as he thanked the lady and took his leave. Five minutes later, mother and son were clutching each other in shared grief before Mary Drake stepped back and looked Francis up and down appraisingly.

'You've put on weight, so someone must be feeding you. 'Ave you finally got married?'

'No, but that's why I came back — to tell you, and to invite you to the ceremony and the feast that will accompany it. I also need to ask brother Thomas if he'll be my groomsman. Please don't tell me *he's* dead as well.'

'No,' Mary reassured him, 'but 'e can't be spared, I'm afraid. 'E's working in the smithy next door, an' the cottage goes with the job. If 'e took the time off to go all the way to Plymouth, we'd all be out on our ears — me *an'* 'is wife an' two wee girls. John, Edward and William's away working elsewhere, so that just leaves me, an' me old legs don't seem to want to move around as much as they used to, so it looks like you'll be the only Drake at your wedding. Apart from the spirit o' you Dad, that is — I'm sure 'e wouldn't want to miss it, seeing as 'ow you finished up the favourite son.'

'Why didn't you let me know that Father had died?' Francis asked gently.

His mother shook her head. 'We made enquiries as to where you might be, afore we let anyone know that your father was fading, but all we were told was that you was out at sea somewhere, and you'd bin gone a year or more.'

Francis nodded sadly. 'That's something else I need to repay the Spanish for. Not to worry — I'll soon find another groomsman.'

'What about John?' Mary asked. 'You was always like brothers, you an' 'im. Or 'as 'e died at sea, like we thought you 'ad?'

'No, he's back in London,' Francis told her. 'He married the daughter of the Navy Treasurer. He may even love her, although I think that her greatest attraction for him was her father's wealth and position. A dedicated follower of riches is John,' he added bitterly.

''Ave you two 'ad a falling-out?' his mother demanded sternly.

Francis dropped his eyes to the floor and nodded sadly. 'It was during our last voyage — he left over a hundred men at the mercy of the Spanish while he gave preference to bringing back his plunder. What sort of Christian man does that?'

Mary bit her lip. 'What sort of Christian man abandons his family and doesn't visit them for years on end? Your dad was aye calling for you after he took to 'is bed, and it would have given 'im great comfort during all 'is pain to 'ave 'ad his favourite son by 'is side. Sorry, but you needed to 'ear that. I remember when you an' John was like peas in a pod — we could never get the pair o' you in for your meals, 'cos you was always down the waterside, looking at ships an' suchlike. 'E were like a brother to you — more than your real brothers was, anyroad. An' do you mean to tell me that you can just throw all that up in the air, just 'cos 'e 'ad to make a decision that no doubt broke 'is poor 'eart? It were John what got you inter sailing, remember?'

'I know,' Francis admitted sadly, 'and I'm on my way to London right now, to see if we can't be reconciled, because I want him to be my groomsman at the wedding. Do you think he'll agree?'

'That'll depend on 'ow you asks 'im, won't it? And if I were you, I wouldn't 'ang around 'ere till you talk yourself out of it.'

'I've only just got here,' Francis protested as he took both her hands in his, 'and I don't know when — or if — I'll be back. This may be the ... I mean to say, we don't know when... Oh, damn and blast it, you know what I mean.'

'O' course I do,' she assured him as she pulled firmly on his hands in order to draw him closer to her. 'So, give your old mam a proper goodbye 'ug, an' always remember 'er in your prayers.'

Cursing the task ahead of him, Francis took the helm as they lowered sail, then dropped anchor in Greenwich Reach and signalled for the rowboats to tow them in. Slowly they inched into a vacant berth, and even fifty yards away Francis could see John standing on the dock wall with a young lad at his side. Francis guessed that this must be his son, Richard, now at a height halfway up his father's thigh, and with the same proud facial expression. Francis's heart softened as he saw the two of them waiting for him, and he forced down the thoughts that assailed him regarding the orphaned children whose fathers had been left an entire ocean away. He instructed Jim Short to see to the moorings and leapt ashore to shake John by the hand.

'How goes Her Majesty's Navy?' he asked by way of an icebreaker.

John grimaced. 'At least you're asking the right man. My father-in-law has seemingly taken to his deathbed, and all the paperwork lies on my desk. I was just beginning to reach the bottom of it when your ship was reported to me as requesting an entrance.'

'Sorry if I inconvenienced you,' Francis replied stiffly.

John's face broke into a smile. 'You only inconvenience me when you plague my conscience. As I try to sleep every night, your last accusing words ring in my head. You voiced what I was thinking anyway when, as commander of our humble fleet, I was obliged to leave men behind. But I shall make it my life's work to get them freed.'

'I have a task for you ahead of that,' Francis told him.

John regarded him knowingly. 'You took your time about it, but if you came looking for a groomsman, you found one.'

13

The fiddle player put down his instrument, and the breathless wedding guests took seats wherever they could find them in the rear garden of William Hawkins' house in St Budeaux. It lay only a few hundred yards away from the parish church in which, several hours earlier, Mary Newman had become Mistress Drake. She was leaning happily on Francis, her arm draped across his shoulders, as John lurched towards them with his latest mug of the local cider. He all but fell into the vacant chair, burped loudly, then addressed them.

'Mary finally got her man, then. My congratulations are overdue to you both,' he slurred.

'Hardly,' Francis corrected him, having opted for a clear head for the night that lay ahead in the spare upper chamber of William's house. 'You have offered us your congratulations as often as you have dipped your mug into the cider vat. You are, in my seasoned opinion, as drunk as a wine-store rat.'

'Harsh,' John chuckled, 'but no worse than my dear lady wife has been canting in my ear this past hour. You will find that married life brings with it certain restrictions to one's natural inclinations.'

'That depends upon one's inclinations, does it not?' Francis countered. 'Since mine is to deprive Spaniards of all their gold, I need to keep a sober head.'

'And my natural inclination will be to keep him at home,' Mary added as she hugged Francis harder and planted a kiss on his cheek.

John's face took on a more serious aspect as he nodded. 'For once, *Mistress* Drake, our ambitions for your husband are as one.'

Francis frowned. 'Married only a few hours, and already my new bride conspires with my best friend to keep me on shore?'

'Needs must, Francis,' John told him in a lowered voice. 'I have promised the Spanish King that we will keep away from those lands he claims for Spain. This is his price for the release of the men we left behind in Vera Cruz.'

'And you pledged my word along with your own?' Francis demanded.

John nodded. 'Forgive me, Francis, but many of those men are your neighbours. I also have the blessing of Sir Robert Dudley.'

'You obviously move in more exalted circles than I, of late,' Francis replied. 'At least I will now not have to choose between putting to sea and organising my new household. And perhaps fathering children.'

'There will be no "perhaps" about that,' Mary giggled. 'But I am with John in urging you to remain on shore, for a while at least. You were lucky to return alive from your last foray into the unknown, and I cannot bring myself to look into the eyes of the wives and mothers of those who did not return with you.'

'Did you promise King Philip that I would remain on land?' Francis asked, seemingly ignoring what Mary had to say.

John shook his head. 'Merely that you would not venture onto land in the Americas that is claimed by Spain.'

'And their treasure ships?'

'You are to stay away from those also. But once we have secured the safe return of our men, it will be different, will it not?'

'And when will this happy event occur?' Francis asked sceptically.

John spread his hands in a gesture of uncertainty. 'There are other matters connected with their release, about which I may not speak, but they are the close concern of Sir Robert and Her Majesty. And I am engaged as the sea captain of choice of the Spanish Ambassador, in which capacity I hope soon to return to Spain in order to pursue the matter. In the meantime, it will assist our plans considerably if you avoid Spanish lands and Spanish treasure ships.'

Francis stared unseeingly at the dancers who were regathering on the grass as the fiddler lifted his instrument back onto his shoulder and struck up the opening phrase. Then Francis transferred his gaze to John, and asked sharply, 'May I presume that if I sail my vessel mid-ocean, put in at no port claimed by Spain, and fire only if I am first attacked, I may continue to put to sea without incurring the displeasure of your new-found courtly friends?'

'You may so assume,' John confirmed.

Mary had heard enough, and she pulled hard on Francis's sleeve. 'Are you minded to seek the approval of your wife?'

'Do I require it?' Francis asked with a mocking smile that faded rapidly as he saw the set of Mary's mouth, with which he was already so familiar.

'You do now,' Mary assured him, 'if you wish to enjoy a happy hearth.'

'I'll just go and see if there's any cider left,' John muttered as he slunk away.

Mary Drake lowered the loaded food basket with a grunt, and sat down heavily next to where Francis was perched on the riverbank, gazing wistfully downstream to where the Tamar flowed lazily towards Plymouth Sound.

'Since you spend your days here, gazing like a lovelorn swain towards the object of your devotion, forgetting both the needs of your stomach and the company of your wife, I thought it best to bring your dinner to you, and remind you that you are now married to a woman, and not to the sea.'

'Is it not a beautiful sight?' Francis asked, oblivious to her gentle chiding. 'The sun reflects off the water, in the same way that it glistens on wave-tops. The sea-birds swirl and clamour for the fish that glide like silver arrows just below its surface, and over all is the constant call of the salt air.'

'Quite the poet,' Mary replied sarcastically as she lifted the cover from the basket, selected a pheasant leg and forced it into her husband's hand. 'To my mind the water smells of rank weed, and the birds are good for nothing but leaving their droppings on my washing when I hang it out to dry in the garden.'

'You are not a sailor, like myself,' Francis reminded her.

'And neither are you, until John tells you that you may resume your perilous life,' said Mary. 'In the meantime, it behoves you to at least *pretend* to enjoy life on land, in the bosom of your new wife, whose bosom grows sore of late. I believe I may be with child.'

When Francis made no reply, Mary shuffled along the grass until her face was directly in front of his and challenged him to repeat what she had just said. 'You said you believe you may be with child,' Francis repeated as he took his eyes off the water and gazed into hers.

'The Lord be praised — he is still with us in this world!' Mary exclaimed as she kissed him full on the mouth. 'Is that not excellent news?'

'Indeed,' Francis conceded without any obvious enthusiasm. 'But if I am to be a father, I must look to the child's future welfare, and indeed to ours. But I know only one way of doing that, and it is forbidden to me.'

'You could build vessels for William,' said Mary. 'He grows frail, and Judith fears that he will soon be confined to the house. There is money in ships, is there not?'

'There is more money in sailing them,' Francis countered as his gaze drifted back towards the water.

'There is also death and capture by the enemy,' said Mary. 'Many a woman here in Plymouth would wish that her man had merely *built* ships, rather than sailed in them.'

'It's in my blood, as you knew when you married me,' Francis offered in his own defence. 'And John said only that I was not to enter a Spanish-held port in the Americas or attack Spanish ships — unless they attack me first.'

'So, what is left available to you?' Mary challenged him, determined to make him concede that for the foreseeable future he would need to play the husband, and hopefully the father. She realised her mistake as a contented smile crossed his face.

'I could realise my first ambition, to sail right around the world,' he replied like a man in the grip of a mirage. 'If I can discover lands that the Spanish have not yet claimed, I may lay claim to them in England's name, and bring back the riches to be worked from them.'

'And what guarantee do you have that such lands even exist?' Mary demanded.

'Therein lies the challenge, and the thrill. At present we know not what lands lie beyond the Americas, but there is a man in London — a wise old man with knowledge of the stars — who offered to partner me in learning what lies beyond the setting sun.'

It fell silent for a long while. Mary continued to hand food to Francis and top up the earthenware mug that she had brought for him to swig the cider from. Finally, she broke the silence.

'Did it never occur to you that I love you with all the intensity that you love the sea?'

'Then I must be truly blessed,' he replied as he leaned forward slightly to kiss her. He then pulled his head back with a puzzled look as he saw the tears forming in her eyes.

Mary kissed him back, then continued, 'It is because I love you so much that I cannot bear to see you so despairing and lost. It is also a true mark of my love that I will not seek to stand in your way, should you wish to put to sea again.'

His mouth opened in an expression of mixed surprise, gratitude and joy. 'You truly mean that? I may return to sea?'

'I am not your gaoler, Francis. Of *course* you may put to sea again. I just ask that you do not do so until our child is born.'

'God bless you,' Francis murmured as he scrambled to his feet. 'I must first visit William, and have the *Pelican* made ready for sailing. Then I must return to London and consult Dr Dee. Come, dearest Mary, and let us to church, to pray for the child you are carrying.'

'And for your safe return,' Mary managed to mumble through the returning tears.

14

Francis gave the order to drop anchor, and when the rumbling noise had ceased Jim Short yelled back up to the afterdeck that ten fathoms of rope had been played out. Francis acknowledged this with a curt nod, then turned his attention back to the chart that John Dee had supplied him with.

The two men had been huddled over it for several days in the upper chamber of Dee's Mortlake residence, and Francis had spent the previous two nights craning his neck upwards until satisfied that the star with the arcane name of 'Ursa Minor' was immediately above the *Pelican*. He had then ordered the helmsman to steer a course south-south-west, and after three days they'd sighted land on the starboard bow. By Francis's estimate, this formed part of the chain of islands that he had last visited with John on the fateful voyage that had ended so ignominiously in San Juan de Ulua.

As he lowered his eyeglass his bitter memories returned, and he renewed his silent vow to take his revenge one day. Not in human life, but in gold, silver, spices and whatever other rich cargoes they carried back to their master in Madrid. For the time being, he could only sit and watch. Watch and plan. And become as familiar with the region they called the Spanish Main as he could.

'Ship on the starboard beam, Cap'n,' Ben Tilney called down from his lookout perch on the forward mast.

'Is she Spanish?' Francis called back up.

'Could be, Cap'n. She's a mighty big carrack, by the looks of 'er, an' 'er flag looks familiar.'

'How many leagues distant?'

'Between one an' two, by my guess. She's headed straight for us.'

'Up anchor!' Francis yelled, and half a dozen hands bent to reverse their actions of a few minutes previously. Francis ordered the helm turned to port, and as the bow of the *Pelican* turned to the left in response to the gentle wheel action, Francis raised his eyeglass again and swore in frustration as he saw the impressive vessel surging towards them, low in the water with what was no doubt a rich cargo of gold, silver and other precious metals. He could have blown her away, or boarded her and plundered her cargo, but he had promised John, and he owed it to a hundred or so of his former shipmates to hold back.

Having ordered the lowering of the Tudor flag from the stern mast, Francis watched with gritted teeth as the Spanish treasure ship passed sedately along their starboard beam and continued on its eastward passage back to its home port. Then he ordered full sail and a course between the two islands visible over their bow, until they were once again in the familiar inland ocean that brought back so many memories. Ahead lay the Spanish Main, and as they sailed sedately across the calm sea they were passed by three more heavily laden Spanish vessels, none of which made any attempt to engage them in warlike action, given that the gunports on the *Pelican* were kept closed in a silent gesture that they posed no threat to other vessels.

Francis watched carefully as each Spanish vessel came into sight. They had clearly all originated from one place, somewhere across the ocean ahead of them. Two hours later they could see the seabirds swirling in eddies above some place on land, and Francis ordered half sail as they cautiously approached it. It revealed itself as a port of some description, and an important one, to judge by the length of its jetties and the number of crude timber constructions behind them.

'What is that place?' Jim Short asked as he handed back the wheel to helmsman Toby Frankling and joined Francis on the poop deck.

'No idea,' Francis replied thoughtfully, 'but it would seem a good place to take on fresh provisions and learn whence comes all the treasure that has passed our starboard beam in recent hours.'

'We land in peace?' Jim asked hopefully.

Francis nodded. 'We have no choice, since we are forbidden to engage in piracy until Captain Hawkins has secured the safe release of the prisoners in Madrid.'

'But if we're forbidden by the Spanish from trading with their outposts, 'ow do we know that we'll be allowed to load fresh provisions?'

'We don't, but until we make a request, we shall remain ignorant, shall we not?'

They dropped anchor in the bay that seemed to serve this newly discovered settlement, and Francis and Jim had themselves rowed ashore, where they sought an audience with the governor. Once it became obvious from their speech that they were English, they were hastily surrounded by uniformed guards armed with pikes and swords, and all but marched like prisoners into the largest building on the waterfront. Here they were confronted by a grim-faced colonial official in a uniform that was ludicrously over-luxurious for the oppressive heat.

They were curtly informed that they had put ashore at a place called Nombre de Dios, and that the English were so unwelcome there that they would not even be granted permission to replenish their supplies of water and provisions. When Francis protested that the common humanity that existed between sailors demanded that they be allowed at least fresh water, their unfriendly host advised them that he was a soldier, not a sailor, and he gave them two hours to return to their vessel or face arrest and confiscation.

Back on board the *Pelican*, Francis was cursing under his breath when Jim Short asked tactfully when and where they might seek to refill their water casks and replenish their meat and fruit stocks.

'We'll just have to put in at every port in this land ahead of us until we find one that's friendly to the English cause,' Francis replied, tight-lipped with anger at their recent treatment.

'And if we don't?' Jim pressed fearfully.

'How much water's left in the casks?' Francis asked. When advised that there was barely a two-day supply, he ordered that the men be put on half rations. 'On the third day we take it, whether it's freely offered or not,' he added with a grimace.

'At least we've seen the last've Nombre de Dios,' Jim muttered.

Francis turned to look back at him with raised eyebrows. 'You think so? Trust me, Jim, if you continue to sail with me, you'll be seeing this place again. And its treasure.'

Two days later they saw smoke rising from some sort of coastal settlement along the near shore of Hispaniola. Believing that they might take advantage of whatever natural disaster had befallen it, they set a course for the distant conflagration. They were fortunate that the jetty remained intact to service the small town that they later learned was called Yaguana, and that the few buildings from which smoke was still rising appeared to contain no hostile Spaniards as they moored the *Pelican*. Francis led a party of twenty armed men up the muddy path from their mooring towards what had presumably once been a colonial office in the centre of the still smouldering ruins. A hundred yards or so before they reached it, an elderly man in a blue frock coat with red flashings stepped out of the sagging entrance. He was brandishing a musket with a bayonet protruding from just below its muzzle, and he challenged them in a language with which Francis was vaguely familiar.

'*Vous êtes Français?*' he asked hopefully.

The man nodded. '*Oui*. Capitaine Bertrand Lefois *a votre service. Ravi de vous rencontrer, si vous êtes Anglais.*'

Francis confirmed that they were indeed English. He then learned from their temporary host that the French had recently recaptured the small port of Yaguana from the Spanish, with whom they were contesting colonisation rights in Hispaniola, which the French chose to call Sainte Domingue. The acquisition of water, fresh fruit and animal flesh was swiftly negotiated in exchange for English coin. The rest of the conquering French contingent lined up on shore to salute a farewell to their English friends as Francis ordered the deckhands to cast off and let the *Pelican* drift out into the bay, ahead of the long journey home.

Back on shore in Plymouth, Francis was a little alarmed to be met, not by Mary, but by William's wife Judith, who smiled determinedly as she embraced him and welcomed him home. 'Mary's not so well,' she told him, 'an' she don't even know you're home. When it were reported that you'd been seen coming up the Sound, we kept the news from 'er, else she'd've insisted on rising from 'er bed, an' the physician sez as 'ow she mustn't.'

'I knew there was no baby,' Francis replied, 'else I would not have put to sea. But is there some other ailment?'

Judith's face fell even further. 'There weren't no bubby, no, but the soreness in 'er bosom that she mistook for one's still there, an' the physician thinks there might be a canker.'

Francis raced home, took the narrow wooden stairs two at a time and rushed to Mary's bedside. She'd been sleeping under the influence of a draught prescribed by the physician, but half opened her eyes sleepily to smile up at Francis.

'Am I dreaming? Is it really you?'

'It's really me, my sweet, home from my voyaging. How is it with you?'

A tear rolled down her face as she gripped his hand harder. 'Sore, but all the better for having you back by my side. Help me up, so I can kiss you.'

'You can do that lying down,' Francis said, leaning forward and pressing his lips on hers.

She looked content for a moment, then her face fell again. 'The physician says I may die, Francis. Please stay with me until I do.'

'Of course, darling one,' Francis reassured her as a tear rolled down his own face. 'The Spanish can wait.'

Francis and John embraced each other as a long-awaited ship came into the Plymouth dock. All around them were shrieks of joy and shouted prayers to God, as the handful of womenfolk welcomed back their emaciated, dishevelled but joyful mariners, most of whom had vowed to the Almighty that if He would only grant them freedom from their Spanish gaol, they would never put to sea again.

'This is not all of them, surely?' Francis asked.

John shook his head. 'The balance of them are on their way to London on the *Gannet*, which I must follow in the *Swift*, along with the Spanish Ambassador. He remains in his cabin rather than witnessing the joy of these reunions, no doubt beset by conscience.' Then he lowered his voice, adding, 'His Excellency is also closely guarding a bag of money that he has brought with him in order to finance an uprising against Queen Elizabeth.'

'This was the price of the release of our men?' Francis asked, aghast. 'A plot against the throne? You will surely go to the block for this!'

'Hardly,' John whispered excitedly, 'since I have been acting throughout with the knowledge of Sir Robert, and he has schemes of his own in hand to seize the rebels.'

Francis shot him a look of disbelief, then remembered something important. 'Mary is laid low, so for the present we cannot resume our activities among the Spaniards. But I believe I have discovered the main port from which their riches are shipped back to Spain, where we may acquire wealth beyond imagining.'

John frowned, then nodded. 'This is as well, since Katherine's father is approaching his last days on this earth, and I have been promised the chance to assume his duties. I shall give priority to the building and equipping of armed men-of-war that we may sea-test on the Spanish scum.'

'Have you grown so high and mighty that you no longer have time to greet your brother?' came a woman's plaintive yell from the harbour wall behind them.

John turned to address Judith with amusement. 'You are not my brother. If you are hiding him behind your skirts, please release him.'

Judith made no effort to stand aside, but simply gestured to where a wizened middle-aged man sat resting on an upturned crate, from which he gave a feeble wave as his face set in a pale smile. John strode over and embraced William, nearly knocking him over in the process. After a brief conversation, John moved back to rejoin Francis. 'Dear God,' he remarked as he did so, 'he looks as frail as my father-in-law, and by the look of him he has the same length of life left in him. It is as well that I have recently acquired the friendship of a shipbuilder in Deptford, since I suspect that no more Hawkins vessels will slide into the water here in Plymouth. But you tell me that Mary has been unwell — what ails her, and when can we expect you back at Spanish throats?'

'Not for some time,' Francis told him glumly. 'But lose no time in returning to London, since it would seem that you hold the safety of our queen in your weathered hands.'

15

Any thoughts that Francis might have been entertaining regarding a return to the Spanish Main had been lost in his concern for Mary's health. Lengthy conversations with the physician who rode to their cottage each day left Francis even more confused, apprehensive and uncertain. His loving bride of only a few years seemed to lurch alarmingly, from seeming robust health to days on end when she would lie in her bed, whimpering quietly to herself when she thought that no-one was listening. The simples prescribed by the physician and delivered by the apothecary in town took away the pains that would beset her on these occasions, but they also served to send her into a deep slumber from which Francis was fearful that she would not awake.

Two years had passed, and Mary was seemingly enjoying a longer than usual respite from her periodic maladies, when she raised with Francis the issue that had hung like a gloomy cloud over the household for the past few weeks.

'When do you intend to put to sea again?' she asked casually above the sound of the bread being kneaded into submission on her baking table.

'Not until I am satisfied that you will still be here to welcome me back,' he replied stiffly. 'Why, do you desire my absence so much that you are eager for me to depart?'

She left off her kneading and slid two flour-powdered arms around him. 'No, dearest, but I know that the sea is your life.'

'So are you.'

'You say so, but I am only in your heart, while through your veins runs salt water.'

'Now who's playing the poet?'

'I mean what I say, Francis. My heart grieves to think that I am all that keeps you here, when you would otherwise be pursuing your dream to conquer all the oceans on earth. It's not as if we have children who could tug at your arms and heartstrings, and it's not as if this humble home is big enough for your restless soul to pace up and down in.'

'You wish for somewhere bigger, my sweet? Somewhere where you could play the lady of the manor, and command a dozen servants?'

'I am content with this cottage, for as long as you are in it with me, my blessed husband. But only if you are happy. You pretend to be content with your frequent journeys to Deptford, to work with John on the design of a new Navy, but I know that in your heart you seek broader horizons and undiscovered lands.'

It was true that John and Francis were working long and hard on the design of new ships that were notionally for commerce, but which were, by secret commission from Sir Robert Dudley, being constructed for the war with Spain that seemed increasingly likely as the uneasy truce between Queen Elizabeth and King Philip limped along without any obvious enthusiasm from either side. Elizabeth seemed obsessed with the problem posed by the continued existence of Mary Stuart of Scotland, a political prisoner being shuffled from one secure manor house to another, always a potential beacon for the hopes of irrepressible Catholic plotters.

From time to time, plots would be uncovered by the wily, and morally incorrigible, Francis Walsingham, and on each occasion it became obvious that the origins of the plot were Catholic in their religion, and Spanish in their loyalties. Elizabeth retaliated by lending support — and occasionally arms and money — to the Dutch, who were forever seeking to throw off the Spanish yoke. Whatever might be their public utterances, Elizabeth and Philip resembled two prize-fighters on a village common, eyeing each other up for the advantage of the first blow.

In this atmosphere of gloom England was secretly adding to its Navy. The ailing Benjamin Gonson had no idea that the new hulls in the dry dock on Deptford Sound were soon to become the foundations of massive carracks the like of which had never put to sea in his day, and which were towed out at night, under the cover of darkness.

It had fallen to Francis to captain each of these vessels on their sea trials up and down the Channel, sometimes as far west as Plymouth, but always as far as Portsmouth, where ordnance could be rolled onto their gun decks. They then returned much lower in the water as they slid back up the Thames, to be kept under cover in a series of sheds in the boatyard of John's business partner and close friend, Richard Chapman.

Even the smaller ships were now armed as a matter of course, and built lower in the water but broader in the beam, so as to combine storage capacity with reduced exposure to cannon fire from the taller vessels preferred by foreign navies. The imposing Spanish galleons now resembled floating cities, with high afterdecks that incorporated impressively dimensioned staterooms for their captains.

Two of these smaller vessels had caught Francis's eye, and were being fitted out not in Deptford, but in the boatyard in Plymouth that William Hawkins had all but abandoned. They were the *Pascha* and the *Swan*, 'square riggers' that could carry double ranks of cannon on their gun decks — four on each beam — in addition to tough, fighting men who would double as both deckhands and brigands when they finally took to sea.

Francis, for all his assurances to Mary, was itching to raise anchor and settle a score with Spaniards in general, and those resident on the Spanish Main in particular.

But it was not just thoughts of Mary that were holding him back. In many a heated discussion over an abandoned supper table strewn with empty wine flagons, Francis and John argued over the future. John might well have given the queen his undertaking not to annoy the Spanish, Francis would argue, but he — Francis — had not. If England was to maintain a flow of illicit wealth that would allow the continued construction of a secret navy, then it fell to Francis to go out and secure it, either by discovering new lands whose minerals could be exploited, or by ripping them from Spanish hands after they had obligingly mined them for England.

John would invariably retort that any overt action by an English seafarer against a Spanish vessel would be deemed an act of war by a Spanish king who currently regarded himself as possessing the stronger of the two navies. He certainly had the greater army, even if much of it was currently committed to the suppression of the Dutch. When Francis countered that Philip of Spain would be much the poorer once he was deprived of the regular flow of gold and other valuables from the Americas, John threw up his hands in frustration and called in Sir Robert Dudley in an effort to make Francis see sense.

To John's amazement and horror, Dudley smiled and enquired of Francis when he could be ready to sail. 'But surely...' John began to protest, but Robert raised his hand for silence and fixed his stern gaze on each man in turn as he gave his ruling.

'Francis is correct that the loss through plunder of his ships would prove a serious blow to the growth of Philip's ambitions towards England — and be in no doubt that those ambitions are of conquest. He has given the Pope his assurance that he will rid Christendom of its perceived antichrist in skirts, and in return the old fossil has promised to wave his shaky ring of office in blessing over Philip's enterprise. This so-called truce has only bought us time against the inevitable — time which you, John, in particular have put to good use in the expansion of our navy. But what we need now is for Francis to attack the source of Philip's wealth.'

'Thereby bringing forward the day when Philip will launch an invasion that we cannot at present withstand, according to your own argument,' John all but yelled triumphantly.

Dudley gave him a look that was almost scornful. 'Do I strike you as a fool, or as someone who is so careless with the life of the woman I have known, loved and worshipped since we were both seven years old?' It fell embarrassingly silent following this intimate revelation, but Dudley carried on as if he had revealed nothing that was not already rumoured throughout the nation anyway.

'Francis should lose no time in transferring Spanish wealth to England, but he cannot do so in the name of the queen. He will be acting entirely in his own capacity, and in accordance with his own motivations. Elizabeth will disown you if you are discovered, Francis, and will take no steps to secure your recovery if you are captured. But you are privily advised that you will cast off with her blessing for a profitable voyage and a safe return.'

As he ordered the sails to be lowered in preparation for the gentle starboard swing into the wide bay that led into Plymouth Sound, Francis was deep in thought, and wrestling between his ambition and his conscience. Every instinct demanded that he lose no time in heading back to the Spanish

Main after equipping the *Pascha* and the *Swan* with all they would need, and recruiting among the lowest alehouses in the town for desperate characters who would risk all for a share of the riches to be ripped from the hands of the Spanish. But he had promised Mary that he would remain with her throughout her malady — one that might herald the end of her life — and how could he live with his conscience if she died while he was away at sea?

He was heartened by the sight of Mary waiting on the quayside, smiling and waving as the *Pelican* slid into her moorings. She seemed not to lack energy as she skipped towards him with open arms and hugged him to her. This was itself encouraging, since there had been times when Mary could not bear to embrace him, such had been the pain in her breast. This time there was not even a wince as she smiled up at him and said, 'We need a bigger house.'

'You are with child?' he asked hopefully, but she shook her head.

'No, dearest, but I grow tired of stumbling around a cottage when I would prefer to do my cooking in a grand kitchen, and gaze through the window glass of my bedchamber at rolling parkland, rather than at the garments blowing in the breeze in the garden of the cottage next door. I have ever craved a country estate, since my early years were spent living above dusty bookshops in filthy streets. And there is just such an estate on offer, or so I am well advised.'

'Where might that be?'

'Just up the road from where we live, on the road to Yelverton. It was once an abbey, but it has been used as a manor house for some years now. You must know of it, since you are from Tavistock, and that is further along the road from Yelverton, up on the moors.'

'You must mean Buckland Abbey,' Francis mused. 'Do you know who owns it now, and are you sure it's for sale?'

'Yes, it is,' Mary chirped back eagerly as they walked arm in arm up the narrow slope from the harbour side into the main street, where there were coaches for hire in which they could return home to St Budeaux. 'I learned this from Katherine, who is still basking in the glory of John being returned to Parliament as the Member for Plymouth, even if it *was* because of the influence of someone at Court. Anyway, John's new honour has opened some more doors around here for Katherine, who has nothing better to do with her time than play the lady at local social gatherings, and she has fallen in with the Grenvilles. It is they who are seeking a purchaser for the old abbey.'

'Sir Richard Grenville?' Francis asked with a sneer.

'Yes, do you know him?' Mary asked anxiously as she looked sideways at the set of Francis's mouth.

Francis shook his head. 'Not the son, who must be about my age. But the father is a rogue of the highest order.'

'In what way?'

Francis took the opportunity to halt for a moment, and lower Mary gently onto the top of an empty barrel outside an inn. He perched on the barrel beside hers and explained. 'I left Tavistock as a boy approaching his ninth birthday, and the whole family left with me. We were reduced to poverty because my father's farm had failed, and he'd left the farmland for sale with a local land agent. We moved on from Plymouth, and my father became the church minister in a village in Kent. When I returned some years later, I learned that the land had been sold to Richard Grenville, whose son of the same name now besports himself in the old abbey, having cheated my family out of the money they were due.'

'How was that?' Mary asked, her hopes all but extinguished.

Francis spat into the mud and completed the story. 'He took possession of our land on a promise that the two hundred pounds or so that it had been assessed as being worth would be paid once his father's estate had been resolved. This was the grandfather of the present Grenville, you understand, and he was regarded as something of a tragic hero after he went down on the *Mary Rose* while defending England against the French. Because of this we lost a lawsuit we brought against the family for payment of the money due.'

'So, the Grenvilles are in debt to you for two hundred pounds?'

'No, we are in debt to them.'

'How so?'

'Remember I said that we lost the lawsuit? This was only because of the standing of the Grenville family locally, and their bribe to the magistrate who judged the cause. This meant that we were due the costs of raising the action — both ours *and* theirs. At the last count this had, by dint of interest, risen well above the original two hundred pounds, which by law we have been adjudged not entitled to anyway.'

'But they do not pursue the debt?'

'Not for some years. But neither are they likely to sell us the abbey.'

'Not even if you offer them much more than it is worth?'

Francis shook his head one more time before taking Mary gently by the hand and lifting her from the barrel in order to continue their joint progress up the street, hand in hand.

'A pity, all the same,' Mary muttered as she snuggled closer to Francis. 'I had quite set my heart on being a fine lady.'

Francis stopped suddenly, pulled her to him and kissed her lovingly on the lips. 'To me you already *are* a fine lady, and if you wish to acquire Buckland Abbey, then it shall be yours. I shall just have to ensure that Richard Grenville does not know who the real purchaser is.'

'And the cost, if you are to offer more than it is worth? Have we the money?'

Francis looked intently into her eyes. 'If you will consent to me putting back to sea, we shall have enough money to buy twenty abbeys.'

16

Everything was prepared, and the seventy men recruited by Francis, and judged by him to be the roughest of the rough, sat with bated breath on the decks of the *Pascha* and the *Swan*, invisible below the gunnels and awaiting the commands from their captains as they nestled their cutlasses, swords and knives close into their chests. The Spanish treasure ship was half a league beyond their bows, cruising sedately towards them on the moderate swell created by the gentle westerly that had filled her sails ever since she'd left Nombre de Dios on her way home to Spain, laden with gold and silver.

Francis steered the *Pascha* to port of the oncoming carrack and called down to Jim Short and his gun crew to stand by the gun ports, currently closed in order not to alert their quarry, but shortly to be opened in preparation for the culverins to be rolled out along their carriages. The smaller *Swan* was well to the rear, and Captain Ben Isles steered her to starboard of the oncoming vessel, but close enough to her line of passage for the lookout on the *Santa Katerina* to shout down a warning to his captain. This was precisely the diversion that Francis had planned, and as the captain and crew of the Spanish vessel began bellowing in alarm at the small but swiftly approaching carrack that seemed to be bearing down on a collision course with them, they were oblivious to the fact that the larger vessel on their starboard beam had opened her gun ports as she drew level.

Francis yelled the command, and one deck down Jim Short repeated it. The culverins were rolled forward, already loaded, and tilted at a slight angle, since their targets were the masts and associated rigging of the Spanish ship. A further barked command from Jim Short and the cannon fired in sequence, ripping away the means of propulsion from the *Santa Katerina*. Ben Isles ordered a hasty lowering of sail, and what little forward motion the *Swan* had been enjoying as she tacked against the westerly was reduced to nothing.

As if by magic, swarthy men with determined grimaces, loud curses and sharpened weapons rose from the deck of the *Swan* in time to throw grappling irons, constructed from small anchors tied to long ropes, onto the deck of the foreign vessel as they drew level. There was a grinding shudder as the two vessels locked together, and the English marauders leapt over the double set of gunnels onto the Spanish deck, where they made short work of the token defence offered by unarmed deckhands taken totally by surprise.

While this had been going on, Francis had ordered the *Pascha*'s gun ports to be closed again, so that the vessel was not swamped when she was turned tightly into the prevailing wind, and steered with only her mizzen mast for power until she also drew alongside the prize. Eager deckhands threw grappling hooks from over her sides into the now blood-smeared deck of the overpowered enemy vessel. Francis leaped across with a drawn sword and demanded, in broken Spanish, that her captain be hauled from where he was cowering in his stateroom, and interrogated, with a knife at his throat, regarding his cargo. Two hours later the hold of the *Swan* had been half filled with gold and silver intended for Madrid, and it was time to seek out another target sailing unsuspectingly out of Nombre de Dios.

They had successfully attacked three more vessels sailing across the wide inland bay until someone on land finally realised what was happening, and a heavily armed warship slipped her moorings in Nombre de Dios and headed for the two English vessels with all guns blazing. They were prepared for this, and in a pre-arranged manoeuvre the *Pascha* and the *Swan* moved half a league apart, tacking energetically against the westerly wind that was driving the *Santa Dominica* across the calm water towards them at such a speed that she flew straight past them, firing salvo after salvo that sailed harmlessly through the air high above both vessels, given their low profile in the water.

Then it was time to counter-attack, and first the *Pascha*, with Francis in command, then the *Swan* captained by Ben Isles, turned hard on their keels and pursued the *Santa Dominica* with the advantage of the wind gauge. Timing their attacks so that the two vessels, on either side of the Spanish aggressor, were not in line abreast as they swooped — thereby eliminating the risk that they would be firing at each other — they sprayed the Spaniard with culverin shot to both her port and starboard beams. Given the height of the *Santa Dominica* out of the water, and the sleeker, lower lines of her English aggressor, the target was impossible to miss. Within minutes she was heading to the bottom of the bay, with Spanish sailors diving off her matchwood decks and swimming for their lives.

There was a small celebration party on board the *Pascha*, during which they considered their options.

'We could set sail for Plymouth with enough gold and silver to last us the rest've our days,' Jim Short enthused as he swilled down his third mug of cider.

Francis was reminded that each of the men had been promised a one hundredth share of any loot, which would be more than many of them had seen in their entire lives, while for his captain and boatswains it would be a fiftieth. But his curiosity was unquenchable, and he turned to Jim. 'I believe that we could acquire three times what we have already in a very short time.'

Jim frowned and enquired what Francis had in mind. 'After all, there don't seem to be any more gold ships tied up alongside the wharves o' that town back there.'

'Precisely,' Francis agreed. 'So where's it coming from? The vessels we looted had come to Nombre de Dios to load their precious cargoes, so somewhere in the town there must be a great storehouse. I say we level the town, then empty that storehouse.'

The following morning, the inhabitants of Nombre de Dios awoke to the sound of English cannon shot blowing off the roofs of their timber dwellings and blasting holes in the side of what Francis believed — accurately — to be the governor's office. It was the largest structure in sight, until it was reduced to a shell by deadly fire from the *Pascha* in particular.

The combined crews then ran up the shoreline, screaming at the tops of their lungs and waving their weapons above their heads. There were a few stray shots from nervously held firearms, then the token guard in front of the shattered administrative headquarters abandoned their weapons and fled. The English had incurred no casualties, and they surrounded Francis, cheering loudly, as he entered the remains of the building with drawn swords, accompanied as always by Jim Short, similarly armed. The governor was swiftly located as he attempted to leave by what was the only remaining door, and his English improved rapidly as Francis emphasised the superiority of his position by slashing the ruff from his ridiculously garish tunic and pointing the blade of his sword at the naked throat thereby exposed.

The governor assured them that while the town did indeed once possess a gold and silver store, until a lucky English cannon shot had blown a hole in its front wall, the store had recently been emptied by the Spanish vessels that the invaders had already captured. Francis's next enquiry was as to the location of the mines from which the valuable ore was extracted, and he was further advised by a trembling governor that there was no mine in the locality, but that the precious metals came by donkey convoy across the narrow strip of land behind them. Since this appeared to consist of virgin forest, Francis was suspicious, and instructed Jim Short to assume guard duties over the governor's throat while he went outside and looked up towards the sky. The sun was rising rapidly, but there was a large coconut or palm tree of some sort in the centre of the square of demolished buildings that had once been a township. Francis put his favourite childhood diversion to good use as he scrambled up it and cast his eyes over the land further west. Then he yelled in delight.

Not only was there a clear gouge mark through the forest that denoted the existence of a crude track along which animals bearing precious loads could be led, but there was glittering ocean in the far distance. Francis's brain reeled with the revelation that the place where they had landed was merely the eastern side of a narrow promontory of sorts. There appeared to be a vast ocean to the west that was simply begging to be explored, and the precious metals that traversed the forest track ahead of being stored in Nombre de Dios must be coming ashore on that far side.

A cursory inspection of the remains of the store in the settlement itself yielded only enough booty to encumber the dozen men detailed to heave it back on carts seized from the rear of the store, down the foreshore and into the hold of the *Swan*. The governor was only too happy to advise his captors that the next caravan of donkeys was expected to emerge from the forest track in a week's time, and he was rewarded for his assistance by being taken back to the *Pascha* and thrown into its hold in order to admire the rich hoard that was already stored there.

Francis, Jim and Ben Isles sat around the table in Francis's cabin and agreed on their next course of action. The hold of the *Swan* was filled to capacity with cargo transferred from the hold of the *Pascha*, thereby increasing its capacity to take more loot once they had ambushed the convoy that was due along the forest track in a few days' time. Ben Isles was then instructed to set sail for home, but to deliver the first instalment of their riches not to Plymouth but to Deptford, where there were secure storage facilities. He was also given a message from Francis to John that this was only the first instalment of a much larger haul, that Francis was alive and well, and that he would be returning in the *Pascha* once they had deprived King Philip of Spain of even more of his wealth. A skeleton crew of thirty sailed on the *Swan*, with many a wave and shouted farewell from their comrades who were to remain in order to conduct the raid on the donkey caravan. While Francis took his brigand party inland, Jim Short was to remain in command of the *Pascha* to keep a close look-out for any Spanish vessels sailing into Nombre de Dios. Any that did were to be blown out of the water.

Three days later Francis and his brigand crew waited as silently as they could in the dense foliage of the mountain forest, swatting at the insects that sought to feed off their sweating skin, peeling the occasional leech off their exposed ankles, and keeping a wary eye on the dense undergrowth for the first warning of an approaching procession. Secreted further back in the trees were the wagons they had brought with them to load up their looted hoard prior to running it back to the township and the waiting *Pascha*. They were mightily relieved on their third day of misery in unfamiliar terrain to hear the distant shouts of what were presumably muleteers, driving on the donkeys whose panniers would no doubt be laden with precious metals.

It was over in minutes, as the terrified native muleteers fled into the surrounding undergrowth at the first sight of ragged, sweating and very frustrated English brigands wielding weapons above their heads, and the handful of Spanish guards were overpowered and ordered to kneel in the mud. They were then forced to transfer the packs from the mules into the wagons that were dragged out to transport them. As one pannier was being pulled from the back of a mule, a pure gold necklace fell to the ground at Francis's feet. He picked it up, cleaned it perfunctorily with his hand, then slipped it inside his shirt. 'No doubt intended for a high-class whore in Madrid, but I can find a more worthy neck for it to grace,' he announced as he gave the signal for the convoy to move off, the Spanish guards dragged along behind it by means of ropes attached to the rear wagon.

Their difficulties began as they breasted the final slope, which fortunately was well hidden from the town of Nombre de Dios, and looked down at a scene much changed since they had set off triumphantly to capture the gold train. There was no sign of the *Pascha* moored at the jetty, but in its place were three massive Spanish warships. Their armed crews could be seen working slowly through the wreckage of the township that the English had created, as if to repair it. Francis ordered an immediate withdrawal into the trees before they were spotted. As they crouched under the overhanging foliage, Francis's leading hand Jack Simmonds sidled up to him, eyes wide with fear and disbelief.

'What 'appened to the ship?' he asked.

Francis hastily swallowed what would have been an angry retort that he was a sailor, not a mystic, and settled for something more restrained. 'My best guess — or perhaps it's my dearest wish — is that they were driven off by those Spanish ships and sailed north.'

'Will they come back for us?' Jack asked.

Francis stared him out for a moment before responding, 'Would you, if you were Jim Short, facing *those* odds?'

'So what we gunner do?' was the next question.

Francis thought hard and quickly. 'We can't go back down, obviously, so we'll have to transfer all this stuff onto our shoulders and cut north through the trees, in the hope of finding where the *Pascha*'s been moored, safely beyond the reach of the Spanish.'

They were fortunate in that most of the more valuable items in the stolen hoard had been packed in saddlebags for easy transportation by the mules. These were quickly lifted out of the wagons and laid across the shoulders of the men, with a double load for their Spanish prisoners, as they struck north through the tangled undergrowth. They hacked a new path painfully and slowly through plants that seemed dedicated to barring their progress with their thorns, all the while keeping an eye out for the wriggling and slithering threats beneath their feet. For two days and nights they struggled on without food or water, until Francis called a halt and looked down the slope towards the ocean. Instructing his men to wait where they were, he stumbled and hacked his way down to the soft sandy beach. After casting a cautious glance to his right, to ensure that they could not be seen from Nombre de Dios, he yelled for his men to follow him down onto the sandy foreshore.

On his instruction they scooped with their bare hands into the deep sand and buried the most valuable-looking items, which still seemed to them to be worth a king's ransom. They then placed a cairn of stones over the burial site, and Francis noted its position as he stepped back into the surf and looked back, as if he were a sailor rowing ashore from a ship moored out to sea. There were several trees to the left that leaned in towards each other in a pattern that reminded him of how his parents would huddle together over the family bible under the candlelight. Committing that image to his memory, he called for volunteers to build a raft.

'What with?' came the predictable enquiry from Jack Simmonds, whose best qualities lay in his muscular arms rather than between his ears.

Francis pointed back up the slope. 'Wood, unless you know some method of shipbuilding out of sand?'

Jack reddened as his comrades joined in the laughter, and he was the first to attack a willowy palm tree with his sword, using it as an axe until it grew too blunt for the task. Others joined in, and within an hour they had a dozen long, pliable tree trunks that they lashed together with strips torn from their shirts. 'Save the largest shirts for sails,' Francis commanded. After a lengthy discussion regarding which of the men was the stoutest, two of the former crew of the *Swan* divested themselves of their undershirts, which Francis lashed to the longest tree trunk. He attached this to the front of the crude raft with the square lashing that was familiar to every sailor. Finally, he lifted the smallest of the remaining tree trunks high above his head. 'This will serve as our rudder, men,' he declared proudly, as he announced that Jack Simmonds and Amos Blunt would be joining him in the launch of their newly created vessel into the swift current that was sweeping north.

'How do we know that they came this way?' Jack asked after an hour or so. His breeches had been soaked by the pursuing waves that broke over the raft, which was being driven slowly north by the wind power behind two discarded mariners' shirts.

'Which route home would you have chosen?' Francis challenged him. 'The wind and current suggest a northerly course, and that way lies Plymouth.'

'Think you to reach Plymouth on this uncertain craft?' Jack asked in his simple way.

Francis burst out laughing, despite their hazardous plight. 'That would indeed be the voyage to end all voyages, but at worst we shall make landfall on some part of this coast that lies in French hands. At best, we shall discover that the *Pascha* has dropped anchor somewhere ahead of us.'

Day followed night in what seemed like a progression that would never end, and Francis was sleeping like the dead when an excited shout broke into his dreams. His eyes flew open, and before he had time to register either his raging thirst or the terrible burning pain in his bare shoulders after days of exposure to the relentless sun, he saw Amos Blunt waving both arms in the air like a man bereft of reason. Francis looked where he was pointing and let out a cry of his own as tears of relief began rolling down his face. The vessel that lay half a league to their north was a small square-rigged carrack, and she was once again flying the Tudor pennant.

Their shouts elicited shrill and excited responses from the rear deck of the *Pascha*. She quickly raised anchor and tacked against both wind and current to where the raft was barely visible above the waterline, such was the strain it had endured, having carried three grown men for three days. Francis was the last up the rope ladder, and as he winced onto the deck of the

Pascha, hampered by the burning sensation in his shoulders, he found himself staring into the eyes of Jim Short.

'Forgive me, Cap'n, but I thought it best to save the cargo and the men from them Spanish ships what entered the bay, afore they began firing at us.'

'You're forgiven, provided that you don't embrace me,' Francis replied, pointing to the raw patches on his shoulders where the skin had peeled off. 'Then I need the longest draught of good Devon cider that you've ever served. If you tell me you've drunk it all, you're in for a dip overboard.'

Jim yelled for cider to be brought on deck, then looked back at Francis with a worried frown. 'Did any of the others escape with you, and what of your venture against the Spanish gold convoy?'

'The others are stranded on a beach south of here, and there is much gold buried in the sand. We must head south and retrieve both them and it. I even have gold down here.'

Jim looked askance as Francis reached down into the front of his hose for the gold necklace he had acquired. 'I have two things for my wife down here,' he joked as he extracted the necklace, 'and this one is pure gold. Now, let us lose no time in heading for home with our hard-won rewards.'

17

During Francis's brief stay in Deptford — just long enough to unload his cargo, since he was anxious to return to Plymouth — he had a lengthy conversation with John regarding whether or not the queen should be offered some of the riches wrung from Spanish hands. John had undertaken to consult Sir Robert Dudley on the matter, since he seemed to know Her Majesty's true wishes, regardless of her public utterances. The matter was a delicate one, Francis was advised, since the queen was making overtures to Spain for a treaty of non-aggression. The Spanish Ambassador Mendoza was constantly advising her that her requests would come to nothing for as long as England supported the Dutch cause, and English pirates continued to assert their right to trade in the Americas.

'So I should delay returning to the Spanish Main for more of that which is being counted and valued, even as we speak?' Francis asked glumly.

John spread his arms in a gesture of uncertainty. 'That is perhaps a matter for Her Majesty to determine. I merely say that your adventures to the west of here are delaying any prospect of a lasting peace with Spain.'

'But those same adventures are ensuring that we shall soon have no need to cower at the prospect of Spanish superiority,' Francis argued. 'The wealth I have already brought back will allow at least ten more keels to be laid. On the subject of which, I would have more vessels like the *Pascha* and the *Swan*, commodious but low in the water. Perhaps a little more towards the capacity of the *Pelican*, but with her bulk in the beam rather than in her height. During our recent encounters with the Spanish, their fire went clean above our rigging, while we had a clear line into their holds. So much so that if we are to rob such vessels of their content, we have to take care to keep our aim high, so as not to send them to the bottom ere we have plundered them.'

'You must meet with my good friend Richard Chapman while you are here in Deptford,' said John, 'since it is his boatyard that benefits from our commissions, to such an extent that it is rumoured abroad that I am lining my own pockets with a share of said commissions. His yard is also an excellent place in which to hide what we have built from spying eyes. If you wish for modifications to our next fleet of ships, it is he with whom you must speak.'

They had left matters at that, and two days later Francis was smiling at the sounds of wives and families welcoming home his eager skeleton crew of Plymouth men as the *Pascha* moored at the Hawkins wharf. He took a coach to St Budeaux to be reunited with Mary.

When he arrived at their cottage, Francis went straight upstairs and tiptoed towards his wife's bed, then leaned down and kissed her softly on the forehead. She murmured gently, and then her eyes opened. 'Do I dream, or is that really you?'

'It is me in the flesh, my sweet. The weary mariner, home from his voyage.'

'God be praised!' she uttered as she raised herself from the bolster and threw her arms around him. 'Are we now wealthy, so that you can remain by my side for my remaining years?'

'As for wealth, close your eyes for a moment,' he replied.

'I fear that if I do, this will all prove to have been a dream,' she objected, although her eyes closed anyway.

Francis draped the gold necklace around her neck and fastened the clasp. 'Keep them closed,' he instructed as he reached across to her bedside table and handed her the looking glass that was always there. He then told her to open her eyes, which widened in disbelief when she saw the pure gold glistening dully in the light from the mid-morning sun. 'There's the answer to your first question.' He kissed her on the lips. 'We are indeed wealthy.'

'And my second question?' Mary teased him. 'How long before you have to set sail in search of more?'

'A good while yet,' Francis reassured her, 'but perhaps one more voyage, if you wish to move into Buckland Abbey.'

He was uncertain whether or not this would be necessary, since the task of valuing the cargoes that his vessels had brought back was still in the hands of Navy clerks under John's supervision. The *Swan*'s cargo had been assessed at over twenty thousand pounds, and most of the sailors from that vessel had already been paid off. Francis had then arrived in the *Pascha* with an even greater prize, and his own rough estimate was that he could safely count on ten thousand pounds for himself.

While Mary was dressing in order to join him for a celebratory dinner, Francis took the opportunity to walk round the corner to William and Judith's house, wishing to enquire of Judith as to the true state of Mary's health.

'Tell me true,' he urged her, 'since she is wont to lie to me and assure me that all goes well with her.'

'In truth it does, most of the time,' Judith confirmed. 'But there are days, sometimes weeks, when this terrible pain afflicts her in her chest — well, her bosoms, to be frank — and she is fit to scream the house down until she receives the simple from the apothecary. It is mandrake, in the main, and her doctor tells me privily that with each onset of the malady it takes more and more of the simple to quell her suffering.'

'So long as it does,' Francis murmured, horrified by what he was hearing.

Judith took his hands in hers as she continued. 'It does, but therein lies the worry, Francis. The physician advises me that mandrake is fatal to the body if taken beyond the quantities recommended by him, and that as her occasions of pain grow stronger, she might be tempted to exceed the dosage prescribed for her.'

'And if she does?' Francis asked, despite his sudden feeling of breathlessness.

'Madness and death,' Judith told him hoarsely. 'Forgive me, Francis, but I felt it my duty to put you wise.'

'And how often does she fall into one of these periods of malady?'

'There were three such occasions while you were last at sea. The third, and most recent, was but a month ago, so there may be some weeks yet before she succumbs again. But if you value her life and her wits, you must not let her exceed what the apothecary advises.'

'So I must sit by and watch her suffer, say you?'

'Unless you want her dead, or in the madhouse,' Judith replied sadly.

Francis walked back home with a mounting feeling of dread. As he did so, he racked his brain for something that would divert Mary from dwelling too long on her affliction, and thereby bringing another bout of it on faster. He had almost reached the front of their cottage when he became aware of the presence of a skinny man dressed in a long brown vestment, sitting by the side of the dusty road with his grubby palm extended.

'Spare something for a fallen brother?' the man asked in a croaking voice, and Francis was reminded of the days when his father would chase any wandering friar such as this from the farm with an angry oath. His father had definitely been a Reformer at heart, and it had ultimately been his salvation. But what had happened to those who had been cast out in the whirlwind that had brought down the Church of Rome, and thrown its thousands of followers in holy orders onto the charity of those to whom they had once ministered? Monks. Monasteries. Abbeys.

Francis searched hastily through the money bag at his belt, found a shilling coin, leaned down and handed it to the beggar. It would feed him, and perhaps afford him shelter, for at least one night.

The man smiled up at him through uneven and blackened teeth. 'God bless you, brother.'

'No — God bless *you*,' said Francis, 'for you have answered my prayer for guidance.'

The following day he took himself down to the chandlery store owned by Geoffrey Montacourt, who had benefitted considerately over the years from the Hawkins family's patronage. He beamed at Francis from behind his counter and enquired after his health.

'Excellent, thank you, Master Montacourt,' Francis replied, 'and I trust that trade is brisk?'

'As ever, Master. Unless the ocean dries up, Plymouth will ever need the services of a chandler, as has your family these many years. What can I oblige you with this fine morning?'

'I wish to purchase an estate,' Francis told him.

Montacourt stared at him. 'From a chandler?'

Francis nodded. 'Through the services of a chandler, certainly. I will make it worth your while.'

'Perhaps you'd care to take a seat, share a glass of wine with me, and explain what it is you require?'

Francis declined the wine, but accepted a mug of cider and advised the still bemused chandler that he wished him to approach the Grenville family with an offer to purchase Buckland Abbey for whatever sum they might have in mind. Francis would in due course supply the asking price, and would pay Montacourt a fee for his services.

'Why can you not approach them yourself?' the chandler asked.

Francis made him aware of the long-standing feud between the families. 'But there will be no dishonesty about it, since you will be the lawful purchaser. It is simply the case that I will buy it from you immediately thereafter, with an additional sum by way of your profit on the re-sale to me.'

Since he could find no argument against this proposal, Montacourt agreed to it, and Francis walked on down to the wharf with a lighter heart. The *Pelican* was out of the water, being scraped, and the *Pascha* and *Swan* were being refitted with sails after the ravages of their last voyage. Francis sat on the harbour wall and thought of those days when, as a young boy, he had gazed wistfully at the vessels at anchor in the Sound, wondering where they were bound — and if perhaps some men of gloom were right, and one day one of them would venture too far and fall off the side of the flat earth. He chuckled at such ignorance, then asked himself what he had done to disprove that theory. For all his wealth, why had he not yet gone around the world and come safely back? Hadn't he learned, during his last time in Nombre de Dios, that there was more ocean on the other side of the Spanish Main? Had it yet been claimed by the Spanish or Portuguese, and if not, why was he still sitting here?

He breezed back into the main ground floor room just as their all-purpose servant, Jenny, was laying the board for dinner. 'Where is the mistress?' he asked, and Jenny jerked her head towards the rear window, through which Mary could be seen picking flowers from the bed on the far side of the narrow lawn, and laying them carefully in her straw basket. Francis walked outside and called over to her. 'They are pretty, but not as entrancing as you.'

Mary turned and smiled palely. 'Even though I grow less each day?'

'You should eat more,' Francis told her as he walked across the grass and took her hand. 'I own that the meals were always more appetising when prepared by your own hand, but you seem to have little appetite of late. Speaking as one who enjoys his food, I have no complaint regarding Jenny's cooking. Perhaps you will have more desire to eat when I tell you that I have just made arrangements for us to acquire Buckland Abbey.'

Mary's face lit up. 'Really? When, pray, and for how much? And can we afford it?'

'As for when, that will depend upon how soon my chosen agent can approach Grenville in the matter. As for how much, that will of course be a matter for Grenville. As for whether or not we can afford it, I must return to Deptford.'

'So soon?'

'I will not be delayed long,' he reassured her. 'I need to learn how much is left for us from the wealth I brought back from my last voyage. John has it locked away in a safe place where others are assessing its value. I left Deptford early, in order to come home to you.'

'Very well,' Mary conceded grudgingly, 'but mind that you come back as soon as you are able.'

Four days later, after John had sought an early audience with Sir Robert Dudley, he and Francis stood nervously in a window alcove in an ornately furnished room, gazing down into a courtyard of Whitehall Palace. Francis gazed up at the exquisitely painted ceiling.

'Sir Robert has excellent chambers,' he remarked.

John shook his head. 'I don't believe that this area of the palace is his,' he said as he gazed across at the two liveried attendants who were guarding the door on the far side, each with a halberd held firmly upright. 'I have been here once before, and through that door…'

He broke off as the door in question opened for long enough for Sir Robert to poke his head through the gap and make a satisfied noise.

'Good, you are on time. Through here, gentlemen.'

'Dear God, not again!' John murmured as he led the way, then stood smartly to one side so that Francis might see the cause of his apprehension for himself.

Robert Dudley walked smartly up to the raised dais and bowed to the richly dressed woman seated on the heavily padded chair with its gilt arms.

'You have of course had occasion to meet the Navy Treasurer, Your Majesty, but may I also introduce Master Francis Drake?'

John and Francis bowed and kissed the extended ringed hand in turn. Then Queen Elizabeth surveyed Francis from head to foot before addressing him.

'The same Master Drake of whom I am constantly bombarded with complaints from the Spanish Ambassador?'

'Your Majesty?' Francis half choked.

'Piracy on the high seas, according to the ambassador. His latest reported outrage is that you sank one of his master's vessels off the coast of some unpronounceable place across the ocean in the Americas.'

'That would have been Nombre de Dios, Your Majesty. It lies on the eastern side of a narrow strip of land.'

'Regardless of the location, Master Drake,' Elizabeth replied with a stony face, 'what have you to say of the allegation?'

'I do not deny it, Your Majesty,' Francis confirmed with a slight bow, 'but did His Excellency also advise you that we were attacked first by this same vessel, when it put to sea to prevent us berthing in the township of Nombre de Dios?'

'*They* attacked *you* before you sank their vessel, say you?'

'Yes, Your Majesty.'

'But if you sank her, how were you able to secure her cargo and bring it back to England?'

'The riches I brought back to England were discovered later, Your Majesty, when I took reprisal action against the township from which the vessel had been dispatched. It proved to be the collection point for the precious metals that were being brought overland from the other side of the narrow strait of land that I mentioned a moment ago.'

'And it was this wealth that you brought back some weeks since, which Dudley here tells me is worth some thirty thousand pounds?' Elizabeth asked.

Francis blinked in amazement, then nodded. 'It almost cost us our lives, Your Majesty. But King Philip will no doubt be chewing his rosary beads in outrage, hence the false complaint by his Ambassador.'

Elizabeth suppressed the smile and converted it into a frown. 'Regardless of the circumstances, and even after making allowances for the fact that you were obliged to defend yourselves, Master Drake, what you did constituted an act of piracy, even if committed on land. The ambassador will

161

demand that I punish you, and I must be seen to do so if we are to appease Philip of Spain. Either that, or the ambassador will demand that you be exiled from England, and I would be loath to do that, since I expect that it will soon need all the sailors of your calibre that it can get.'

'Perhaps a heavy fine, Your Majesty?' Francis grinned. 'Shall we say thirty thousand pounds, to be assigned over to the Treasury from where it currently lies in the Navy vaults?'

This time Elizabeth couldn't hide her smile, and she clapped her hands daintily while allowing herself a ladylike chuckle. 'I can see that we shall become good friends, Master Drake. Robert, would you arrange suitable accommodation for Masters Drake and Hawkins here at Whitehall? That way they will be free to join us for supper, along with yourself and Cecil. Please also invite Sir Christopher Hatton. You may now all withdraw.'

'That could have gone a lot worse,' John observed once they were back in the outer chamber and breathing more easily.

'Could it?' Francis demanded testily. 'I am thirty thousand pounds poorer, and I shall require more investors ere I can set sail in search of more wealth. And Mary is hoping to move into Buckland Abbey.'

'At least you retain your head,' was all that John could offer by way of consolation. 'And when we both return home, we can boast to our wives that we took supper with the queen.'

'I'd rather be eating fish pie with Mary in Plymouth,' was Francis's grumpy response.

Francis began to relax and enjoy the sumptuous supper as the conversation drifted to a subject dear to his heart.

'Sir Christopher is not just a member of my Privy Council and Vice-Chamberlain of my Household,' Elizabeth announced as she languidly selected her third sugared almond. 'He also shares an interest with you, Master Drake, in that he would wish to invest in a voyage that will see England claim the oceans and lands that may lie beyond the Americas.'

'Truly?' Francis asked as he put down his knife and abandoned the slice of venison that was impaled on the end of it.

'Truly,' Sir Christopher Hatton confirmed as he raised his goblet in a silent toasting gesture, 'but I am no sailor like yourself, Master Drake. My interest is purely financial. I am already wealthy, as you will learn if you enquire of my many enemies here at Court — including Sir Robert here, although he hides it admirably — but I would acquire more. I can offer ten thousand pounds to see your fleet properly equipped, and your cousin Hawkins can no doubt lend you some of the worthy vessels being constructed in secret downriver in Deptford. What we will require of you will be the sailors and the navigational skills, if you have learned more from Dr Dee than how to make gold from base metal.'

'I did indeed learn much from him,' Francis confirmed, 'but in truth I learned the most important fact from my previous expedition. There is an ocean on the far side of the Americas that lies west of that land, but — if I am correct in my belief — it will prove to lie to the east of us, so that by sailing round the foot of the Americas and proceeding in what will seem to us like a westerly tack, I will eventually return to England from the east.'

'Thereby proving beyond peradventure that the world is not flat, as I have had occasion to demonstrate to Her Majesty,' said Dudley as he took her hand.

'Yes, thank you, Robert,' said Elizabeth, tactfully withdrawing her hand. 'I well recall your little trick with the orange. But Master Drake must realise that if he is to discover new lands, he must ensure that they are claimed in my name, and to that purpose I shall equip him with Tudor pennants, brass plates and other items that shall leave no-one in doubt that what is done by Drake the explorer is in the name of Elizabeth of England.'

'I would be honoured to have such a noble task allocated to me,' said Francis, 'but what of the Spanish? When we spoke earlier, you all but advised me that Philip of Spain seeks my head on Tower Hill for my engagement of his vessels, and my insistence on my right to trade in New Spain.'

'You must do nothing to provoke him further, understand?' Elizabeth frowned. 'On this you may rely: if ever it becomes a choice between England's safety and your head, I can soon find other sailors.'

'But none of the calibre of my cousin,' John observed as his first contribution to the conversation, only to be pierced by an angry glare from Elizabeth.

'Be that as it may,' she continued, 'I wish Master Drake to be in no doubt as to where his best interests lie, since they are also the best interests of England.'

'And if I am attacked by resentful Spaniards?' Francis asked.

Elizabeth's expression softened as she turned back to address him. 'That is, of course, another matter. But I have yet to hear you say that you will accept this commission.'

'If the expression on my countenance does not speak loudly enough,' Francis said, beaming, 'then let my words make up for my lack of gratitude. I accept with all my heart. Your Majesty may rest assured that the English pennant shall soon grace half the foreshores of the undiscovered world, while the Tudor flag on my stern mast shall be seen in oceans as yet unknown to Spain.'

Francis's excitement and commitment wavered in the face of the reaction from his wife Mary when he broke the news a week later. She sat down heavily at the large table in their main room and stared straight ahead without a word.

'Are you not pleased, my sweet?' he urged her. 'I get to fulfil the dream that has possessed me since boyhood. I do so with the queen's blessing and the patronage of one of the wealthiest men in England, and I shall return with more than enough money to purchase Buckland Abbey, *whatever* price Grenville shall demand!'

'As for your lifelong dream,' Mary replied coldly, 'I am of course pleased for you that you are able to pursue it. That you do so with the queen's blessing also adds to the pleasure. But in that it will take you away from me yet again, for what may be the only days left to me in this life, do not expect me to share in your joy. As for Buckland Abbey, should I be in this world when you return, you may move into it alone, since it has been the cause of your desertion of your sick wife.'

There seemed to be no reasoning with her, and with a sad heart he walked outside into the garden and stared down at the flower beds that were now past their best. When he wandered back inside to the sound of the board being laid for dinner, he was advised that Mary had taken to her bed, complaining of a headache, and he left it at that. When he tiptoed gently into their bedchamber late that night, after downing twice his normal amount of cider, Mary's face was turned resolutely to the wall. He slipped silently in beside her and listened to her rhythmic breathing as he slowly fell asleep.

Her sullen mood didn't alter for the next few days, so Francis decided that since matters could not get any worse between them, he might as well lose himself in the necessary arrangements, beginning with the acquisition and fitting out of the necessary ships. The first four vessels answering his latest specifications had already been floated down the slipway of Richard Chapman's shipyard, and they had been named the *Marigold*, the *Christopher*, the *Elizabeth* and the *Swan*. The *Pelican* had been chosen as the flagship, and Francis sailed in her to Deptford, the remaining vessels in his fleet following in line, to select his remaining captains and crews. He would also load as much armament as each vessel could carry, given the hope that most of the hold capacity of each vessel would be required for precious metals and other cargoes with which to reward Sir Christopher Hatton.

Their patron took considerable interest in what was going on in Deptford, and one afternoon he arrived by barge with a large bundle under his arm. He strode purposefully up to where Francis, from the quayside, was supervising the loading of cannon shot below decks on the *Pelican*, shook his hand and handed over the bundle — a roll of cloth with eyelets set into it.

'This is your leading vessel?' he asked as he nodded down at the *Pelican*.

'Indeed, she will be commanding the fleet that sails around the world in order to secure my reputation and your fortune,' Francis answered.

'Then it is only appropriate that she carry what is now in your hand,' said Hatton, and Francis unfurled what he had already guessed was a flag of some sort. The emblem was a deer painted a garish yellow, and while Francis was admiring the skill that had gone into its creation, Hatton added, 'I would that you fly this on one of your masts, perhaps below the Tudor banner. It is my family crest of a golden hind, and I would that it be seen wherever you venture.'

'It would be an honour,' Francis assured him, 'and hopefully there will be times when it proves necessary to remove the Tudor flag. With your yellow deer on our mainmast, we shall look like a harmless merchantman — until we open the gun ports, that is.'

'It's a golden hind, not a yellow deer,' Hatton reminded him. 'But mind the queen's warning — if you are captured, she will disown you.'

'But I wager that she won't disown us when we return triumphant, laden with riches, whomsoever they may once have belonged to,' said Francis.

Once the five vessels were fully fitted out — and with two-thirds of their crews hired from among the available mariners who always frequented the local alehouses, seeking further voyages — they set sail in a proud line down the Thames on an outward tide. Their departure was acknowledged by a burst of cannon fire from the river wall of Deptford Dockyard, of which John was now both the Treasurer and Controller, following the death of his father-in-law Benjamin Gonson earlier that year.

The return to Plymouth was more subdued, and Francis discovered why when Mary eventually got around to talking to him again. She had marked his return with the same sullen silence that had marred his departure to Deptford, but as the days approached the chosen departure date for the voyage 'to prove that the world is round', as local gossip had it, Mary would occasionally, and grudgingly, make some comment or other. This time it was, 'You realise that I'm the most reviled woman in Plymouth?'

'Why might that be?' Francis asked, glad that she was speaking again, but concerned by what she had to say.

'Because it is believed that you are taking local men to their deaths.'

'By those who also still believe that the earth is flat, you mean?'

'No — by those who remember how few came back with you and John *last* time. At least if you are killed this time, I will have something in common with those who snarl when I pass them in the street.'

Thoroughly alarmed by what he had learned, Francis called on Judith and William and asked them if what Mary had complained about was true. Judith sat him down with a mug of cider and explained.

'Some are saying that, it is true. But you must have seen for yourself how Mary is all but destroyed by your seeming disregard for her. You set sail for foreign parts at every excuse.'

'I do so in order to make us rich,' Francis protested, but there came a faint snort from old William, safely seated in a wide chair from which he could not fall, such was his frailty these days.

'You do so out of vainglory, Francis. You were always the same, even when I had to teach you the basics of shipbuilding. Your only interest was in putting to sea and playing the hero.'

Things did not become any more promising when Francis called in at the premises of Geoffrey Montacourt, the chandler who had undertaken to make a bid for Buckland Abbey in his own name, in order to conceal Francis's interest in the place. Geoffrey shook his head sadly when asked if there had been any progress. 'There is another who is also interested in purchasing it, and he is Sir George Sydenham, the High Sheriff of Somerset. I fear that Grenville will play the middle game between us, in the hope of raising the price.'

Francis frowned. 'We shall see who has the more wealth available when I return. In the meantime, do continue to fight my cause.'

On the morning of the departure, barely two weeks before the Christmas of 1577, Mary made a point of getting up late, and only appeared downstairs after Francis had finished what might well be his final breakfast at his own table. The silence was unbearable, so Francis rose and put on his cloak, and stood waiting expectantly for some acknowledgement from Mary that, in her mind at least, this might be their final farewell. 'Do I at least get a kiss?' he asked eventually.

'I suppose so,' was her surly response, along with a reluctant dab on the lips from her dry mouth. Without another word he turned and walked away, and by the time he'd reached the end of their frost-covered lane, there were tears streaming down his face.

Then he heard a faint call from somewhere behind him and turned. Mary was racing after him, her bare feet raising faint clouds of frost as they pounded closer and closer. She was screaming, as if in pain, and when she finally hurled herself into his arms, she almost bowled him over.

'Forgive me, my sweet!' she implored. 'I love you more than my life, and I cannot bear for us to part like this! If only you knew the pain in my heart, to have treated you thus these many months. But say that you still love me and will return safe! Then I'll come with you — to Buckland Abbey, or to the ends of the earth if needs be! Just reassure me that I'm still loved!'

'Could you ever doubt it?' Francis replied through his own tears as he hugged her to him. 'But you will catch your death out here in the cold. Let me carry you home to our warm hearth.'

'No!' Mary insisted. 'I could not bear to see you leave through that door again! Just hold me tight, remember this moment as you risk your life on an evil ocean, and come back to me here, where I swear before God that I will treat you as a wife should. Just promise me!'

The tears were frozen on Francis's cheeks as he reached the waterfront, where scores of other women were seeking similar assurances from their departing menfolk. He was reminded that he was carrying their hopes and fears as well as Mary's as he gave the command to cast off, and deliberately kept his eyes fixed ahead as Plymouth Sound slid beneath their keel.

18

Six months later, the remains of Francis's fleet were moored in the gloomy windswept bay of Puerto San Julian, and like his predecessor, the fabled navigator Ferdinand Magellan, Francis opted to winter there. They were well south of the Equator, and had therefore followed winter into the Southern Hemisphere, and there was need to take stock of their perilous circumstances. They were down to only three ships, but not as a result of the unforgiving ocean that they had spent half a year crossing. Instead, it had proved necessary to scuttle the *Christopher* and the *Swan*, after stripping everything serviceable from them, because insufficient men remained to crew them effectively. They had died from disease, by accident, or at the hands of fellow sailors as boredom had led to brawling on board. Francis was thankful that most of those who had perished had been Deptford men, and that their surviving captains, John Chester and Thomas Moone, were still available to take the helm of any enemy vessel they might encounter and plunder after steering it into the nearest port for unloading.

This left the *Marigold*, commanded by John Thomas, and the *Elizabeth* under John Wynter, along with the *Pelican*, Francis's flagship. His decision to move on was due partly to his own frustration at the enforced indolence, partly his curiosity regarding what he had learned from a rare copy of Magellan's log of his voyage around the south of the Americas loaned to him by Dr Dee, and finally because the weather appeared to be in their favour. Although the wind was still bending the sparse vegetation almost horizontally in its eagerness to sweep past the coastal outpost, the snow flurries had ceased, and the visibility was icily clear down the relatively narrow channel that disappeared to their right as they looked out of the harbour into the bay. According to Francis's chart, this was the eastern end of the passage that Magellan had taken around the foot of the Americas, in order to emerge at the other end into clear ocean.

It looked as if they had indeed reached the southernmost point of the long continent whose eastern seaboard had been largely claimed by Spain. If Francis was to do the same for its western seaboard in the name of Elizabeth of England, he had to first lead his fleet of three through the forbidding gorge of swirling water, with towering cliffs on either side. In places it appeared to be little more than five leagues wide, to judge by the promontories that were visible even from the shoreline of San Julian if one looked west. To make matters worse, the wind was blowing consistently from that direction, which would necessitate that the English ships tack from side to side in order to make headway.

Since this would pose too much of a risk to vessels either alongside each other during the passage, or too closely in line astern, Francis opted to take the *Pelican* through first, to be followed, at half-day intervals, first by the *Marigold*, and then the *Elizabeth*. After taking on a month's supply of water and fresh food, Francis ordered the *Pelican* off the moorings it had occupied for six months and took the wheel himself as he called out the settings for the sails that would be put into effect by sweating, cursing deckhands working in shifts.

They were, by Francis's guess, halfway through the strait when the true danger of what they had embarked upon became apparent. The narrow channel, down which they were weaving in long tacking sweeps that were each approximately an hour in duration, lay between two mighty oceans. Each of those oceans had a tidal current, and they met somewhere in the middle in a series of whirlpools that swirled and splashed in waves that approached ten feet in height as the two oceans fought with each other for dominance.

It took three men to hold the wheel steady as wave upon wave smashed into the sturdy beams of the *Pelican*, and spray came in torrential waves over the bows and gunwales, threatening to swamp the vessel, knock her over on her keel, or sweep the grim-faced deckhands over the far side of the ship. Any man overboard would be forever lost in this unforgiving maelstrom, and even Francis was praying to a God he had not given a great deal of thought to since he'd been obliged to listen to his father's sermons half a lifetime ago.

Another fear was that the beams would be ripped clean off their ribs by the relentless battering, and Francis gave thanks to God that they had nothing in the cargo hold that could be displaced by the constant rolling. Then he remembered the cannon on the gun deck, and he prayed that the balls would not be dislodged from their cases, as they would roll around the lower deck and possibly breach the vessel on its water line. At the very least, he thought, the powder would be thoroughly soaked by the salt water that was pouring down through the gaps in the hatches. It would need to be brought up on deck to be thoroughly dried, if they survived.

Francis was startled out of his prayers by excited chattering from his men, and looked up to see that the ocean ahead of them was less stormy. They must, he reasoned, have passed into the calmer waters that lay on the other shore of the Americas. As the channel ahead of them widened in the sinking rays of the afternoon sun, he spotted a small island off their port bow and steered the *Pelican* towards it. There was no sign of any harbour, but a natural inlet appeared to offer shelter. He ordered that the anchor be dropped, and that the crew take stock of any damage they might have suffered.

'We lost the ship's nameboard,' he was told by Jim Short as they sat below decks, sharing a rare rum cask with the senior crew. This was only to be expected, since the nameboard had simply been nailed onto the upper bow, and had clearly been worked loose by the thrashing waves they had just navigated their way through.

'I shall offer a prize to the man who comes up with the best alternative name for the *Pelican*,' Francis joked, addressing the handful of men who sat around him, 'since we seem to have left our identity behind us in that Devil's cauldron back there.'

That was to be by no means their only loss. The *Pelican* had survived, not only as the result of brave and instinctive seamanship by its commander, but because her one-hundred-ton capacity provided sufficient resistance to the towering waves. Half a day behind her — and sailing by night into the worst sea that Captain John Thomas had ever encountered — was the *Marigold*, whose mere thirty tons was insufficient to withstand the battering. She broke up within the first hour, when she was barely through the worst of it, and still in the eastern half of the mountainous turbulence. Her wreckage therefore floated back with the ebbing tide on the Atlantic side, and was spotted by lookouts on the third vessel in the line, the *Elizabeth*. This was under the experienced, and cautious, command of John Wynter, who ordered that all sails be lowered and the anchor dropped, while they looked glumly at the pieces of wreckage that drifted past them.

Wynter had just convinced himself that he owed it to his men not to venture any further when one of his deckhands gave a distressed yell, raced back amidships for a boat hook that lay propped up against the starboard gunwale, and hastened back to the port side, over which he appeared to be fishing for something. With a shout of triumph he pulled hard, and a ten-foot length of wood clattered down onto the deck on the end of the hook, water cascading from it as it lay on the boards.

'What is it, man?' Wynter demanded.

'A nameboard, Cap'n,' came the awestricken reply. 'The *Pelican*.'

'God rest their souls,' Wynter muttered as he ordered the vessel back to San Julian, ahead of a return to Plymouth with the awful tidings.

Francis's crew waited for three days before concluding that the *Marigold* and the *Elizabeth* had either been lost in the watery hell that the *Pelican* had miraculously survived or had turned back for their own safety. During that time, Francis had made use of the first of the brass plates that had come from the royal armourer back in London, and had himself rowed ashore, where he placed the plate under an overhanging rock. He then loudly declared that the land that lay inside the bay was now English soil, and was named Elizabeth Island.

It was then time to push north and explore the far side of the long land mass of the Americas, but there remained the matter of the new name for their vessel. Sailors were a superstitious bunch, who would murmur nervously among themselves that the gods of the ocean had clearly expressed their disapproval of the name *Pelican*, and would take additional vengeance on their frail craft if they defied those gods by pushing on with the same name.

There had been some suggestions for new names, few of them rising above the obvious choices of loved ones back home in England. But *Lucy*, *Amy*, *Katie* or *Martha* somehow

175

failed to sufficiently dignify the momentous event that was unfolding. Francis was at a loss until he looked up at the pennant supplied by Hatton, primarily in order to assess the wind direction as it fluttered on the main mast. Then inspiration struck, and he yelled down to Jim Short, who was lining up the men in anticipation of the order to raise anchor.

'Jim, we have our new name! See yon pennant, supplied by our patron?'

'What, the yeller deer, you mean?'

'Yellow deer be damned — she's a "golden hind", according to Sir Christopher. As of today, we voyage on the *Golden Hind*. Raise anchor, and let's find ourselves some easy wealth!'

The wind gauge for once worked to their advantage as they sailed north with sails filled by a south-westerly — or perhaps it was best described as 'south-easterly', Francis mused as he tried to come to terms with the fact that England was now months away on their port beam. Whatever name one gave to it, they were being driven swiftly along a barren mountainous coastline that seemed to stretch forever beyond their bow. As they kept a safe few leagues from the rocky coastline, occasionally they would pass inlets and islands that appeared to possess vegetation. They slipped swiftly past them on their northward passage, and only began to study the passing land with greater intensity when the water barrels were running low.

It was then that they discovered that Spaniards were not the only hostile inhabitants that they might encounter if they made landfall. On the fifth day they began to notice increased greenery off their starboard beam, and the reason for that became apparent when they saw, to their delight, a substantial waterfall cascading from a cliff top through the dense trees of a forest. This then formed a substantial lake whose waters emptied into the ocean along a wide estuary. They dropped anchor and put ashore in their cutter, loaded with water barrels, which were already part filled from the crystal-clear stream that flowed seawards along the stony beach on which they had made landfall.

Five days later the forward lookout shouted down that there was a sail in sight ahead of them, and Francis leapt up to the bow with his eyeglass, then yelled back excitedly. 'A Spanish merchantman, by the look of her! If she's already loaded, ahead lies our fortune, lads!'

It soon became apparent that they were rapidly gaining on the ponderous carrack with the high stern and broad beam that were both suggestive of a successful merchantman. Francis ordered the taking in of half the sails, in order to slow the *Golden Hind* down. The only flag they were flying was the one donated by Sir Christopher Hatton, so as they came slowly alongside the Spanish vessel, whose stern name plank identified her as the *Nuestra Señora de la Concepción*, the Spaniards had no idea that the vessel approaching theirs was in fact an armed English ship. Francis ordered that the anchor be half lowered in order to reduce their speed to the same as that of the caravel alongside them, then gave an order for the gun ports on the starboard side to be opened to reveal their four cannon.

When an ornately dressed man appeared on deck in response to a horrified cry from his helmsman, Francis yelled across to him in his crude Spanish.

'*Armas! Cuatro! Rendirse o fregadero!*'

The mention of guns, surrender and the threat of sinking all in the same sentence was sufficient for the captain to yell back, '*Si — rendirse!*'

This was all the invitation Francis needed. It was the most civilised act of maritime robbery he had ever engaged in, and also one of the most rewarding. By the time that the contents of the holds of the *Nuestra* had found their way into the hold of the *Golden Hind*, they had acquired eighty pounds of gold, twenty tons of silver, and case after case of coins, jewels and raw pearls. So far as Francis could ascertain from friendly conversations with the Spanish captain during the four days that it took his men to effect the transfer, they had intercepted a vessel travelling from several Spanish mines further south of the narrow isthmus of land that Francis had last visited when he'd robbed the mule train in Nombre de Dios. Regardless of where it had come from, they had almost no room left in the hold of the *Golden Hind*. Jim Short was all for heading home until Francis reminded him that they had been commissioned by Her Majesty not as pirates on the high seas, but as explorers and discoverers of new lands.

For the next few weeks they allowed the prevailing wind to drive them north, past thousands of leagues of virgin landscape, with the occasional settlement that they took to be Spanish clinging to a foreshore alongside a freshwater inlet. Elsewhere, as they sailed past distant plains that swept down to the edge of the sea, they occasionally caught sight of clusters of hide tents, around which they could, when they employed an eyeglass, see groups of natives. Driven once again by the need for water, they dropped anchor in a wide bay surrounded by gentle wooded cliffs and rowed ashore with some trepidation.

They found that a large mound of stones had been erected at the point from which they had disembarked from their cutter the previous day, and on it lay another deer carcass and a pile of fresh fruit that was unfamiliar to them. It had a nutty taste that was most acceptable, when the inner core of flesh was cut from around its outer skin.

Francis suspected a trap of some sort, so he hastily ordered that this gift from the gods be loaded into the cutter and rowed back to the *Golden Hind*. Then curiosity got the better of him, and he sat on the stone pile watching the small boat being rowed back out into the bay until, as he suspected would happen, a curious face peered timidly at him through a cluster of bushes to his right. He stood up and beckoned with his hand, holding his other hand open for inspection to demonstrate that he had no weapon.

The body attached to the face appeared from round the side of the bushes. The man was another native of the type that had attacked them some weeks previously. But this one seemed much friendlier as he approached Francis with a hand raised to the sky, palm outward, in some sort of gesture of greeting, which Francis returned. Then the man pointed, first at the cairn of rocks from which the ship's crew had removed what was probably meant as a peace offering, then at the departing cutter. He spoke a few terse words that were unintelligible to Francis, who simply bowed formally, in the hope that the man would interpret this as a gesture of thanks. Ten minutes later their palms had met in greeting, and England had completed its first encounter with the indigenous Miwok people.

By Francis's calculation they spent four months in that place, by the end of which they had not only co-existed peacefully with the local native people, but had also begun to learn from them how best to hunt the local wildlife, which fruits were edible and which were poisonous, and where the sweetest water could be found. They had also constructed a wharf of sorts near the point at which they had first come ashore. They used trees felled from the forests that fringed their chosen settlement and bound their trunks together using a tough form of vine that the natives seemed to favour for their own tent straps. The two communities now spoke a few words of each other's language, and when Francis announced that the shortening days were warning them of the approach of another northern winter, and that they should lose no time in setting sail for home, he learned that eight of his crew wished to remain, having formed relationships with the local women.

'Since this seems destined to become an English colony,' Francis declared, addressing the entire ship's company on the wharf, where the *Golden Hind* was being provisioned ahead of her departure, 'we shall need to name it, then claim it for Elizabeth, if indeed she remains our queen. I have given the matter some thought, and have chosen the title "New Albion" for this furthermost part of Elizabeth's lands. I shall leave this plate fixed to the tallest tree, and when it falls, as in due course it must, it shall be the duty of those left behind to ensure that another tree proudly bears this symbol of English settlement. We depart at daybreak on the morrow.'

Much of the remainder of the voyage home became something of a blur in Francis's memory, since so much of it was unremarkable, with one island after another floating past their beam as they tacked hard against both the current and the tide on a course that Francis judged by the sun to be south-westerly. Almost weekly they stopped off at a promising-looking settlement in order to trade coins or pearls for fresh food, and to refill their water barrels. As they journeyed, they noted the changing faces of the people they encountered. Francis grew proficient in sign language, and their coins and precious stones did most of the talking for them.

The *Nuestra* proved to be the last Spanish vessel they encountered, although they had to negotiate with a Portuguese trader for the available harbour space in a place that they learned from his English-speaking boatswain was part of 'The Spice Islands'. He also advised them of the existence of a large land mass further west that they would need to skirt at its tip, but whose waters were a churning hellhole.

Greatly heartened, Francis calculated that this presaged that they would, when they sailed around this land mass, be less than six months from home. He set a course south-south-west, in the same way as he had skirted the foot of the Americas almost two years previously.

There were apprehensive mutterings from the men on deck when their bow was finally pointed towards a seething cauldron of water that was once again the result of the meeting of two mighty oceans. Francis yelled down that they had a choice: either push forward on full sail, and hope to ride out this second swirling mass as they had done the previous one, or turn back and spend another two years or so retracing the route that had brought them this far, including the even worse conditions they had encountered at the foot of the Americas. 'If we push on with God in our hearts, we shall make Plymouth inside a six month!' he promised them, and the muttering became mumbled prayers for their deliverance.

Even Francis had his doubts as they crashed down from each crest into a boiling pit of angry foam, then lurched back up at a speed that left their stomachs at their knees to meet the next crest that broke over their bows. The majority of the men had been ordered below, with Francis and Jim Short clinging doggedly to the wheel in order to keep her bow pointed into what lay ahead. After an hour of bucking and heaving, Francis finally accepted in his own mind that their only hope was to plough on at top speed, thereby reducing the vessel's exposure to errant currents and minimising the time it took to force their way through the saltwater mountains. He ordered Jim Short below, but he politely refused. 'Better to go to me grave "up top" 'ere, than drown below decks,' he said.

After what seemed like half a day, the wave crests seemed to get smaller, and the first cautious face appeared from under the main hatch. The man called down to his companions in gleeful tones, and within minutes the entire crew was back on deck, sliding around on the slimy residue left by the waves, and laughing as they tried to grab the remaining fish that were writhing their last on the wooden deck.

Francis was the first to recognise that his men required a period of rest after so long on the open ocean, so as they began to glide up the western shore of the land mass whose foot they had just skirted, he kept his eyeglass focused on the shoreline over their starboard beam. The following afternoon he spotted a wide bay over which a strangely shaped mountain loomed, like a giant flat-topped rock mushroom. He dropped anchor in the bay and ordered double rations all round, before retiring to his cabin and falling on his knees to thank God for preserving himself and his loyal crew from yet another potential watery grave.

Two weeks later they had replenished their water barrels from the clear lake that lay less than a mile inside the scrub that lined the shores of the bay, and they had brought down enough deer-like animals to ensure that they had meat for a month. While the hunting had been going on, Francis had accompanied the ship's carpenter, Thomas Brindley, into the fringe of a nearby forest, where they found a fallen tree that most closely resembled an English oak. From this, with the assistance of two spare deckhands, Brindley cut a section that he carved into a long oval, before chiselling the name *Golden Hind* into its interior surface. He then polished the entire section and highlighted the lettering with the small amount of silver that remained from his store. The section was then proudly affixed to the rear of their vessel, high on the outside of the poop deck, and hopefully clear of any crashing wave action. Francis called all the crew on deck, authorised the breaching of their final cider barrel, and led the toast. 'To the *Golden Hind*, the finest vessel in Queen Elizabeth's navy, and the pride of Plymouth. Now, let's head back there to our families, boys!'

It was late September 1580, two months short of three years since the *Pelican* had set sail, when rumours began to circulate in Plymouth of a ghost ship seen in the Channel off St Austell, Fowey and Looe. She was identical in her rigging and dimensions to the ill-fated *Pelican* that had set out on a foolhardy search for the ends of the earth. The commander on her main deck, visible through a powerful eyeglass, bore a strong resemblance to the valiant but misguided fool who had been the cause of so many Plymouth families being rendered destitute. She was, it was reported, heading for Plymouth with a ghostly captain at her helm, and was surely a ghastly visitation from God sent to haunt those families that had loaned men to the blasphemous endeavour to prove that men could oppose His divine will.

This no doubt helped to explain the eerie silence as the vessel now known as the *Golden Hind* nudged her way into a vacant berth on Sutton Wharf. The ropes were thrown towards the bollards, but this time there were no eager boys racing forward to earn a few pennies by hooking them on. Several cursing deckhands leapt onshore and completed the task, observed fearfully by the handful of locals huddled in a doorway across the lane, who had come to watch in case the 'ghost ship' began to unload the wraiths of their loved ones.

One woman edged slowly across the rutted mud towards the quayside as she recognised the returning spirit of her man, the father of the three children left at home with her sister's family. The man looked up and gave a cry of pure joy as he raced across and crushed her in his arms with loving endearments and promises never to go to sea again. The woman struggled to free herself from his grip, then reached out and touched his wind-burned face. Then she turned to the others in the doorway behind her and yelled, 'This ain't no ghost — it's my Amos, back from wherever he's been all this time! I'd know that smell anywhere!'

Others came out to join her, and most of them were rapidly and tearfully reunited with men they had mourned for the best part of three years. The news travelled rapidly through the narrow streets of the town, and the laneway alongside the wharf was soon crammed with shrieking women whose returning menfolk were only too glad to confirm that they were indeed back home alive.

It would be a while before the news reached St Budeaux, and the sun had lost most of its late afternoon heat when Francis finally accepted that his only way of being reunited with Mary was to walk home. But he could hardly leave such a rich cargo unattended, and the sooner they set off again for Deptford the better. He couldn't ask any of his loyal crew to delay their joyful reunions for one day longer, so it would be down to him. Whispering an apology to the absent Mary, he loaded two matchlocks and sat on the outer ledge of the poop deck, from where he could command the clearest view of the hatch covers. He was almost nodding off to sleep in the descending twilight when he heard a woman's voice softly calling his name, and he looked towards its source.

There was a woman wrapped heavily against the evening dampness, standing on the edge of the wharf, as if about to board the *Golden Hind*. He leaped up in eager anticipation.

'Mary?' he croaked, but the woman shook her head.

'No, Francis — it's Judith.'

'Is Mary on her way down?' he asked, and Judith stepped unsteadily down onto the port gunwale. Francis ran forward to offer his hand as she stepped down onto the deck, then looked up at him pleadingly, tears rolling down her face.

'Please forgive me for what I've to tell you, Francis, but no-one else was prepared to come down here and do it. We all thought you was dead, you see. Leastways, that's what John Wynter told everybody when 'e come back on the *Elizabeth*, an' said as 'ow you'd all gone down in a whirlpool. 'E even 'ad your boat's nameboard, what'd floated down with the rest o' the wreckage.'

'We survived that, as you can see,' Francis said reassuringly, 'and now the vessel's been renamed the *Golden Hind*. It's good to know that Wynter and his men got back here safely. Any news of the *Marigold*?'

'Lost, they reckon. But you got to know something else as well, Francis.'

'Mary? Did she think I was dead? And will she give me one of her stern sermons on the evils of putting to sea?'

Judith's face fell, then she looked bravely back into his eyes. 'That's what I come to tell you, Francis. When the news came from John Wynter, she took to 'er bed, and never got up again. She died last February, Francis — they reckon it were a broken heart.'

19

A shattered Francis finally wrestled his conscience to the ground as a watery sun rose palely over the rooftops to the east of where he sat motionless on the top of the poop deck, a pistol lying loosely on each thigh, and barely within his grip.

It was, he reasoned, definitely his fault for neglecting Mary yet again in his relentless and selfish ambition to be the world's greatest mariner, and for that he would never forgive himself. But as for her death, he could hardly be blamed for the false reports that had reached Plymouth regarding the loss of the *Pelican*. He could just about live with himself for that, and he *had* returned with many of the local men who had entrusted their lives to him. Perhaps he owed it to both Mary and himself to continue with the mission that had deprived her of her life, and himself of the warm comfort of a woman's company. Or was he simply finding yet another justification for his burning need to be the best on the ocean?

There was a polite cough, and he glanced down at the main deck. Jim Short stood looking up at him with an apologetic smile, and holding out something wrapped in cloth.

'They told me you were still 'ere, Cap'n, so I brought you some breakfast. It's only bread an' cheese, mind, but better than some o' that swill what we were forced to eat when we was at sea. I'll take over your watch, if that's agreeable to you, then you can get home an' get some sleep. You were dozing off there, by the looks o' things.'

Francis nodded. 'Thank you, Jim, but I've little enough to draw me back to St Budeaux.'

'Yeah, sorry to 'ear about your missus, Cap'n. Lucy told me when I got home, an' it were 'er what sent you this breakfast. A sorta thank you for bringing me home safe.'

'I was just thinking about all the men who *didn't* get back home, Jim,' Francis sighed. 'My conscience tells me that I've killed enough men already and should perhaps find a living on land.'

Jim gave a short, ironic, laugh. 'Who're you kidding, with all due respect, Cap'n? You couldn't no more settle on land than I could, if the truth were told. We've both of us got saltwater for blood, an' Lucy's already saying as 'ow I should be signing up with you again, rather than getting under 'er feet an' showing the kids a bad example with me table manners. So where to next?'

Francis gestured down towards the hatch cover of the main hold. 'We need to get all our riches back to Deptford first, then we can decide what comes next. Could you round me up a crew for sailing on tomorrow's tide?'

'An' who'll guard them riches while you're back home, catching up on your sleep?'

'I'll only need a few hours. Then I'll come back and relieve you, and you can set about recruiting a crew, although I imagine that very few of those who came back with us yesterday will be willing to put to sea again quite so quickly.'

'You're forgetting that they hasn't been paid off yet,' said Jim. 'The minute they 'ear as 'ow the cargo's off to London to be valued, they'll want to be there, trust me on that.'

Jim's prediction proved to be entirely accurate. Five days after she'd made landfall at Plymouth, the *Golden Hind* was being berthed in Deptford Sound, and Francis was yelling instructions from the foredeck for an armed escort for the contents of her cargo hold. 'And see to it that the Treasurer is instructed to have it listed and valued!' he added, just as he caught sight of a grinning John among those on the jetty, and laughingly apologised. The two men embraced once Francis had scrambled hastily ashore, then John held Francis at arm's length and looked him over.

'You look remarkably well for someone who was reported dead, dear cousin!' he enthused, then his face fell. 'Have you come by way of Plymouth?'

'Indeed, I have, and you need not tremble that you have to advise me of Mary's death,' Francis assured him sadly. 'I fear that I was not the best of husbands.'

'You at least followed your dearest dream,' said John, 'and Her Majesty will be well pleased that you are safely returned. How much do you assess your cargo to be worth?'

'I have no idea, since there is so much of it,' Francis replied. 'We should have time for dinner before your assessors have finished the task. Did anyone advise you that I have been around the entire world?'

'How could they, since you are only just back among us? But you must be ready for a good meal, instead of that dreadful weevil pie, not to mention that goat's piss water from the bottom of the barrel. Come, let's go in, and Katherine can tell you what a fool you were to set sail, while Richard drinks in stories from his greatest hero.'

Francis had been back at Deptford for over a week, inspecting the sleek new vessels being slipped down the quay at the nearby shipyard of Richard Chapman, when the royal dockyard received a visit from Sir Robert Dudley. He'd been sent by the queen to congratulate Francis on his safe return, learn of the new lands he had discovered, and assess the wealth that he had brought back. Robert invited Francis to walk with him as they inspected the new English Navy vessels in

Chapman's yard. They had been constructed along the lines Francis had proposed following his encounters with the larger Spanish galleons, and great care had been taken to keep them as low in the water as was consistent with the load they were intended to carry, of men, cargo and cannon.

'Did you agree what percentage Hatton was to receive of your booty?' Robert asked casually.

Francis shook his head. 'He invested ten thousand, so it is to be hoped that he can be awarded three times that amount as his reward for his confidence in me.'

'Francis,' Robert replied quietly as he pulled gently on his tunic sleeve so as to bring both men to a halt in a quiet spot along the quayside, 'I must swear you to secrecy regarding what I am about to tell you. The riches you brought back in your one vessel are assessed at almost twice the value of the nation's Treasury income for an entire year. Her Majesty has instructed me to claim all of it in the name of the Crown, but I am here to advise you to take from it what you require, and what is due to others, before we give Elizabeth the final valuation assessment.'

Francis wasted no time in extracting, from John's Comptroller of Accounts, the money needed to pay both Sir Christopher Hatton and his own surviving crew, with a little extra for any destitute widows that he might learn about when he returned to Plymouth. Then he took ten thousand pounds for himself, mindful of the fact that he still had to acquire Buckland Abbey. He had originally enquired about it in order to please Mary, but since he doubted that he would be able to face the memories that would assail him when — and if — he returned to their former home in St Budeaux, it seemed appropriate to pursue his original interest in the place.

Francis had been staying for just over a month as a guest in the sprawling house that went with John's official post under the Crown when he received another visit from Robert Dudley. He advised him that Her Majesty wished to inspect and dine on board the *Golden Hind*, the vessel that had proved to Spain that it did not own every ocean in the world. Francis was also advised that he was to be rewarded by Elizabeth for the honour and riches that he had brought to England.

When the day of the queen's visit arrived, Francis stood apprehensively on the deck of his now famous vessel, hoping that the special ramp that had been commissioned to enable Her Majesty to make her way from the quayside down to the main deck would prove effective.

A double line of Gentlemen Yeomen from the Tower across the river was ferried into Deptford Sound by special barge. They stood sternly down the quayside with their halberds at their sides as the stately procession, led by Robert Dudley in his role of Master of the Queen's Horse, made its way down the quay to the deck of the *Golden Hind*, where Francis stood waiting. He was somewhat at a loss to understand why Elizabeth appeared to be accompanied by a dapper little man in full finery, who minced alongside her as if he were her lapdog. They came down the specially constructed ramp to stand before Francis, who bowed deeply, then looked enquiringly at the gentleman by her side.

'This is the Marquis de Marchaumont, Master Drake,' Elizabeth told him. 'I have invited him to accompany us today because he is the French Ambassador, and he has a certain function to perform that involves you.'

'I thank you for not bringing along the Spanish Ambassador, Your Majesty,' Francis jested, 'for I feel certain that I know what function *he* would wish to perform on me.'

'On your knees, Master Drake,' Elizabeth commanded him, and fearful that he might have overstepped the mark Francis did as commanded. The queen then reached behind her and took a sword from a cushion on which it had been borne along by one of her retinue. She then handed the sword to the ambassador and took this opportunity to show off her command of his native language.

'*Monsieur L'Ambassadeur, placez cette épée sur l'épaule gauche, s'il vous plaît.*'

The ambassador took the sword and lowered it onto Francis's left shoulder. While Francis was sighing with relief that it had not been employed in order to remove his head, Elizabeth issued another instruction.

'*Et maintenant, l'épaule droite.*'

The sword was transferred to Francis's right shoulder, and Elizabeth smiled down at him with what looked like genuine affection.

'You may now rise, *Sir* Francis Drake.'

A rousing cheer went up from the many onlookers on the quayside, among whom were John, his wife Katherine and their son Richard. Elizabeth allowed the cheering to subside, then reminded Francis that she had been invited to dine on board.

'Indeed, Your Majesty,' said Francis, still reeling from the honour that had just been bestowed upon him, 'but you will find the accommodation cramped, even in my state cabin.'

'This is all to the good,' Elizabeth replied. 'It will serve to acquaint me with the appalling conditions that brave men such as yourself endure while bringing such honour and glory to the nation.'

They were soon seated, facing each other on either side of Francis's chart table, which had been draped in damask cloth and was now doubling as a banqueting board. This was spread with bowls of the queen's favourite sweet dishes, such as sugared plums, almonds and dates. The ambassador himself, along with almost all of the retinue who had accompanied Elizabeth to Deptford, were now being feted in the hall of the Admiralty Building as guests of John and Katherine. Only a Queen's Lady and a couple of pages remained in order to preserve the proprieties, and they gazed wistfully down at the treats on the table.

'Might I enquire why the French Ambassador was chosen to dub my shoulders, Your Majesty?' Francis asked.

'The answer to your question is two-fold, Sir Francis,' Elizabeth replied. 'First, and perhaps foremost, we are grateful to the French for their support for our interests in the Low Countries, and their resulting animosity towards the Spanish. The second reason follows on from the first; since the French Ambassador was a very public participant in your knighting, and since King Philip of Spain has conceived a fierce hatred of you, it was a studied insult to both Spain and its King.'

'Forgive me, Your Majesty, but I was of the belief that we do not wish to provoke Spain at this time.'

'Nor do we, Sir Francis, but I may tell you that thanks to your many endeavours in bringing riches into my nation, freeing half the oceans of the world for English ships, and designing new warships, we are now much stronger against Spain than we were previously. But you must swear an oath of silence regarding how much you actually robbed the Spaniards of in your latest venture, since we are not yet quite prepared to tweak Philip's nose to the extent that he launches his massive armies at us from across the Channel.'

'I so swear, Your Majesty,' Francis replied, 'but does this mean that I must remain confined to harbour, which to me would be worse than being incarcerated within the Tower?'

'It does, but I have another commission for you to conduct during your confinement on land — one that I believe will interest you greatly, since it involves Plymouth.'

'And it is?' Francis asked eagerly.

Elizabeth waved for her wine goblet to be replenished. 'Your worthy town, and the home of so many of your brave sailors, is currently without a mayor. We should, in the normal course of things, consult the residents before selecting its next mayor, and in one sense we have already done so. Sir Robert sent out commissioners to make enquiry of the stout folk of Plymouth as to who they would wish to be their new mayor, and, as we suspected before we began the process, they came up with one name repeatedly. It was yours, Sir Francis — do you wish to answer your fellow citizens' call?'

Three months later Francis was installed in his new office, after a welcome home that made him blush with embarrassment while swelling with pride. The son of a failed Tavistock farmer had now ascended to the highest office that Plymouth could offer. This was shortly augmented by Francis's appointment as the local parliamentary member for the town of which he was now the mayor.

One of the many long-standing, and highly controversial, projects that awaited his attention concerned a proposal to divert water from a river high on Dartmoor in order to provide Plymouth with a greater supply for both drinking and fire-fighting. The difficulties encountered were not restricted to matters of engineering and cost, but also opposition from farmers in the neighbouring county of Somerset, who drew essential water supplies from the headwaters of the river whose normal flow would, particularly in dry months, be impeded by the diversion.

Francis had little to occupy what few leisure hours he was able to rescue from his civic duties other than thinking about his coveted move to Buckland Abbey, and the renovations that he would make in order to render it more habitable. From time to time, and at increasingly short intervals, he would present himself at Geoffrey Montacourt's chandlery and demand news of his progress in purchasing the abbey as Francis's secret agent. On the most recent occasion, Montacourt had shrugged with embarrassment and said, 'If anything, sir, it gets worse. Your rival Sir George Sydenham has, it would seem, raised his bid to some twelve thousand pounds, which I would respectfully suggest might be beyond your means.'

'Twelve thousand?' Francis bellowed. 'The old ruin can't be worth half that outrageous sum. Why is it so important to the old fool?'

'He's no fool, sir, but the High Sheriff of Somerset. It may be that he's using your desire for the old abbey to bargain with you regarding the proposed leat from Dartmoor, since some of his tenant farmers are threatening to abandon their leases if there's insufficient water.'

'And how did he come to know that I was the other interested party?' Francis demanded.

Montacourt's gaze dropped to his shop counter. 'Forgive me, sir, but he quickly came to suspect that the other notional interested party, a mere ships' chandler, was unlikely to have been in a position to raise the bid to the ten thousand that I offered. He demanded that I call on him at his inn when he was last here, and threatened to have my business closed down if I did not tell him who my silent principal was. I have a wife and three children, sir, and as you will appreciate…'

'Yes, yes,' Francis replied testily, 'but we can only hope that the Grenville family haven't learned the same thing. It's high time that I had audience with this Sydenham irritant.'

On the pretence of discussing the conflict over the proposed diversion of river water from Dartmoor, Francis sent word to Sydenham's mansion at Combe Sydenham, some miles beyond Taunton, that he wished to meet with him. A week later, a distinguished-looking middle-aged gentleman was admitted to Francis's mayoral chamber, where he announced that he was Sir George Sydenham, and was not accustomed to being summoned to meet with men of Francis's station in life.

'You came, nevertheless,' Francis said impertinently.

Sir George allowed himself a smile. 'A man of spirit, clearly. You would seem to be as courageous and incapable of being overawed as your reputation would suggest.'

'Regardless of my reputation,' Francis went on, 'you must judge me as you find me. And despite my lowly origins, I have sufficient about me to wish to ensure that the people of the town of my adoption have sufficient water for their needs. This is what I have called you here to discuss.'

'And we shall, but over supper,' Sydenham replied. 'I am currently staying at The Kestrel with my daughter, and you are cordially invited to join us this evening, should your duties permit.'

Later that evening Francis was reminded of another occasion on which he — along with his cousins — had taken supper in a private dining room all those years ago, with Benjamin Gonson and his daughter Katherine, who was now John's wife. This time, he was dining in the presence of another lady — his host's daughter, Elizabeth Sydenham. She was strikingly handsome, if not quite pretty, and seemed to be only in her early twenties. Francis and Sir George talked for some while about Francis's experiences on the high seas, and the foreign lands that he had visited ahead of the Spanish, before his host broached the topic that had led to their meeting.

'You must be aware, Sir Francis, that your plans to divert the river from the Moor will deprive some of my tenants of the necessary water for their animals and crops.'

'Not during the wet season,' Francis pointed out. 'And in any case, I care more about the need for adequate fresh water in my town, to ensure that my citizens are not reduced to boiling what they take from the estuaries, and that they have sufficient access to a ready source of water should a fire break out. The houses are built close together, as you will be aware, and a fire in any one of them could result in it spreading to a whole line. In case I have not made my position clear, let me add that I prefer people to cows.'

He caught a flicker of amusement on the face of Elizabeth Sydenham, who had so far not uttered a word. Her father caught her look and gestured with a slight jerk of his head that she should take her leave, which she duly did after pleading a slight headache due to the tedium of their journey from the adjoining county. Once she was out of the chamber, Sydenham turned to look at Francis, who was seated to his left.

'What thought you of my daughter, Francis?'

Francis was somewhat taken aback by the bluntness of the question, and the conspiratorial tone in which it had been delivered. 'In truth, I hardly had opportunity to form an opinion, Sir George.'

'Let us dispense with the formalities, Francis. You may simply call me George.'

'Even if I may, I still have formed no opinion. She seems pleasant enough, but she spoke not a single word, as I recall.'

'She is not one for idle prattle,' George replied, as if seeking to excuse his daughter's lack of social skills. 'She finds most conversations between gentlemen of our status to be tedious and lacking in purpose.'

'So we are now of equal status, are we?' Francis countered. 'Earlier today you were at pains to remind me of my lowly origins.'

'You have earned your status through bravery and dedication to England's cause, Francis. Something that Elizabeth would greatly admire, should she be asked her opinion.'

'And why would we need to ask her opinion?'

'Allow me to tell you something about my daughter, *Sir* Francis. She is well past twenty, and because of my wealth she has had many suitors. She is not uncomely, you must agree, and several of her suitors were handsome, as well as wealthy in their own right. But she has rejected them all. Why do you think this is?'

Francis reddened slightly as he offered the only response that came to mind. 'Perhaps she prefers the — the — the *company* of women?'

George shook his head. 'I too thought that, but after a most embarrassing conversation with her on that very point, she advised me that this was not the case. What *was* the case was that all the men I had introduced her to were, as she described them, "limp, boring and lacking in manly qualities." Do you regard yourself as possessing "manly qualities", Francis?'

'I had never considered the matter,' Francis admitted.

George leaned towards him, lowering his voice and looking behind him to ensure that they were not overheard. 'I wish Elizabeth to be married without further delay, in order that I may become a grandfather. My wife died some years ago, and we had only the one child. I could of course order Elizabeth to marry whomsoever I chose, but I wish her to be happy. This is why I am planning to buy her a large estate, in order that she might marry someone she actually wants for herself — someone who possesses the sort of manly qualities that she can admire, and perhaps one day come to love, even though they may not be wealthy.'

'Forgive my presumption,' Francis replied after coughing with embarrassment, 'but am I to understand that you consider that I might be that man?'

'That rather depends upon whether or not you wish to reside in Buckland Abbey, does it not?' When Francis stared blankly back at him, George continued, 'I am well aware that you seek to acquire the estate — I have been ever since I learned that there was another interested party, and made enquiry of that rather grubby tradesman who was your somewhat unconvincing agent. Then I made further enquiry and learned that there is a long-standing dispute between you and the current owner, Sir Richard Grenville, and that he would be unlikely to sell to you. This suited my ambitions for my daughter admirably.'

'In what way?' Francis asked nervously.

'It is simply agreed, is it not? You are currently without both a wife and an estate. You have the wealth available to purchase the estate, and there is a young lady who I suspect would require little persuasion to become your wife. When she agrees to acquire that status, I shall withdraw my offer to purchase Buckland Abbey. Then your chosen agent may purchase it, before selling it on immediately to you.'

Francis took a deep swig of wine while considering the proposal, then raised the objection that came most immediately to mind. 'How do I know that Elizabeth will entertain my suit?'

'You do not, clearly,' George agreed. 'But you did not know what lay on the other side of the world until you made enquiry, and bravely hazarded your life in the process. I feel sure that paying court to my daughter will present less of a hazard, and you may call on us at our home, Combe Sydenham, in a week's time.'

20

'My father has ordered you to propose marriage to me, has he not?' Elizabeth Sydenham asked bluntly before she and Francis had even reached the line of yew hedges that marked the boundary between the courtyard and the ornamental gardens. They and George had just shared a somewhat subdued dinner, remarkable mainly for the awkward silence that had hung over it like the faint aroma from a distant midden. George had then suggested that Elizabeth might like to show their honoured guest around the grounds, and here they were, like over-energetic children sent out to play.

Francis stepped sideways to free Elizabeth's hand from the crook of his arm, then fixed her with a stern stare. 'Firstly, no-one, but no-one, orders Francis Drake to do anything, mistress. Secondly, what put it in your mind that he might be so anxious to find you a husband?'

'Because he has done nothing these past two years but try to put a husband in my path. He seems not to appreciate that I will have no concourse with any of the feeble apologies for manhood that he parades before me.'

'Do I strike you as yet another "feeble apology for manhood", Mistress?'

Elizabeth's face reddened somewhat, then her gaze fell to the dusty ground beneath her boots. 'I fear that you have caused me to blush. No man has done that before.'

'And *this* man did not do so intentionally, Mistress. You must forgive me my blunt manner of speech, but much of my life has been spent with rough sailors upon whom polite twittering conversation appropriate for noble supper tables would be wasted. And you do not answer my question.'

'I hardly know you well enough to comment on your manly qualities, Sir Francis. Perhaps I should do so before I make any further unguarded observation regarding suitors.'

'There is one obvious and ready way in which that might be achieved, Mistress.'

'Elizabeth. Please call me Elizabeth, and I shall henceforth call you Francis, if I may do so without seeming too forward or presumptuous.'

'Nothing could surely be more forward than declaring your belief that your father had ordered me to propose marriage,' Francis replied mischievously.

Elizabeth giggled as she tapped him playfully on the nose. 'I can see that we shall become well suited, Francis — even if your reason for paying court to me is the acquisition of that tumbledown old abbey that my father is acquiring in the hope of providing a honey hive around which the bees may buzz.'

'I can well afford to purchase Buckland Abbey for myself,' Francis assured her. 'And when I do, whether or not it will contain a daughter of Sydenham lineage may well depend upon just how well suited we prove to be.'

'That's agreed, then,' Elizabeth replied. 'Let us return to the house, before the evening mist begins to drape its dreary mantle over the hills that surround us, and I shall inform my father that I have not yet totally rejected his latest choice. But please ensure that you visit again without undue delay.'

Francis was both fascinated and repelled by Elizabeth's forthright manner and underlying allure. He seemed compelled — almost despite himself — to demonstrate that he would do whatever she demanded of him, even to the point of marriage.

The betrothal was announced — by *her*, no less — one dinner time as they returned from a long walk in the woods on the edge of the estate, during which Elizabeth had informed Francis that his claim on her affections was rapidly wearing thin. He found himself proposing marriage to her like a man in the grip of a dream. Once they were officially betrothed, Sir George withdrew his interest in Buckland Abbey, and Francis acquired it for a considerably reduced sum, via his agent Geoffrey Montacourt. The wedding was celebrated with great splendour in a local parish church, and Francis was soon to discover that his second marriage was to be nothing like his first.

Gone was the dependency he had experienced from Mary, along with her reluctance to let him out of her sight, and her heart-wrenching pleas for him not to put to sea. By contrast, Elizabeth never seemed happier than when he had naval matters to attend to, and she could stride to the stables, demand the saddling of her favourite stallion, and thunder off for the day into the surrounding woodland. She was sometimes sighted miles away on the gorse-covered slopes of Dartmoor, like some phantom white lady of bucolic myth. Even in the bedchamber she liked to take command, treating Francis almost like some talking stallion, and he was fortunate that he was able to live up to her expectations. Had he not, he had no doubt that her scorn would have been withering.

But above all she encouraged his involvement in the commissioning and strengthening of a new English Navy, in association with his cousin John. This was all to the good, and perhaps just as well, given the way in which events were playing out in England's long-standing and terse relationship with Spain.

It was now 1585, and no-one was more delighted than the socially astute Elizabeth Drake when the arrival of the Earl of Leicester was announced at Buckland Abbey. Francis strode out into the courtyard and shook him warmly by the hand like a long-lost friend as he dismounted, along with the handful of attendants who had accompanied him. Robert Dudley had enjoyed his grand title for some years now, but that did not diminish Elizabeth's pride when she witnessed her husband and the queen's favourite embracing like brothers, and jesting light-heartedly over a hastily ordered dinner. The centrepiece was a huge side of venison that the cook had been preserving for some suitable occasion.

As the sweet courses were tactfully removed from the board — a sign that the servants would be grateful for a break before they set about the delivery of supper — Robert lowered his voice. 'I would speak with you privily, Francis,' he said, glancing at Elizabeth, who was beaming her satisfaction at having such an honoured guest at board for a meal that had gone off so splendidly.

'Do not concern yourself on my account, my lord,' she announced grandly as she rose from her seat. 'I have no doubt that you need to discuss great matters of State with my husband. I shall take myself off into the gardens, there to admire the finest blooms this side of Taunton and walk off some of that excellent venison from our home estate. Should Francis wish to share with me later those matters that he has been authorised to disclose, he may do so. And so I bid you a good afternoon.'

Robert followed her with his eyes as she glided sedately from the room, and then turned to Francis. 'A fine spirited filly — where, pray, did you find her?'

'You might say she came with this house,' said Francis. 'But as I judge, you are not here to discuss my marriage.'

'Indeed not,' Robert confirmed as his face fell. 'I come in England's best interests, but without the knowledge of Her Majesty. In that sense, I should of course be grateful — as ever — for your discretion regarding what I have to impart.'

'You have it without asking,' Francis assured him.

'As you are already aware, Elizabeth — which of course means England — has long expressed her support for the Dutch in the Low Countries in their attempts to throw off the yoke of the Spanish, who have occupied their lands for some time now. But Philip of Spain has recently strengthened his grip, and has begun a course of persecution against Protestants. This has occasioned a petition from the "States General of the United Provinces", who are what passes for a government in the Low Counties, seeking England's more direct intervention.'

'By force of arms, say you?' Francis asked.

Robert nodded. 'A treaty was signed last month to that effect, and Elizabeth has commanded that I lead her armies.'

'For which you require ships to transport you across the Channel? Has John requested my involvement?'

'That, certainly, but there is more, hence my reason for journeying here today. Although the queen is anxious to be seen to support the Dutch, she is, at the same time, apprehensive that by doing so she will provoke Philip into attacking England. My orders are, in effect, to march my forces over there — largely men of my own, financed by me personally — make a great deal of noise, but refrain from engaging Spanish troops, lest this be taken as a declaration of war against Spain.'

'Surely, Her Majesty has placed you in an impossible position?' Francis objected.

Robert spread his arms in a gesture of helplessness. 'She relies too much, I fear, on that old woman Cecil — or Lord Burghley as he must now be addressed — and his is ever the voice of caution. But I am not here to seek your advice in matters of diplomacy, for which you are not highly regarded, if I may say so without giving offence.'

'You may,' said Francis, 'but what is it you require of me, apart from the transport of your army into Antwerp or wherever?'

Robert grimaced. 'I have a feeling that Philip is seeking any excuse to invade England, under pressure from the Pope, who as you know excommunicated Elizabeth some years ago, and called upon those of what he calls the "true faith" to remove her from her throne. Philip is a fervent Catholic, and wishes to ingratiate himself with Rome by being the means by which England is returned to its fold. Whether I engage the enemy or not, Philip will use the presence of English forces in the Low Countries as the justification for diverting his army under the Duke of Parma, and crossing the Channel.'

'Has he the ships?'

'Our spies in Spain advise that Philip has been amassing a vast navy suitable for the transport of men, horses and ordnance. We believe that it will be used to bring seasoned Spanish men-at-arms across the Channel, where we have no army large enough to oppose them. Unless, of course, they can be prevented from doing so. Now you may perhaps guess why I am here.'

'You wish me to command the naval force that will keep the Spanish from making it to the Dutch mainland?'

'Whether you command it or no, Francis — and that will be a matter for Her Majesty to decide — I wish you to build it.'

In the weeks and months that followed, Francis was almost permanently absent from home as he travelled between Plymouth, Deptford and Portsmouth. He took stock of what vessels were already available, ordered that they be brought up to the highest standards of seaworthiness, and commissioned the construction of others to a specific design based on the *Golden Hind* — low in the water, broad in the beam, square-rigged with an extra set of sails, and loaded with cannon. He and John were reunited in their joint efforts to produce, almost in secret, a flotilla of ships that could repel the largest floating war machine that the world had ever witnessed.

They had been engaged in this task for almost two years, and had vessels hidden in every marine estuary in the south of England with enough depth at low tide to conceal warships, when Robert Dudley returned in disgrace from the Low Countries. His relationship with Queen Elizabeth was more unstable than it had ever been. Not only had he accepted the title of Governor-General of the United Provinces when Elizabeth had insisted from the outset that everything he did in the Low Countries was to be in her name, but he had also engaged the Spanish with force of arms, losing the strategically important town of Grave to them.

The queen had reacted angrily, refusing to send any funds to supplement Dudley's private expenditure. He was already financially ruined when he learned, to his ungovernable rage, that Elizabeth had been secretly negotiating with Spain for a peace treaty during the entire period that he had been risking life, limb and fortune on her behalf. Dudley made an official request to be relieved of his post, and long before this was grudgingly granted he was sulking back in England, blaming the entire fiasco on Cecil and his spymaster Francis Walsingham.

It was Walsingham who sought admission to the upper chamber in the Trinity House building in Deptford that was home to the Hawkins family late one February night in 1587. John and Francis were sitting in front of the fire, drinking mulled wine and discussing their progress in recreating a navy that had been sadly neglected for as long as Elizabeth had been on the throne. Walsingham was relieved of his cloak by the senior usher who had guided him up the staircase, and was invited to join John and Francis by the fire.

'What news from Spain?' John asked, well aware of the extent of Walsingham's network of informers, paid or otherwise.

'That is why I am here,' Walsingham replied in a conspiratorial tone, 'since I was privily advised that Sir Francis was here also, and England has need of his services.'

'Am I to ferry more soldiers across the Channel?' Francis asked coldly, fully aware of the involvement of Walsingham in Dudley's unjust downfall, and unwilling to assist the silent snake from the hole he appeared to have dug for himself.

'No, Sir Francis, but I am commanded by Her Majesty to commission you to sail to the coast of Spain, and report back on the state of preparation of Philip's navy.'

'And why might that be, assuming that to be a matter deemed worthy of knowledge by the mere Comptroller of the Queen's Navy, whom you have so far ignored?' John asked bitterly.

Walsingham smiled coldly. 'Forgive me, but it is more the state of *Spain's* navy that brings me here this evening.'

Francis's curiosity was instantly tweaked. 'Are we to expect an invasion?' he asked.

Walsingham shrugged. 'We believe that this will be Philip's reaction to the latest event.'

'Which is?' John asked, not wishing to be excluded from the conversation.

Walsingham sighed. 'The Scots Mary was executed this morning. Not here in London, but in Northamptonshire, so it will take some time for the news to travel abroad. Her Majesty has been advised, and her rage is currently terrible to behold, or so I am advised.'

'Did she not give her consent?' Francis asked.

Walsingham shook his head. 'She signed the warrant but gave strict orders that it was not to be employed until she gave final approval. She fears that Spain will use the excuse to invade, hence my attendance here, in order that we may be advised of Philip's state of readiness.'

'We?' Francis queried suspiciously.

'Myself and Lord Burghley. You may rest assured that you have Her Majesty's approval also, but only to the extent of assessing the size and readiness of Philip's fleet. It lies mainly in the harbour at Cadiz, but with other vessels at the port of Lisbon.'

'And should I learn that Philip's navy is about to set sail, while our fleet is all over the south of England?' Francis demanded angrily.

Walsingham shrugged. 'I am no sailor, clearly, but if you could find some way to buy us the time to regroup...'

'It will require much more than that,' Francis insisted with a glare. 'We may — and I repeat *may* — have sufficient ships, but we have barely a third of the captains and crews that will be required. Even when they are identified and recruited, they will require training. Opposing Philip's navy in our current state of preparedness would be like sending a farm labourer armed with a scythe to do battle with a horse-borne and heavily armed knight!'

'I clearly have no answer to that, Sir Francis,' Walsingham murmured deferentially. 'I was merely sent as the messenger in this matter, and I have achieved that which was entrusted to me. And so I bid both you gentlemen a respectful good evening.'

He bowed at the door and then scuttled swiftly down the staircase, leaving Francis and John staring at each other in disbelief.

'What will you do?' John asked Francis, who chortled in sheer delight.

'What I have been waiting these many years to do! If I do not die in the attempt, the queen will surely have my head, but it's time to settle an old score regarding some of our Plymouth comrades who never came back from our voyage to the Americas.'

21

Francis chuckled as he looked through the narrow straits into the wide bay of Cadiz's inner harbour, where a great fleet of carracks had been assembled. He was on the poop deck of the *Elizabeth Bonaventure*, his command ship, and one of the royal galleons put at his disposal by the queen. Slightly behind him were the *Golden Lion*, captained by William Burroughs, the *Rainbow* under Captain Bellingham, and the *Dreadnought* under the command of Captain Thomas Fenner. A further twenty merchantmen and armed pinnaces made up the fleet, and it was armed to the teeth with as much ordnance as they had managed to cram onto the gun decks and into the holds.

On their starboard beam was the town itself, on a promontory that was intended to guard the entrance to the wide deepwater bay beyond, but as the cannon on shore began blasting away at the invaders, Francis ordered full sail and yelled down to Jim Short on the gun deck to give back as much as he got. The town guns fell silent as several of them received direct hits from the starboard culverins of the *Elizabeth Bonaventure*, and the towers of several imposing-looking buildings flew into thousands of pieces. Then it was onwards into the bay, where Francis could count at least sixty Spanish carracks sitting at anchor.

He signalled for the vessels under his immediate command to fan out in line abreast — a tactical move whose purpose became obvious as the first of the Spanish vessels raised anchor and lumbered into action, heading out of the bay with guns blazing. But the poor design of these enemy carracks had resulted in their only being able to fire in a forward direction, and the smaller, fleeter English warships slid down either side of them and blasted them to shreds. Screaming sailors dived overboard into the bay, where they swam furiously through the wreckage of spars, sails and dead bodies to seek the safety of the shore. Within minutes, the entrance to the bay was hazardous with sinking hulks.

This intense barrage lasted for most of the day, with the Spanish ships either trapped where they sat in the bay or blown into memory if they attempted to break the blockade of English warships. Towards late afternoon, Francis changed tactics and began sending armed merchantmen alongside the ponderous Spanish carracks and boarding them. The captured cargoes were transferred into the holds of following vessels, and token crews remained on board the captured Spanish vessels until nightfall, when the second part of the overall plan was executed.

The bay was still thick with Spanish galleons whose captains had declined to run the gauntlet of English cannon, and they made a perfect target for what came next. Each of the boarding crews that had captured an enemy vessel gathered up all the remaining ordnance they could find on board into a massive central pile, then poured as much tar, oil and other flammable substances as they could find all over the upper decks. Then a long, slow fuse was laid down into the gun decks, and the ships' wheels were jammed into a fixed position pointing back into the bay before the boarding crews lit the fuses and leapt back overboard, to be picked up by supporting pinnaces, leaving the blazing captured ships to creak slowly towards the Spanish at anchor.

As the flames became visible in the clear night sky, the captains of several enemy galleons that lay in their path ordered their gunners to open fire at the approaching vessels.

This had been Francis's plan all along, and the exploding 'hellburners' sent torrents of flaming wood among the rest of the anchored fleet, while their still-burning hulks, most of them now minus their rigging, drifted inexorably towards their targets.

As the sun broke cover the following morning, it was obvious through the smoky haze that the original Spanish fleet was considerably reduced. Francis made a rough calculation that they had put paid to half the fleet that had been assembled by King Philip in preparation for an invasion of England by way of the Low Countries.

It had fallen eerily silent in the town of Cadiz, as the English fleet sailed back out of its bay, heading for the open ocean. Francis, with the aid of his eyeglass, could see much coming and going in the narrow streets that overlooked the entrance to the bay itself. With great satisfaction he realised that all the activity was in preparation for a feared attack on the town itself. But land conquest was not his ambition — sea conquest was, and if the information he had been supplied by Walsingham was correct, there were more Spanish vessels to be found to the south, in Portugal.

There were also, Francis guessed, more Spanish merchantmen on the way back to their home ports from the Americas, laden with rich cargoes that would enable Philip to finance more ships that would replace those that he had lost. Francis ordered the fleet out into the open ocean, where they sat and waited, after replenishing their supplies by means of a successful raid on the Portuguese castle at Sagres. Here the men were allowed ashore for refreshment, pillaging and other activities to which Francis turned a blind eye — the last thing he needed was a mutiny.

By the time that the sated seamen had been rowed back to their vessels, a fleet of incoming carracks had been spotted off the starboard beam, and Francis ordered his vessels into battle order. They were offered little resistance once their culverins had shot the rigging from the incoming merchantmen, and eager English boarding parties leaped onto the foreign decks in anticipation of more gold, silver, sugar, spices and pearls. Instead they found only barrel staves. Thousands of them, packed tightly into the holds of the vessels that had sailed, not from the Americas, but from other ports in the Algarve to which the seasoned wood had been delivered ahead of its shipment north to Spain, where the staves could be converted into barrels.

Francis was initially livid that their efforts had not yielded further riches, but then he began asking himself why such a fundamentally valueless cargo would have been sent north to Spain in such large quantities. It was Jim Short who answered that question. 'There'll be a few Spanish coopers that'll be regretting the loss o' that lot,' he observed, then wondered why his captain was leaping up and down with delight.

'Of course!' Francis yelled back. 'Barrel staves mean barrels, and without barrels there's nothing to store water, wine, fresh fruit and fish in! This lot were clearly intended to be made into barrels with which to provision Philip's navy!' Then he remembered that Jim had once told him of his former apprenticeship to a cooper before he ran away to sea. 'How soon could another supply of staves like this be made available to King Philip?' he asked eagerly.

'Not for another year at least,' said Jim. 'It 'as to be seasoned wood, you see, like the staves we took out o' them Portuguese ships. Afore wood can be called "seasoned", it 'as to be left to dry out for a year an' more. If you tries to make barrels outa "green" wood, it just leaks out all over the place.'

'So without all these staves we've captured, Philip can't provision his ships for another year at least — is that what you're telling me?'

When Jim nodded, Francis ordered that the fleet's holds be emptied of every single stave they'd looted, and that they be ferried onshore and lit. Then he authorised raiding parties to journey further inland and bring back cattle carcases to roast in the series of bonfires that lit up the beach for half a mile on either side of the plundered wine casks from the castle. It was as well that the men were not required for immediate further duties against the enemy, because some of them were ill for days afterwards.

Back in Deptford, ahead of sailing back to Plymouth, Francis dictated a note by the hand of a Navy clerk, and gave an order that it be delivered to Queen Elizabeth personally. After the preliminary pleasantries, Francis wrote:

I had hoped to remove the head of King Philip of Spain, but I have merely singed his beard. Be assured that although I have set back his plan to invade our shores by many months, he will be even more determined, by my actions, to press ahead with same. We must prepare our island for invasion, and do so strongly. My actions have bought us time, but time that may only be employed in bolstering our sea defences against that which must one day come.

After reading Francis's note five times, Queen Elizabeth was still in two minds as to how to react. Drake had disobeyed her order not to engage the Spanish in any aggressive way, but merely to observe the size of its assembled fleet. He had been even more disobedient than Robert Dudley, and she had punished him severely, even though they had been close friends — and occasionally something more — since childhood, and he was the Earl of Leicester. She must clearly find some very public way of bringing this arrogant and headstrong Devon commoner down to his rightful level.

On the other hand, he had served England well, by delaying any Spanish invasion at a time when England was ill-prepared to oppose it. She had no army worthy of the name, and the ability of her navy to prevent Spanish troops being ferried across from the Low Countries depended almost entirely on men like Drake. She needed the advice of the two men she most trusted to give her wise counsel.

Cecil and Walsingham responded to her summons within minutes, since they had been huddled together in Cecil's ground-floor chambers asking themselves the same questions that Her Majesty was now about to put to them. Annoyingly, they were accompanied by Dudley, who had been seeking an audience for the past hour in her outer chamber, and had slipped in alongside the two senior statesmen.

'Well, gentlemen?' Elizabeth asked haughtily. 'What are we to do, given that this latest attack on Philip's fleet in his own port has been taken by him as an excuse to invade England?'

'You can hardly blame him for that,' Cecil offered as humbly as he could, even though he still had his fingers crossed behind his back, 'and we knew that he was planning to use the slightest justification to declare war on us. He had a fleet all ready to sail.'

'A fleet that Drake has bravely reduced in size, thereby delaying any invasion,' Dudley added with a smile that was erased immediately when Elizabeth pierced him with an angry glare.

'I might know that you would applaud a man who disobeys my orders, Dudley!'

'Be that as it may, Your Majesty,' Walsingham intervened diplomatically, 'we must deal with the situation as it currently presents itself, and not as we would have wished it to be.'

'This is why I summoned you and Cecil here,' Elizabeth retorted as her face grew redder, 'although I don't recall granting audience to you, my Lord of Leicester.'

The three men exchanged uncomfortable looks, each one daring the other two, with his eyes, to be the one to advise her. Eventually it was Cecil who weakened first.

'Clearly we must meet the challenge at sea, Your Majesty, since our army is much reduced.'

'Our army is non-existent, thanks to Dudley,' Elizabeth snapped. 'What is worse, his recent failure to overcome Parma's forces in the Low Countries has revealed to the enemy just how little resistance they can expect if they succeed in landing on our shores. And now, it seems, we are reduced to relying for our defence on his pirate friends Drake and Hawkins. They have served England well by plundering Spanish treasure ships, but can they take on those massive floating cities that I'm informed the Spanish employ to transport their soldiers?'

'We will not know until they are commanded to try, Your Majesty,' Walsingham replied tactfully, 'but Hawkins at least will be needed immediately, if we are to build up our navy to the necessary level. He has begun commissioning more of those sleeker, faster vessels that can come alongside the Spanish galleons, and below the level of their gun ports. He hopes, by this means, to go among the enemy's fleet and send them to the bottom before the men that they carry can grapple his ships and leap aboard, which I am informed is the way that the Spanish fight, given the opportunity.'

'So, if Hawkins has the fleet commissioned, when will it be ready? Do we have the men to serve on our ships? How well provisioned are they?' Elizabeth demanded in a quick-fire succession of questions.

Walsingham swallowed hard. 'We are likely to have no shortage of men, or so I am assured by Hawkins, but as for provisions — and, in particular, gunpowder — perhaps more taxation?'

'Out of the question!' Elizabeth retorted. 'They must fight with what they have.'

'Very well, Your Majesty, but I must emphasise the importance of giving what limited resources we possess to the exclusive use of our navy,' Walsingham insisted. 'Our best intelligence is that the Spanish fleet is intended only as transport for Parma's forces to cross from the Low Countries. Our only hope lies in preventing that from happening.'

'And when can we expect this invasion, say you?' Elizabeth swept all three men with an imperious gaze, leaving it to Cecil to take up the briefing.

'Our spies in Spain assure us that Philip is still recovering from the blow delivered by Drake, but that he has ordered that no expense be spared in rebuilding his fleet. We can expect him to launch into the Bay of Biscay well within the year, and probably closer to eight months.'

'And what steps may we take to alert ourselves to this happening?' Elizabeth demanded.

Walsingham was anxious to reassure her. 'As to that, Your Majesty, I have commissioned a series of faggot stacks along the high points of our southern counties. Philip is seemingly amassing his new fleet at Corunna, since it is more easily guarded against attack. When we receive word from our spies there that this fleet has set sail, each stack can be lit when it is actually sighted from a distance away, and will act as a beacon, both to advise us of the progress of the enemy, and to alert those manning the next most easterly stack to keep a close watch out to sea.'

'And where will we intercept them?' Elizabeth demanded, and all three of those in attendance on her looked uncertain, before Walsingham proved the bravest of the three.

'That is perhaps best left to those who will command your navy, Your Majesty.'

'And who shall that be, pray?'

'I had thought Sir John Hawkins, Your Majesty — or perhaps Sir Francis Drake,' Walsingham suggested tentatively, to a loud snort from Elizabeth.

'I will not have it spoken abroad that in its greatest time of challenge, England could do no better than commission pirates to defend it. By all means grant line commissions to Hawkins and Drake, but who among our senior nobles has experience at sea?'

'If we are mindful of rank rather than actual experience,' Cecil replied acidly, 'then perhaps the Lord High Admiral. He is also the Earl of Nottingham, and your cousin.'

'An excellent choice,' Elizabeth concurred, oblivious to the sarcasm. 'Let it be proclaimed throughout the realm that our brave fleet shall be commanded by Lord Howard of Effingham — but, as a matter of common courtesy, ensure that he is advised first.'

It was left to Robert Dudley to explain to an outraged Francis that a nobleman with little experience or understanding of life at sea had been selected to command the naval defence of

England against the Spanish. Dudley had tactfully chosen, as the moment to break the news, his first supper as the honoured overnight guest at Buckland Abbey, with Elizabeth Drake in attendance, playing the gracious hostess.

'It's not a matter of my personal pride!' Francis protested unconvincingly. 'It's also a matter of ensuring that the nation is best served by a man who can make the most effective use of a makeshift navy, cobbled together at the last moment, under-supplied with ordnance and crewed by men who have but lately been dragged from their farms and town trades — men who know as much about naval warfare as I do about needlecraft. They need to be led by men who know what they are about.'

'This is all well known to Her Majesty,' Dudley assured him softly, 'which is why I am authorised to commission you to command one squadron of this new navy, with the rank of vice-admiral, and your cousin John as rear-admiral.'

Francis was pacing up and down the south terrace, still muttering angrily, when Elizabeth walked out to join him.

'What did you expect?' she asked. 'You're not ennobled, and therefore…'

'No-one enquired as to my birth lines when I was bringing riches into the nation, or sending sailors to their likely death at Cadiz, where we set back Philip's invasion plans by many months!' Francis exploded. 'Where were all the nobles then?'

Elizabeth placed a consoling hand on his sleeve and gently steered him back into the house. 'It will soon be dark, dearest, and we cannot leave our honoured guest to amuse himself. Nor would it be seemly for me to entertain him alone, so you are at least required to command your own great hall.'

Far from mollified, Francis nevertheless allowed himself to be guided back into Dudley's company. An uneasy silence fell between them, broken only when Dudley coughed politely and enquired if Francis had opted to live his life on land until the Spanish invaded. 'I hope not,' he added, 'since it is Her Majesty's wish that you and Sir John Hawkins assemble the new navy.'

'The new navy that some wobbly-legged fop can send to the ocean floor with his incompetence?' Francis growled.

Dudley shook his head. 'The new navy that will save England from foreign invasion, thanks to you and John. The queen may think that she knows what is best for England, but I know better.'

In the months that followed, keel after keel was laid in both Deptford and Portsmouth, as John Hawkins commissioned yet more galleons in the English style, varying in capacity from two hundred to four hundred tons, wide in the beam but low in the water. Along with these were over one hundred and fifty armed merchantmen of varying capacities, the largest of which were designed to carry over forty culverins apiece. To Francis fell the onerous task of supervising the ordnance fit-outs, then sea-testing each vessel as it slid down the slipway and was towed into mid channel in its home port. His was also the responsibility of recruiting men who could be called upon when the time came to man the upper and gun decks, and organising the training of those who would be responsible for raining cannon fire on enemy ships whilst ensuring that the vessels on which they were sailing did not suffer any mishaps in the process. Francis raved, swore and blasphemed when advised that the men he had taken such care to train were not to be retained full time, but had to return to their former trades or their work on the land, because the queen was not prepared to pay the meagre few pence a day that would ensure their ongoing training and experience. Likewise, Francis was advised that the armoury at the Tower of London had finally been emptied of what ordnance and explosives had been available, and that even ordnance training must be limited.

'I am preparing to defend England with both arms tied behind my back, and a blindfold over my eyes,' he complained bitterly to his wife as they sat on the south terrace, sipping wine and admiring the blooms in the flowerbed that confirmed that the spring of 1588 was well advanced.

'Is that not why you were chosen to defend England?' Elizabeth asked warmly. 'If any man can do so under those conditions, it is Francis Drake.'

'*Sir* Francis Drake,' Francis corrected her with a smile. 'I may not be a noble, but at least I was knighted. And now I feel within my bones that I must soon earn even that grudging honour all over again.'

22

Corunna Harbour was a mass of sails, hulks, ropes, carts and shouting men who were ordering provisions onto the gently heaving decks from the arms of lesser men who sweated in the noonday sun. Deckhands unfurled ropes by the mile, ships' mates yelled up the order of the rigging, first officers looked to the hoisting of the flags of war, and powder boys struggled with the loading of barrels down onto the gun decks.

Captains and other higher ranks sat watching the noisy action from the windows of quayside hostelries, quaffing their final draughts of Jerez and toasting the good health and long life of the King who had finally ordered the invasion to set sail. Within weeks they would be adding to the wealth of their ancestral estates with the rich plunder to be found in English coastal towns.

The more religiously inclined among them made the sign of the cross and prayed for their own safe deliverance as they drove the English bastard from her usurped throne, and restored the true religion to that Godforsaken land in return for saintly blessings for themselves. The less confident had left money for Masses to be sung for their souls in the churches of their home estates. Fortune or misfortune, the long-awaited *Grande y Felicisima Armada* would slip from the outer harbour on the outgoing tide, and the Duke of Medina Sidonia would command the finest, strongest and most invincible naval invasion the Christian world had ever seen.

After some delay, and a brief setback while a storm threw the vessels out of formation, the invasion fleet set a course northward out of the Bay of Biscay, heading for the western approaches to the English Channel. In all there were about one hundred and thirty ships, containing between them some eight thousand sailors and over twice that number of soldiers. They would soon be augmented by another thirty thousand currently awaiting them in the Low Countries to be ferried, for the final leg across to England, in specially commissioned troop barges that would be protected by the warships.

They had arranged themselves in a crescent formation. Twenty mighty galleons were interspersed between the centre of the line and its tips, guarding and shepherding the remainder of the fleet, which consisted of heavily armed carracks and troop and supply vessels. It creaked and bucked northwards, hastened on its way by a stiff westerly that its pious commander took to be another sign that God was on their side, and had honoured the blessing bestowed on the Armada by Pope Sixtus. After many days at sea, the Spaniards cheered at their first sight of The Lizard, England's south-westernmost point, either not knowing or not caring that this also made them visible to the enemy on whom they were rapidly advancing.

Francis stood looking out to sea from his position on Plymouth Hoe, idly noting with annoyance that the hundred or more vessels that lay in the Sound with their bow ropes fully stretched were still pointing towards the open ocean, denoting an incoming tide. The scudding clouds above him also betrayed the steady westerly that was likely to hold the fleet in harbour for some time yet, while giving the wind gauge to the Spaniards whose invasion fleet was expected any day now.

Behind him, Lord Howard, Admiral of the Fleet, was seated while watching a leisurely game of bowls, having wagered a sum of money on the outcome with one of his sycophantic hangers-on. This was perhaps as well, since Francis could barely bring himself to speak civilly to the old fool who had been given command of the entire English fleet when, by the look of him, he would be hard put to command even a horse.

It had been like this for several days, since word had come of the launch of the Spaniards from Corunna. The English fleet had been assembled from various ports across the south of England and had been divided into squadrons. Francis had line command of his own squadron of twelve, with the *Revenge* as his flagship, and it lay furthest away from his vantage point, out beyond Mount Batten. The squadron immediately behind it, and closer to shore, belonged under John's command. The remainder of the fleet lay closer inshore, within easy reach of the Plymouth waterfront from which Lord Howard could be rowed to and from his luxurious *Ark Royal*, from the stateroom of which he would no doubt presume to issue orders for the entire English Navy, after first seeking advice from Francis.

Since Howard was paying close attention to the game, it was Francis who first became aware of the ragged youth racing up the path leading from the town, clearly in a hurry for some reason or other. He came to a breathless halt as his feet skidded on the rough stones, and he was looking from side to side, as if searching for someone to whom to deliver important news.

'What is it, boy?' Francis demanded.

The youth looked up at him hopefully. 'Lord Howard?' he asked.

Francis nodded towards the white-bearded older man seated on the bench. 'That is Lord Howard, but I am Sir Francis Drake. If you have news of the approach of the Spanish, you must share it with me.'

The youth nodded, and the two of them walked to the bench on which Howard was seated. The breathless messenger delivered the news, before pocketing the coins that were his reward.

'My lords,' he announced between breaths, 'a sea captain called Fleming moored at the harbour not an hour since, claiming to have spied a wall of sails off the Isles of Scilly, set on course for the Channel approaches. He says also that the beacon has been lit on The Lizard.'

'We must put to sea at once!' Howard announced as he rose to his feet with the aid of his ornate walking stick.

Francis allowed himself an insubordinate smirk. 'Good luck with that, my lord,' he gloated. When Howard demanded an explanation, Francis turned to face the sea once again and took great delight in explaining, as if to a five-year-old, 'You will note that the clouds are passing us on a course from right to left. Since to our right lies the west, while to our left is the east, it may safely be concluded that the wind is westerly. There is also a full tide running into the harbour.'

'So?' Howard demanded.

'Anyone with the slightest knowledge of seacraft would be aware that for a ship to leave this harbour, it requires either an ebb tide or an easterly wind, and preferably both. We currently have neither.'

'So when may we set sail and take on the enemy?' was the next question, to which Francis had another impertinent answer.

'In the same way that Her Majesty did not place me in command of our fleet, likewise God did not place me in a position from which I can control the elements. But, if my instincts born of years at sea do not betray me, this westerly will continue for at least another day.'

'By which time the Spaniards will be halfway down the Channel!' Howard reminded him. 'Is there nothing we can do other than await a fortunate shift in the wind?'

'Again, it helps to have some shipboard experience,' Francis went on. 'If you would give the order for all the vessels in the fleet to lower their sails and raise their anchors once the tide changes course, we may float out on the ebb. However, since this will be after nightfall, it would be as well if each vessel were to run a stern light, if we are to avoid collisions. Then it would be my respectful advice that they once again drop anchor until daylight, then tack westwards.'

'The Spaniards will be well past Plymouth by then, will they not?' Howard demanded.

Francis nodded. 'Indeed they will, but we will have the wind gauge when we pursue them.'

'Your meaning?'

'My meaning is that we shall be able to sneak up behind them in two formations, to the north and south, and sink them in our crossfire.'

'It sits uneasily with me, to be doing nothing to meet the enemy head-on,' Howard pouted.

Francis turned away. 'That is how one fights on land perhaps, my lord, but at sea we are much more devious. In any case, you will hardly be doing nothing. First you must settle up for what looks like your losses on the bowling green. Then you must give the order for the fleet to slide out into the Channel on the ebb tide, under the cover of darkness. By then, the beacons should tell us how far the enemy have progressed in their attempt to reach Calais.'

In the captain's state cabin in the stern castle of the Spanish flagship the *São Martinho*, a furious argument was being waged once it was realised that the English were confined to harbour by the elements. The only man with any real sailing experience was Admiral Juan Martínez de Recalde, a naval veteran who was second in command to Sidonia, an army martinet whose entire training and experience had reinforced the view that an order was an order.

His order, direct from the mouth of King Philip, had been to sail direct to the Low Countries, and there provide a naval escort for land troops in barges who would enforce the will of Spain on England and its heathen queen. In vain de Recalde argued with Sidonia, sometimes at screaming pitch, that were they to turn into Plymouth Harbour they could destroy the entire English fleet while it was still at anchor, in retaliatory memory of what had been done to them by Drake in Cadiz.

By the time that de Recalde stormed out of Sidonia's cabin in a helpless rage, he had been informed that they were, instead, to sail into the last available deep-sea English anchorage — the Solent, between the Isle of Wight and Portsmouth. There they would establish a land bridge before sailing on to their rendezvous with the land troops of the Duke of Parma across the water in the Low Countries. But even that second-rate alternative was about to come to nought.

The wisdom of hanging back, and in fact furthering their distance from the Spanish by tacking into the westerly in the direction of The Lizard, was fully vindicated by the middle of the following day. Francis took his squadron south, close off the French coastline, and turned hard east, allowing the strengthening westerly to drive his squadron of twelve at full speed in pursuit of the slower, more lumbering, Spanish hulks. Never before had he taken such great advantage of the wind gauge, and as the sails of the Spanish came into sight further down the Channel, Francis ordered Jim Short below with his gun deck crew. They were given instructions to load, prime and be ready for the yelled command down the gun hatch. Then he smiled as he looked aft, and saw that Lord Howard, for want of any better idea, was following the English shoreline behind them, and could open up with another salvo on the port beams of the Spanish vessels, once Francis had done with them.

With the *Revenge* in the lead, proudly flying the Tudor ensign from her stern mast, they came alongside the rearmost of the Spanish vessels, the galleon *San Salvador*, and Francis yelled the order down the hatch. The *Revenge* rocked from side to side six times as the port side culverins under Jim Short's command barked into life, sending cannon shot into the top rigging of the enemy vessel, which veered heavily to port in an evasive action. They were clearly too far away from the Spaniard for Jim to assess the correct angle of fire, but Francis was reluctant to close in further and risk the armed men who were screaming curses at them from the deck of the *San Salvador* being able to leap onto the decks of the *Revenge*, as they had been taught to do. In any case, the wind gauge was taking them past the enemy galleon at too great a speed for their culverins to be deployed again safely, so Francis yelled down for Jim to reload, but hold his fire.

As they sped onwards towards a massive transport hulk flying Spanish colours, Francis looked back from his position on the poop deck. He grinned with satisfaction as he saw the *San Salvador*, having steered too hard to port, colliding with the carrack it had been protecting, the *Rosario*. Even from that distance, and with the air full of gunpowder residue, he had the satisfaction of hearing the sickening crunch of a mid-ocean collision and seeing massive holes being driven into the beams of both vessels. There were a few moments of shouted Spanish commands, and feverish running backwards and forwards on both decks, before men began diving overboard in order to swim clear of the listing vessels. But Francis had spent long enough building ships for his Hawkins cousins to realise that the vessels were unlikely to sink, and that once abandoned they would make simple targets for piracy.

For the next few hours, English and Spanish gunners blasted away at each other as the rest of Howard's fleet caught up with the action, and the Spanish were being harassed along both their port and starboard beams. But as night began to fall, not a single vessel on either side had gone to the bottom, and Francis calculated that his would not be the only vessel to run out of ordnance if it kept up at this pace. The *Revenge* had almost overtaken the leading Armada vessels anyway, and he ordered the lowering of sail as he looked landward across his starboard bow and saw the twinkling lights on the spires and towers of Boulogne up ahead.

On board the *São Martinho* de Recalde pushed angrily past the attendant guarding the door to Sidonia's state cabin, and wrinkled his nose against the smell of vomit that betrayed the fact that the supreme commander of history's greatest naval invasion force had succumbed to yet another bout of seasickness.

'What means this idiocy?' he screamed. 'The inland waterway of which you spoke is well to our stern. According to my charts, there are no further deepwater anchorages between here and Calais!'

'Then it is perhaps as well that Calais is our destination, is it not?' Sidonia replied weakly as he dry-retched yet again into the bowl at his side.

23

Francis stood with a defiant smirk in front of the table at which Lord Howard was attempting to consume his dinner while venting his wrath over his vice-admiral's disobedience. Francis had not even been offered a seat, let alone invited to partake of dinner, but it seemed that nothing would make him admit that he had been guilty of mutiny.

'Thanks to your treasonous actions, half the fleet is spread in disarray along the Channel!' Howard thundered.

'Since the wind still lies westerly, they should all end up in the sea-roads leading to Calais, where we may rejoin them,' Francis replied with a flippancy that would have earned him a flogging, followed by a hanging from his own yardarm, had he been of a lesser rank.

His orders had been to guide several squadrons of vessels down the Channel in pursuit of the Armada, under cover of darkness, but displaying a stern lamp that would ensure that all the vessels remained in formation behind the *Revenge*. However, the temptation had proved too great, and he had ordered that his lamp be extinguished as he turned and tacked back westwards in search of the abandoned *San Salvador* and *Rosario*. He had found them just as the dawn highlighted their wallowing in the shallows off Le Touquet, and he had sent boarding parties onto each vessel in turn, carrying off a considerable quantity of gold, coins and other valuables, in addition to what had been his main target. In the confusion caused by the absence of his guiding stern light, the following vessels had wandered listlessly around in the dark, and there had even been two minor collisions before the abandoned squadrons found themselves both separated and leaderless.

'Even when England lies in grave danger of being invaded, you could not resist falling back into your pirate ways, could you?' Howard yelled.

'Pirate ways that have made victory over the enemy even more likely,' Francis assured his commander. 'Thanks to the tightness of Her Majesty's hand upon her purse, we had little left in the way of ordnance with which to send Spanish ships to the bottom. On board the two vessels that had been abandoned, we found large quantities of gunpowder, and many twelve-pound balls that will fit within our culverins. Without those, we would have been reduced to firing lamprey dumplings, greatly reducing the size of your dinner.'

'Get out of my sight until you have some meaningful plan to further engage the enemy!' Howard shouted and returned to his meal. A minute later, aware of Francis's lack of movement, he looked up angrily. 'Well?' he demanded.

'I already have that meaningful plan, my lord, which is why I did not withdraw from the presence,' Francis told him. 'But I shall require your authority to destroy some of the ships that Her Majesty entrusted to your care.'

'Where are those soldiers we were meant to transport?' de Recalde demanded testily as he stood looming over Sidonia's chart table in the stateroom of the *São Martinho*. 'And how is it proposed that they be guarded by us as they cast off in their barges, since the waters between us and the shore are too shallow to admit vessels with draughts as deep as ours?'

Sidonia sighed. 'The more immediate question, Admiral, is whether they are aware of our presence, and if they are ready to set sail. So far there has been no sign of them.'

'Did anyone even bother to advise them that we were on our way?' de Recalde asked. 'As for whether or not they are aware of our arrival, we must surely be visible on land for ten leagues on either side of Calais. The more pertinent matter is whether or not they know *why* we are here.'

They could have argued all day over who was to blame, but de Recalde had a valid point. When contact was eventually made with the Duke of Parma and his Army of Flanders, as it was known, it was reduced to sixteen thousand instead of the original thirty thousand, due to disease among the lower ranks. Even then, word was sent back that there were at present insufficient barges available to transport even such a reduced force, and that the Armada that was to protect the land troops would need to remain at anchor for at least six more days. The reality — which was not confided to Sidonia — was that the Dutch and Flemish had begun to repay the English for their loyal support in the way in which they were best equipped. This involved guerrilla tactics.

Because of the low-lying nature of much of their homeland, the people of the Low Countries had become adept in the construction and navigation of what were known as 'fly boats' — flat-bottomed barges that could navigate the shallows around Dunkerque and Gravelines. When it became known, through a network of spies that had infiltrated the Spanish ranks, that an invasion of England was being planned making use of a larger, more reinforced, version of such vessels, Flemish saboteurs began entering the boatyards in which they were being constructed by night, and setting fire to them. When the Spanish increased the armed guards on the boatyards, the local response was to slow down the construction process while pleading lack of available tradesmen or materials, a ploy that worked so successfully that there were still only half the required number of transport barges available.

Nevertheless, Sidonia was nervously aware that his fleet was exposed to English cannon-fire for as long as it lay at anchor. He therefore sent word ashore that Parma should begin the embarkation of his available troops, in order that at least some of the Armada could complete its voyage across the Channel. This was when the Dutch, under Lieutenant-Admiral Justinus of Nassau, showed that not only could they build flyboats, but they also knew how to sail them in the shallows that the Spanish soldiers would be required to navigate in order to access the deeper waters between the Low Countries and the English south coast, in which they would be protected by Armada vessels.

The blockade of the waters immediately off Gravelines and Dunkerque led to a stalemate, in which both sides of the intended Spanish invasion force looked on with mounting frustration. The land-locked troops were unable to put to sea because of the heavily armed and threatening flyboats that awaited them, and the Spanish fleet were unable to move into dangerously shallow waters in order to blast the flyboats away. It was then that Francis made efficient use of a tactic already horribly familiar to Spanish sea captains.

He finally prevailed upon Howard to decommission several English carracks, which were first emptied of both contents and men, and then coated with pitch, tar and brimstone. Their holds were crammed with gunpowder looted from the *San Salvador* and *Rosario*, and in the early hours of the morning these hellburners were torched and left to drift on the prevailing westerly current towards the Armada ships at anchor. Shouts of alarm from Spanish lookouts became screams of panic from the captains whose vessels were in the way, and a considerable number of them ordered the urgent cutting of their anchor ropes, rather than wasting time hauling them in. This was to have serious consequences for the fate of the fleet as a whole.

Sidonia, in his flagship, and the senior naval officers in the largest of the galleons stubbornly remained at anchor and concentrated on the hazardous task of diverting the flaming ships off their destined course. Those vessels whose anchor lines had been cut were carried further east by the prevailing wind and current, completely out of formation and incapable of halting their inexorable progress down the coastline of Holland. They travelled past the hazardous Flemish shoals from which the Dutch had removed the warning markers, then out into the lower North Sea as the wind turned a little more from the south.

On Francis's insistence, and since Howard could think of no reason against it, the English warships then began a fast run at the remaining Spanish vessels at anchor off Gravelines. Previous wasted shot had revealed that the thickness of Armada hulls was such that English culverins needed to be within a hundred-yard range of the enemy. However, they had to avoid closing in any further, lest the Spanish were able to put to good use their preferred tactic of sending soldiers over the gunnels of enemy vessels in murderous boarding parties. The English were also woefully short of ordnance, so every shot had to count.

Francis had also learned from his forage onto the gun decks of the captured carracks that they were seriously overloaded. This explained something else he had noted during the engagement the previous day, namely that the Spaniards could only fire once, and their cannon could not then be run back for reloading because of all the below-decks clutter. He therefore ordered Jim Short, on the *Revenge*, and other master gunners in the fleet, to tempt the enemy into firing their precious first fusillades, and then move in for the kill with a barrage of shot at close range, aiming for the high-decked galleons and carracks as low in the water as was possible.

Within minutes of the English bearing down on the remaining Spanish ships at anchor, the air was so thick with choking clouds of gunpowder residue that it was difficult to breathe. Shouted orders were drowned out by the constant roar of culverins, and it was impossible to see more than a few yards ahead. Keeping only slightly inside the one-hundred-yard range, each English warship swooped in with cannon blazing once the Spanish had fired their one shot, and were elated to note how the strong westerly swell would periodically, and obligingly, lift the enemy vessels several feet further out of the water on their seaward beams, exposing more of their lower hulls to English master gunners. By late in the afternoon there was no returning fire from the enemy, and word reached Francis that the English had nothing left to fire with. He therefore ordered a withdrawal and led the *Revenge* back though the lines of English warships that had obeyed his command. Each set of decks was lined with cheering mariners who threw their caps in the air as they marked his progress back towards the *Ark Royal*.

'What next?' Howard demanded sternly, determined to maintain the appearance of command, even though he was relying on the sturdy, ruddy-faced Devon man to advise him on appropriate tactics.

'We allow the elements to do their worst,' replied Francis.

Howard's eyebrows rose in disbelief. 'Your meaning?' he demanded.

'You will of course recall that westerly wind that you thought so inconvenient when you were losing money on the outcome of a bowls game on Plymouth Hoe? Well, it blows still, and the Spanish have run out of sea lane. Their invasion fleet is also dispersed, with half of them floating easterly, well beyond the point at which they can offer cover to soldiers on land, even were they able to make their way through the Dutch barges that lie in wait for them. I suggest that we also divide our fleet; you remain here with the bulk of the warships, preventing any movement away from the Flemish shoreline, while I chase the remainder further away.'

'But you tell me that we are out of ordnance,' Howard objected.

Francis nodded. 'You and I know that, my lord — but do the Spanish? And should we be fortunate enough to capture more enemy vessels, we can make good use of what is stored below *their* decks.'

'Can we not simply let those enemy ships that have fled the encounter return home?' Howard asked.

Francis stopped himself from delivering the rude riposte that came to mind. 'The captains of the enemy vessels that have already fled have a limited range of options, my lord,' he argued. 'Without sail, they will drift further away from us on the westerly current. If they hoist sail, they will be driven eastward even more quickly. If they turn about and tack back westerly, they will — so far as they are aware — do so straight into our waiting guns. My concern is that they may hoist sail so as to steer into the Thames, where there is no army to meet them; even the few soldiers they have carried ever since they

left Spain would be sufficient to take London. I suggest —
with your consent — that I take my squadron and harass them
up the English east coast until they are way beyond any
prospect of making meaningful landfall.'

Howard was still considering this bold plan when a message
was brought down into his stateroom by one of his junior
officers on board the *Ark Royal*.

'My lord, the remainder of the Spanish have raised sail, and
appear to be heading east.'

'Why would they do that?' Howard asked Francis.

'Their commander clearly wishes to reunite with the rest of
the fleet, in the belief that there is safety in numbers.
Presumably you would care to join me in escorting them from
the rear, to ensure that they never enter the Thames?'

Howard agreed, since there would seem to be little
alternative. For the next two weeks, they followed the
shattered remnants of the once proud and mighty Armada,
looking for all the world like a pack of dogs harassing a herd of
sheep, until they were well north of the border with Scotland,
and the last navigable port of any size — Leith — was well to
their stern. Martin Frobisher, the commander of one of the
four English squadrons, was allocated the hazardous task of
harassing the Spaniards even further north in worsening
weather, while Francis, John and Howard turned south and
began the long tack home against the still prevailing south-
westerly.

They parted company off Margate, with Howard setting a
course back up the Thames after promising to advise Queen
Elizabeth of the 'sterling service' that Francis and John had
given in the repulsion of the Spanish threat. John politely
reminded him that his home was also in London, and that he
had a wife and son awaiting him in Deptford. John and Francis

embraced on the deck of the *Revenge* before John was to take his cutter back to his own ship.

'We've come a long way since our boyhood pranks around Plymouth, Francis,' he said. 'Even then you were the more adventurous of the two of us, and that mischievous humour of yours has served England well. Thank God that our noble commander allowed you your head.'

'He had little choice,' Francis grimaced, 'since his only experience of the sea was on diplomatic missions to France, and even then he was merely a passenger. It would seem that Her Majesty knows even less about the art of naval warfare, or she would not have entrusted our fleet to that land-lubbing elderly fop. No doubt he will be given further titles for his alleged service to England, while those of our men who lost arms, legs and eyesight in the encounter will be left to beg in the gutters.'

'Time I rejoined my vessel and sailed for Deptford,' John muttered as he shook his head disapprovingly, 'ere I become infected with your treasonous mood.'

A week later the familiar sight of Salcombe Head rewarded Francis's eager squint through the spray off his starboard beam. Through the rapidly rising mist that was being dispersed by the mid-morning sun, he also became aware of a flotilla of sails ahead. They proved to be those of small fishing vessels that had taken advantage of the ebb tide at daybreak in order to sail out to welcome the returning local hero, for word had come to Plymouth from returning coastal carracks that the *Revenge* had been sighted the previous evening as it made its stately way past the Isle of Wight.

The cheering could be heard faintly on the northerly wind as Jim Short ordered several modest tacks through the Outer Sound, then lowered sail as they passed Mount Batten on their starboard beam and lazed towards Sutton Wharf on mizzen sail only. The Hoe, and every available headland close to the town itself, was crowded with townsfolk who had gathered to welcome home their mayor. Francis surveyed the yelling crowd on the wharf, but he could not see his wife among them, and concentrated instead on ensuring that the *Revenge* bumped gently and safely into the berth that had been specially cleared for it. The ropes were secured to bollards, then his deckhands jumped onto land to embrace their waiting families, leaving Francis unsure what to do next.

'The coach is waiting in the next street, Master,' coachman Ed Jarvis from the Buckland Estate advised him as he peered down to where Francis was seated on a coiled rope in the centre of the main deck. 'The Mistress didn't want to risk getting trampled by the mob,' he added by way of explanation.

With a whispered word of thanks, Francis leapt ashore and made his way to where the coach was waiting. As he got to within a few feet of it the door was opened by a heavily ringed hand, and out came the instruction, 'Get in, Francis — I'm eager for my dinner.'

As they rumbled up the Yelverton Road on their way home, Francis was reminded of that day, now long in the past, when he had travelled in the reverse direction on the front board of his father's farm cart, with his mother and brothers seated behind them surrounded by everything they possessed, on their way into Plymouth and the start of a new phase in Francis's life.

'Did the queen grant you any title in return for your valiant efforts?' Elizabeth asked.

Francis shook his head. 'Why should she? All the glory will go to that idiot Effingham.'

'So when will you be putting to sea again?'

'I've no idea, but I'm suddenly in no great hurry,' Francis replied as he leaned across and kissed her. 'Even I've seen enough of the ocean for the time being. But I suspect I'll only be on land for a brief while, until England once more requires the seagoing skills of a farmer's son.'

A NOTE TO THE READER

Dear Reader,

Thank you for taking the time to read this novel; hopefully you enjoyed it, since there are two more in the series.

There are certain facts we all remember from our school history lessons, however badly they were taught. For example, that the Norman Conquest was in 1066, that Henry VIII had six wives, and that Charles I was executed in public. But other things that we vaguely remember cannot be verified by the records kept at the time, such as they were. So, we learn with disappointment, we cannot be certain that King Alfred burned the cakes, that Robin Hood fought a guerrilla war against the Sheriff of Nottingham in Sherwood Forest, or that Francis Drake paused for a game of bowls before taking on the Spanish Armada.

In fact, if put to it, we can only remember one fact about Francis Drake, and that is that he defeated the Spanish Armada. Even that is not strictly accurate, since the English fleet that boldly sent Philip of Spain's invasion fleet packing was in reality commanded by Lord Howard of Effingham. But Francis Drake has become as much a popular hero hidden from clear view behind the mists of time as Robin Hood. This makes him — like Robin Hood — a convenient icon representing the spirit of the age in which he lived.

The middle years of the reign of Elizabeth I were the age of exploration. John Hawkins opened up the English trade with those parts of the Americas that were already dominated by Spanish and Portuguese explorers, Francis Drake became the first English mariner to circumnavigate the world, and Walter

Raleigh promoted English colonies in the New World to which, in the next generation, the Pilgrim Fathers sailed in search of religious freedom.

Drake and Hawkins are ideal subjects for historical novelists such as me, since so little detailed knowledge of their lives was recorded for posterity. John Hawkins was the second son of a shipbuilding family in Plymouth, while Francis Drake was the oldest son of a failed farmer from Tavistock who dreamed of putting to sea ever since boyhood holidays spent with John Hawkins, his second cousin. That much we know, along with the bare facts of the dates of their marriages, the fact that John had a son called Richard, and the likelihood that Francis left no legitimate children. It is also a matter of record that Sir John Hawkins was Comptroller of the English Navy at the time of the Armada, while Sir Francis Drake was for some time the Mayor of Plymouth.

Onto this bare frame may be weaved such tapestries as are conjured up by the imagination, and I hope that I have done both men justice. I was able to take considerable liberties with Francis's marriages, and most notably the first, since beyond the bare fact that his first wife was named Mary Newman little else is known about her.

The vast majority of the characters who feature in this novel actually existed, and performed the actions described. Only the lesser characters such as the sailors who ploughed the seas under Drake and Hawkins are fictional, although they undoubtedly reflect those who must have existed. It was a hazardous life in those days, and hopefully I've captured something of the drama of exploring unchartered seas with the ever-present peril of enemy attack adding to the underlying risks attendant on taking on mighty oceans in wooden vessels equipped only with sail.

As for the fabled events that legend ascribed to Drake on Plymouth Hoe, I again used my imagination. There is no doubt that he was there when the impending arrival of the Armada was announced, since it afforded a commanding view of Plymouth Sound, but Drake's delay in putting to sea had less to do with any game of bowls in which he might have been engaged, and more to do with the state of the wind and tide.

I'd love to receive feedback on this novel, in the form of a review on **Amazon** or **Goodreads**. Or, of course, you can try the more personal approach on my website and my Facebook page: **DavidFieldAuthor**.

Happy reading!

David

davidfieldauthor.com

Sapere Books is an exciting new publisher of brilliant fiction and popular history.

To find out more about our latest releases and our monthly bargain books visit our website:
saperebooks.com

Printed in Great Britain
by Amazon

44519152R00136